A Break In Time

The 2ⁿᵈ book in the A Moment in Time series

A Break In Time

(Book 2 in the "A Moment In Time" series)

By

Margot Bish

Author's Note

Although I have used the names of real historical people, I have no knowledge of their real characters. It has been interesting attaching characters to, for instance, men best known for their part in the gunpowder plot and pointing to their possible motivations, but these are entirely fictional, based on factual documents of the time, but applying modern reactions to the facts of the situation which may well be incorrect. This was a time of strong religious beliefs and, sadly, a great deal of persecution leading to violence on both sides in the desire to uphold their beliefs, as well as political motivations as powerful families tried to gain favour with the queen.

I find myself unable to judge the rights and wrongs of these people, only wish that, in our present time we could find a way to live in peace, regardless of our religious beliefs, nationality or background.

For those who would like to follow the characters' journeys, Feckenham's location is at 52 deg 15' N1 deg 59' W, with Coughton Court at location 52 deg 14'N 1 deg 53W. My thanks to the owners of Shurnock Court for allowing me to use their property as the central location of my story.

Chapter 1

It's difficult to know where a time travel story begins, but I think this one begins with an eight year old girl discovering a note, brittle with age, tucked behind the skirting board in their old manor house parts of which were built before the Tudors ruled England. The note looked old too.

It was raining waterfalls outside, as it did now every day from the beginning of November until the end of February. Occasionally it was replaced by snow, so that the water filled fields and the moat froze and became a series of skating rinks divided by snow sculptures designed and created by the howling wind. Surreal.

It was November now and, because it was impossible to do anything in the torrential rain outside, the family knuckled down to indoor redecoration. This year was skirting boards.

Fishing the note out carefully, she unwrapped the folds, trying not to breathe or tremble for fear the paper would fall to pieces in her hands. She laid it flat on the floor. The writing was only a little faded by time. The darkness of the secret space had preserved the ink. Only some of the words were lost in the failing foldlines. It said:

"If you find this note after 2019, my name is Margot Bish. Please contact my mother....."

Jemma frowned hard over the next words, distorted by

the crease in the paper but could make no sense of them except that they might have been an address. She skipped to the next clear words.

"It may seem crazy but I have fallen back in time and can't get back. I am healthy and safe. I miss those I love."

She sat back on her heels and stared in amazement at the browning ink. Was this for real? The paper looked genuinely old but much thinner than she would have thought "old" paper would be. The writing looked like biro, but then, a modern person would maybe have had her own pen and paper. How could she tell if this was someone having a joke or a real cry for help? It didn't say when she had fallen back to. Victorian England? Tudor? Maybe only the world wars in the 1900's. Jemma flicked her eyes around the walls that sheltered her. To lie safe behind the skirting board it must be after the skirting boards were fitted. So what? After Henry VII she supposed. She did some sums. It was now 2034. The paper could be more than 500 years old. Well, maybe the paper was only 15 years old, but it had been in its place for about 500 years.

Her dad glanced across from his painting on the far side of the hall.
"Come on Jemma. No daydreaming or I'll catch you up. Tea break in twenty minutes. See if you can keep going until then."
Jemma turned her head in his direction, but it took her a while to focus.
"Look what I found," she said, waving her hand in the note's direction.
Carl sighed and clambered stiffly from his knees to his feet, stretching his spine as he stood and then walked

across the room. He bent to scoop up the note with an indulgent smile.

"No,no," Jemma gasped. "Don't try to pick it up. It's old."

Carl sighed but obediently bent to a crouch and studied the note, twisting his head to read the upside down writing. He shook his head.

"It must be a joke. People can't travel in time. Come on. Let's see if you can sand to the door before I reach that corner."

He pointed across the room. Stretching back to standing, he turned, grinned over his shoulder at his kneeling daughter and. as he set himself into a race start position, said."On your marks....Get set....Go!"

He ran the five paces across the room, paint brush in hand.

"But Da-ad," Jemma began.

Her dad shook his head and pointed the paintbrush at her like a gun. "Work now, talk at tea break, OK?"

Jemma nodded glumly but returned to her sanding, casting glances at the faded paper. She sanded now automatically while her mind considered what she could do next to unravel the mystery. Could she check the history books looking for a Margot Bish in time? She shook her head frustratedly. Why hadn't she said which date? Too many centuries to search. Well, maybe she could find this Margot in 2019 and see what she looked like. Her mind lit up excitedly. If she had got back, maybe she was still alive and Jemma could find her.

Electricity was rationed now in an effort to save the struggling earth. If only the sun would shine, there would be plenty of energy generated by the solar panels on the roof. She smiled, remembering the fight her dad had had to get permission to fit them on a listed building despite the desperate need for green energy to replace fossil fuels. He had made his points so forcefully that the councillors had blushed with embarrassment and given in. The common sense argument that the building need not be damaged under the cosmetic blight but without solar panels, the whole building and the whole population might be destroyed seemed to be the clincher.

The pouring rain should create hydro energy but only once the water-levels dropped and the rainwater could run more forcefully to the sea. So, right now, she was limited to only one hour a day of web-time except for school. She wondered briefly if she could claim historical research was educational and counted as school time......probably not. The time had passed. Carl gave a cry of triumph.

"I won," he yelled."And two minutes to break time."
Jemma had forgotten the race. She had almost reached the door, could feel the odd breath of air from under it as the wind gusted in a stronger puff outside the house. "Only just," she retorted.
She turned and studied her dad's work, hoping she could spot a bit he had missed, but he was too much of a perfectionist to be able to disqualify him.
""You finish off," Carl said, "And I'll go make the drinks".

He limped out of the room, still stretching out the stiff joints and pins and needles from too much shuffling along on his knees. Jemma shrugged to herself and set to with the sanding block. Just a couple of centimetres to go. How was she going to keep that note from falling into dust? Almost, she wished she hadn't found it, hadn't disturbed it from its centuries old nest but on the other hand, November could be pretty boring with no one else to play with. It would be good to have a challenge like this to unravel, even if it was some kind of hoax. After lunch was schoolwork and then she could work out her strategy. Yes, she thought, I like that word, strategy.

It was science and woodwork this afternoon. Her Mum said just ten years before, everyone went to a special building called school and did lots of learning of subjects all together in classes, but then a disease came along and made it safer for everyone to learn at home and straight after that, the flooding and droughts had got worse and first, lots of schools closed because they were flooded or the roads were flooded and no one could get there and then, everyone realised that driving to school was adding to the climate problems, but so was using the computers for learning from home so now everyone learned from books at home and there were just a couple of zoom sessions with teachers to deal with questions and let everyone meet up.

They did meet up for some lessons in Spring and Autumn, to go through anything that needed lots of questions and answers and to learn new team games, maybe act out a play and then new books were handed out and old books handed back in, and everyone said goodbye for another five months. Jemma could hardly believe things could change so much, but she quite liked being able to choose which subjects to do when, and be allowed to start early in the morning and have a break doing something not for school in the middle of the morning. The only thing she would have loved to have was a friend to play with, really touch and share toys and games with. Now she would have to choose whether to chat on the web with Sonya, her best friend or save her web-time to find this Margot. "Maybe I can get Sonya to help find her," she said to herself as she picked up a chisel and mallet to make a small boat which had all the lines ready drawn. She rubbed the wood, feeling the grain and inhaling the wood smell of the room where her uncle and dad did most of their repairs and project work. Looking across the room, she could see a cog wheel held in a vice, complicated drawings pinned to the wall. "One day, I'm going to be able to make things like that," she promised herself and set to on her boat which seemed a bit of a waste of time, when she could be learning to make machinery for sluice gates or growing crops...... her mind wandered on as her hands chiselled and sawed and the little boat took shape. One day, she would be a structural engineer or an electrician like Uncle Seb and help make Shurnock "run like clockwork", like Uncle Seb said. She liked learning about science and doing experiments and Uncle Seb liked doing them with her. Sometimes it was hard to stop him doing all the work she was supposed to do and other times she found he had tweaked a project and made it work better than it was supposed to. Today, he was out in his waders and waterproofs, fixing one of the dams so she could work on her seed growing project in peace. Her lettuce seeds were in the kitchen and sprouting nicely. She turned the tray to make sure they all got the same amount of heat and light. The kitchen smelled good, warm smells of pastry, onion and bread as her Mum cooked a pie for their evening meal which would help keep them warm at night. She couldn't help sniffing but it made her Mum laugh.

"You can't be hungry already. You've only just had lunch," she said.

"I know, but hot food always smells nicer," Jemma said.

"Aren't these lettuces lucky to live in the nice warm kitchen with the lovely smells and not be the poor straggly ones in the dark draughty porch?" She looked sad for a moment. "I wish I was allowed to swap them over."

Her Mum gave her a fond glance. "Maybe you can do that when the project is over and you've written your results. We might even find room for them all in the kitchen, but don't get too attached to them. Remember we will be eating them one day."

Jemma sighed and poked at a germinating leaf. "Poor things," she said. "I hope they can't hear what we are saying."

Jemma carefully wrote out her results on the number of growing lettuces in each of the locations around the house but she already knew which lettuces would win the race – those in good soil with warmth and light. Some of the school lessons seemed to drag behind what she already knew. Uncle Seb said all the books needed to be rewritten by the children in the next class above and some of the lessons needed to be scrapped altogether. Who needed to know poetry these days? Mum liked art and poetry, though, and singing, which is poetry to music and said we needed it as stress release. Jemma didn't know who was right but liked to listen to the banter, Mum's voice growing higher in exasperation, Uncle Seb's dropping to a muttering growl if she out-debated him.

Lessons done, Jemma said, "I'm all finished. Can I use the laptop for something?"
"Talking to Sonya?" Mum asked.
"Well, some, but also, I found this note and I want to look for the person who wrote it," Jemma replied.
She had flattened the note between two pieces of wood, screwed lightly together and now showed it to her Mum.
Beth put down her rolling pin so that she could concentrate better on what she was looking at.
"The paper looks old, because it has browned and gone brittle," Beth commented, having washed her hands and dried them carefully before looking closely.
"But that's not old ink and the flow is even, like a biro. How odd. Well Jem, you might be disappointed if you find it's a hoax, but go ahead. It will be good exercise for your logic muscles and teach you how to research and question what you read. Remember, though, only one hour so don't waste it going off at a tangent."
"I know," sighed Jemma. "You were lucky when you could just browse all day. I mean before the climate got so bad."
She went over to the small study, sectioned off so that the kitchen heat would keep the room warm but the damp from cooking would not damage the equipment and switched everything on, both internet connection and laptop. She had thought carefully about what she must do. First a search engine for the lady's name in 2019 and Worcestershire and

then another in 2020. If there was time, she might then have a picture and be able to see if she was still around now. Then she would contact Sonya and show her the evidence.

The internet was annoyingly slow. All the northern hemisphere storms and rain were destroying the radio masts and distorting signals from the few working satellites. She had set a timer for 45 minutes so she would have time to chat to Sonya. The name, Margot Bish came up at last with some person in America. Huffing, she added Feckenham and realised that was a mistake because she knew all the Feckenham families and so did Mum and Dad and there were no people with that name. She deleted it and tried Redditch and a newspaper headline came up.

"Missing woman. Has anyone seen this person?"

Jemma gasped. So quickly she had made a link. The article explained that the lady had gone missing one weekend in 2019 and her last known intention was to garden at Shurnock Court. Jemma gasped again and her eyes grew wide. Here!

Her bicycle had been found but no sign of the lady. Any sightings should be notified to the police and could be anonymous if required. A telephone number was given. Jemma rubbed her nose thoughtfully. Well, she had disappeared, but was the note a decoy to disguise some other crime, like a murder or a kidnapping? It seemed a funny thing to do but then, maybe this lady had just wanted to start a new life and thought the note, if found would make people give up looking for her. No. There were better ways of doing that. Just a letter saying I'm off on a new life, please leave me be, or something. Jemma kicked her feet against the chair in excitement. Now what? Did she get back? Jemma searched for follow up articles but it seemed the police were flummoxed. She saved the picture and tried the name with 2020. Nothing new, only a webpage offering gardening services but that was from 2018. The timer bleeped. Time to contact Sonya. It seemed her friend had been waiting for her to link up and they chatted about other things for so long that the computer timed out for the hour before she had mentioned the mystery.

"Oh Sonya, I have to tell you about a lady who disappeared when we talk tomorrow," Jemma gabbled as the screen counted her last seconds down and blacked out.

In the next few days, Jemma searched the web and found two new links. She sat back in the chair, hands together in a clasp of jubilation. First, in 2020, a report that she had been found but the police were unable to piece together what had happened in 2019, and then a newer advert offering gardening services in 2021. Then, nothing. No death reported or anything. She just dropped out of the public eye. Maybe she was out there still, somewhere for Jemma to find. She glanced out of the window.....When the rain eventually stopped. The next question was, if she really fell through time, how did she do it? It must have been at Shurnock Court. Could it still happen? She did get back so it must be possible to travel backwards and forwards. Was that exciting or terrifying? Jemma started to think what kind of emergency kit you might need to survive in any time you fell back to. What did a person really need? To eat and drink and keep warm and dry, so, a cup, and a knife. You couldn't count on batteries so, matches or a magnifying glass to light fires. What about waterproofs? She looked down at the moccasins she used for slippers and wondered if she ought to wear shoes all the time. Just in case. String would be useful, and needle and thread. Money? She laughed, thinking how it would be to offer a travel pass with an expiry date 100 years ahead. Carefully, she assembled her kit, even a roll up waterproof jacket. When she could get supplies, she would add some of those dehydrated food kits that last for years. She fastened the kit to her belt and felt safer.

"Jem? Are you upstairs?"

That was Mum calling. Jemma looked at her watch. Gosh, half past four, and she hadn't fed the hens or the pigs.

"Just coming, Mum," she called, and clattered down the stairs and into the kitchen. "Sorry, I lost track of the time. I'll just feed the animals and then I'll help with the food."

She grabbed her big overcoat with its peaked hood and shoved her feet into wellingtons whilst feeling for the armholes in her coat. Arms in, she zipped up as she hurried back through the house and out of the front door, turning left to stay under the house eaves. She could hear the water running down the downpipes and into the massive underground storage tanks which could hold 10,000 litres of water and still overflowed by February. Peering through the perspex inspection hatches she could see the water churning and rippling beneath her feet. She passed the ancient willow and danced across the raised and covered path to the barns where the hens clucked amongst the hay bales and Mayberry the sow suckled her newest batch of piglets while Pegasus, their dad, snuffled and grunted in the adjoining sty.

Jemma scooped food from the barrels and dished it out, the hens running with their sideways kicking stride to the centre of the barn. Aldebaran and Cassie, the shire horses waited patiently for her to bring them oats and hay and offered their noses for a pat and stroke before she refilled their water buckets. Jemma loved the feel of the barn, warm with the heat given off by the animals, the hay bales acting like insulation. Uncle Seb, with his quirky mind had altered the roof design to cool it in Summer and retain heat in Winter, but also retain good ventilation. He had shown her how water pipes like the elements in kettles could move water around changing the heat at different levels.

"Wow," thought Jemma, whenever she looked at them. "How did he work all these things out and then find a way to build them?"

She thought her family were lucky to have him, even though

they all had important skills – Mum was brilliant at growing plants for food and medicines, Dad had trained as a vet but then studied natural medicines and all three had been aware of the climate clock ticking and the need to find a place that wouldn't flood but where they could grow all the food they needed and store water against the Summer drought and fire season. As she stroked the two shire horses towering above her, she thought they were all pretty amazing.

She suddenly remembered she was already late doing her chores and, with a final pat to Aldebaran sprinted back to the house as best she could in wellingtons that clomped as she ran. Kicking them off in the stone porch, she hung up her coat, barely wet, on the hooks by the wood-burner and hurried off to help her Mum with the meal.

Mum said it was good always to work as a team with everything because that way everyone learned new skills and could fend for themselves if they needed to. Jemma thought Mum said some odd things sometimes. Like, who was going to have to fend for themselves when they all looked after each other? But then, Mum always looked a long way ahead. Dad said it was Mum who knew most about global warming and had been proved right over and over in what was going to happen next and that was why they were all so well prepared and comfortable here at Shurnock Court. It was Mum who saw that the Arctic icebergs melting and the meltwater evaporating in Summer would change the weather systems so it would rain all Winter and flood so much of the country from the rainfall running into the rivers. This was going to cause much more danger than the sea level rising, she said. It was Mum who worked out that the heat of the sun would evaporate any Summer rainfall so they would have to store all the Winter rainfall underground to survive the Summer, using it to irrigate crops and prevent wildfires burning both the crops and the trees they needed for fuel. Jemma smiled to herself remembering her dad and Uncle Seb digging out the reservoirs and when Mum said, "Dig bigger," they grumbled

and growled and said, "You'd better be right after all this," and Mum had smiled quietly and confidently and said,
 "You'll thank me, one day."

 Jemma had reckoned she was about five then, and now Mum was right.
"What are you smiling about?" Beth asked, handing her a saucepan of potatoes to dish out.
"Oh, just remembering," Jemma said, and suddenly, without warning, she had another memory following on from the first of Uncle Seb dashing off round the house for a pick-axe and then, a lady appearing in strange clothes, incredibly long skirts, almost hiding her shoes. The lady had smiled at her from the corner of the house and then turned away, a black and white cat at her feet, they disappeared, not around the corner, but before they turned the corner.

Jemma's smile slipped. Had that lady been a ghost or was it this Margot coming forward to 2031? Or had someone else used the time change thing? Jemma had smiled back and not been frightened and no one else had seen her because they were looking at the digging. "Come on Jem," Beth said, "Taties will be cold by the time they're on the table if you don't shift on."
Jemma hurriedly tipped potatoes onto plates.
"Mum, did you ever see anyone from the past here?" she asked.
"Ghosts do you mean?" Beth asked.
Jemma hesitated. "I'm not exactly sure," she said as Beth handed her peas to add to the potatoes. "Maybe just, well, someone watching us from their time, or something,"
It was Beth's turn to pause. "I wouldn't say seen exactly, but felt, yes."
 She brushed a stray curl from her forehead in embarrassment. "I thought I passed a man on the stairs once, but as a feeling, not a sight. I think he might have hesitated like he sensed me too. Why do you ask?"

Jemma swallowed. "I saw a lady once when you were all busy digging, and now I'm wondering if it is to do with that note I found. Mum, do you think it's possible to fall back in time?" Beth thought carefully as she served out walnuts and thin slivers of pork."There are hundreds of things in the world that we think are impossible and then find can happen. Just look at electricity and solar panels or genetic modification, so, although I can't think how someone could travel in time, I won't say it couldn't happen." She grinned. "You have to have a brain like your Dad's to be that confident, only believing in what you can see and prove."

"Huh," retorted Jemma, seeing Carl and Uncle Seb entering the room.

 Uncle Seb was rubbing his hands together in anticipation. They climbed onto the bench seats by the table and held out their hands to take their plates, Carl ginger bearded and green eyed, Seb much darker with brown eyes and a straight flopping fringe, both broad shouldered from much physical work with as little use of power as possible. They smiled identical grins born of working in the natural elements and succeeding in the challenges nature sent their way. Jemma slid onto her bench, her Mum beside her and they ate quietly, enjoying and appreciating each mouthful of home-grown food.

As Jemma stood to clear the plates, Carl noticed the time survival kit for the first time.

"What's that?" he said, waving his fork with the last mouthful of potato attached.

"Nothing," Jemma said airily.

"Hmm, definitely looks like a something to me. In fact, lots of somethings all packed together," Carl commented.

Jemma knew he wouldn't give up until she told him, so, blushing a little, she said, "It's a time slip survival kit, in case I accidentally fall back in time."

She turned hurriedly away with her hands full of plates and went to the sink, allowing water heated by the cooker to run onto the washing up and scrubbing fiercely. Her cheeks burned with embarrassment.

"Oh, right. Um. What's in it?" Carl asked, half teasing, half interested in what his daughter considered important.

"I'll show you later," Jemma said, determined not to be laughed at. "After I've cleaned the dishes and you've put everything away."

Seb laughed. "That's put you in your place," he said to Carl levering himself to his feet. "My night off so I'm off to draw plans of my new invention."

He went first to the pipe valve above the cooker and altered the hot air pipes so that the remaining heat from the stove would warm the main hall and the bedrooms – no heat wasted. Carl hurried to tidy the utensils away while Beth took hot water bottles to the bedrooms, also warmed by the stove. As soon as everything was tidied away, they all congregated in the hall, close to the warmth of the wood-burner. Jemma reluctantly took off her kit and Carl poked through it. He smiled crookedly at his daughter.

"This is pretty good," he said. "What about first aid, though? You might want a dressing or two with antiseptic powder, and how about tools? Pliers might be useful, and a folding saw might be better than that knife."

He paused and rolled over on his back, gazing at the ceiling high above, and not at his treasure of a daughter. "Are you frightened you might fall back like that other lady?" he asked. Jemma considered. "A little bit," she admitted, "But also a bit, well, almost hopeful, It would be quite exciting."

Carl rolled onto his stomach and smiled at her.

"It probably won't happen, really," he said. "But if it does, be sure to write us a note to say you are OK."

Jemma smiled and nodded and they said together, "And tuck it behind the skirting board."

They looked into each other's eyes, read the laughter and burst into giggles and guffaws. Nevertheless, Jemma added the dressings to her kit and promised herself she would save her pocket money and buy a folding knife when she could.

18

Jemma wasn't exactly obsessed by her mystery but she watched for intruders from another time and trod carefully, trying to sense openings to another time. Sonya and she surfed the net hunting for references to Margot Bish but found nothing, except for one picture of a climate protest in Birmingham in 2024, which her Mum recognised.

"We were all there, your Dad, Uncle Seb and me, and that lady you are looking at looks a lot like your Margot lady so I'd say she was there, too. Of course, you weren't born then. That was the demo where we suddenly knew the leaders of the world, and particularly the UK weren't going to save us. By the time they would do anything, it would be too late, so we would have to save ourselves. There were three young speakers there who seemed to just know what would happen and told us what we must do......"

Beth paused, looking back in time to that demonstration. "One of those girls looked a lot like my cousin. Quite odd, like I knew her from somewhere else, and how amazing we were so close to your time travel lady without knowing."

Jemma found herself becoming more and more interested in history and devoured history books as if she was starved of information. Uncle Seb, who used to have a permanent small shadow trailing him found he had to ask for her company to help with his engineering and she talked often as they worked of how the Elizabethans or Victorians would manage a similar task. "I think you are going to be a genius like me," he said, giving her a hug. "You just sponge up the information and apply your brain to the hows and whys. You're only eight ..."

"Nearly nine," Jemma interrupted.

Seb nodded seriously and grinned inside, "Nearly nine and you already know how to create a waterwheel to grind corn and a solar panel to make electricity, given the right materials. In case you do go back in time, maybe I'd better show you how to make the right materials and you can then create electricity and completely change history."

Jemma shook her head seriously. "I'm not sure that would be a good thing," she said. "If I did that, the world might get hot

even earlier and I might not even get born."
Uncle Seb rubbed his eyes and eyebrows, hiding his laughter. "I never thought of that," he said.

Chapter 2

Time passed and Jemma grew to nineteen without falling through time. During the Summer, when the solar panels generated more than enough electricity and it was too hot to work outside she spent hours trying to trace the history of her home and the nearby village of Feckenham and slowly the people of the past took on personalities and became real people in her mind.

Just twice, she thought she felt an echo of the past overlying her own time. Once she had seen fighting men, soldiers retreating hastily, full of fear across the yard and over the moat, armour scuffed and worn, some bleeding, others scarred and limping, fear in their gasped breath. She had pulled back from her stride and crouched hidden at the corner of the house, physically gripping the stonework until all was quiet and still and then she found herself unable to cross the yard until she had gone back indoors and convinced herself it was just imagination.

The second time, all she saw was a single man on a midnight black horse who passed her, oblivious of her existence, from behind. The land in front of her shimmered with his passing and the dykes and raised banks of her time disappeared to be replaced by a plank bridge over the moat. She watched the horseman cross the bridge and eventually turn onto The Saltway, a road as ancient as the Romans, and vanish behind the trees. She stepped slowly backwards and the scene faded. There was sweat soaking her shirt to her body and she felt nauseous but it was OK, she had not slipped into his time, only watched it surround her, shimmer and fade away. Shakily, she returned to the house, so pale, Beth ran to support her, sit her down and hold her tight while she told what she'd seen.

The world of her own time was changing fast. Every Summer they survived on the land of Shurnock Court, by careful irrigation, gradually letting loose the water stored in their massive underground tanks from the winter floods. Crops were rotated just like in Victorian times to get the best use of the soil. There was no waste, even the chicken droppings and the ash from the stoves fed the land. Uncle Seb had invented solar panels so tiny you could carry them round and use them to heat water and cook, even attach a laser cutter to cut wood or metal, although that drained the power awfully fast. Jemma had added two to her survival kit which she still carried, part habit, part superstition. He'd also improved the hydro electric plant, creating a reservoir area with ten sluice gates so that they could continue to turn the turbine even when the land around them was flooding.

When she had finished school at 16, Jemma had learned from Uncle Seb how to create turbines and generate electricity from wind and water. He was brilliant at explaining the importance of blade angles and curves and insisted on perfection in making them.
"Every tiny, miniscule mistake reduces the number of watts you can generate. We can't afford any waste," he explained, pointing out a tiny dent not sanded out in the wind foil she was creating.
There were also watermills and windmills used to grind corn and even cut wood.
"Why put all that effort into creating electricity when the raw power will do the job more efficiently?" Uncle Seb had said with a grin as he allowed Jemma to feed another

log through the cutting blades and watched the log basket fill.

It was December and Jemma was putting tinsel, saved from childhood, around the doors and windows of the great hall. A tree already stood sparkling with metallic and wooden ornaments in the corner.

 Unexpectedly, the porch door banged open and Seb staggered in, leaning hard against the door to shut it against the howling wind. He was holding the sleeve of his jacket tight around his arm and blood was seeping through his fingers.
Jemma dropped the tinsel and ran to him, shouting, "Mum, Mum, Seb's bleeding."
He was pale and breathing hard as he stumbled across to a chair. He looked into Jemma's frightened eyes.
"It'll be OK," he reassured her. "Just push with your fingers, here, and hold my arm up high. I couldn't do that outside or I'd have overbalanced in the wind. That's why there's so much blood on my jacket. And don't laugh imagining me falling over in the wind! "
Jemma half laughed, her mouth bending awkwardly at the mixed emotions trying to take control. Seb smiled as she did as she was told, pushing hard on the artery in his arm, to slow the bleeding and give it a chance to clot but still the blood was pumping and throbbing warm and sticky as it ran over her hands.

Beth erupted into the room carrying a first aid case and hurried across to them.
"We might try a tourniquet," Seb said, trying to make light of the gaping gash between elbow and wrist.
Beth dropped the case in her haste to grab a dressing.
"What happened?" she asked as she tore off the wrapper,

23

slapping the dressing on and wrapping the ends round, once, twice before twisting the rest of the strapping to make a cord that could be tightened between the main artery and the slashed skin.

"Number 3 sluice bust just as I was shutting it down and the metal door came flying at me. I put my arm up to stop it taking off my head.....and this is the result."

He grimaced. "Now the water's piling through, flooding the bottom field. I managed to shut the next sluice up so we won't drown, but what a waste of power and water. I think maybe I lost a bit of blood while I was shutting the other sluice, so now I'm feeling a bit light-headed.......I'd better lie down on the floor," he added.

"Oh Seb!" Beth said as he slid floorwards off the chair.

"It'll be OK," Seb repeated. "Keep that tourniquet tight, now."

Beth clenched her teeth and twisted the cord hard. Seb shut his eyes as the room seemed to spin above him, Beth's face swimming in and out of focus. He could feel sweat on his face, but he was determined, he was not going to be sick. It was undignified.

"Jemma," Beth said. "Time me. Ten minutes and then we ease the tourniquet. Go get Carl. He's in the barn and run back. You can do that in ten minutes."

Jemma let go of Seb's arm and sprinted out of the house, headed for the barn along the raised walkway that could float like a pontoon if the area flooded. The wind howled, pushing her sideways and making it difficult to breathe.

Carl was watching the newest batch of piglets as they sucked at their mother's teats, making tiny grunts and squeals as they drank. He turned quickly as Jemma skidded through the doorway and puffed out,

"Dad, Seb needs you....Cut badly."

She swung back through the door and pounded back towards the house, Carl passing her half way, calling urgently as he came into the porch.

"Where are you?"

"In here," Beth shouted and he pushed off the wall to ricochet into the hall. With one look at Seb, he said,

"Get my bag," and was gone again to grab his vet's case with needles and thread and other lifesaving tools from the workshop.

He almost collided with Jemma as he returned. Her watch began to beep, counting down the last ten seconds and Beth eased the pressure bandage. The dressing was red and more blood soaked into the weave as she let the blood flow back into his arm, carrying the oxygen needed to keep the cells alive. It was Carl's turn to issue instructions.

" Bowl of ice, Jem," he said, tersely, as he pulled out a needle and threaded it up.

He turned back to Beth, "Got to take off the dressing to sew him up. That'll break the clots so we need to put on the pressure again, OK?"

"Too soon," she said, "We might lose his arm."

"Better that than his life," Carl said quietly.

Seb didn't open his eyes but, licking his lips, he slurred, "I can hear and speak, you know. Don't I get a say in this?"

"Later, we can discuss things," Carl half laughed, "Right now, it's me making the decisions,'cos I'm the expert."

"Ah, right," Seb said. "Carry on then.... Expert."

Carl glanced at Beth who took a breath and twisted the tourniquet tight again. Jemma reappeared clutching her bowl of ice and Carl took a piece, rubbing it over the dressing to loosen it and cool the skin, forcing the capillaries to contract and reduce the blood supply. Gradually the dressing was cut away and Carl sprayed on

25

an anaesthetic, but without waiting for it to take effect, began to stitch.

"At least the rain and blood has cleaned this," he commented. "Not a chance of infection."

Seb had winced at the needle's first touch but now seemed to be sliding into sleep.

"Keep with us, Seb," Carl said firmly. "No sleeping on the job."

Jemma had quietly set her watch for another ten minutes, but Carl was finished in five. He wrapped a clean dressing on with firm pressure and knelt back on his heels.

"Let go, now," he said, holding another pad ready, "But keep his arm raised."

Beth slowly eased the pressure, involuntarily holding her breath. There was no spurt of blood, but Seb was chalk white, his breath shallow and fast.

"Just keep that arm up. I'm going to make a frame to support it. You did well, Beth, Jem. I think he'll be alright," Carl said.

Beth rubbed a blood stained arm across her face, unable to stop the tears seeping from her eyes as the stress shivered through her body.

"Oh God, Carl. I was so frightened. Why was he so careless?"

She sounded angry but knew it was just a stress release reaction and almost laughed at herself. She turned and hugged Jemma who was also silently crying. "Well done, my love. You were just brilliant."

She stood back, checked Jemma's face, kissed the top of her head and held her tight again, still holding Seb's arm high with her other hand as Carl bustled round, creating a frame, taking Seb's blood pressure and then adding a drip. With his work almost finished, he said, "I think we all need a sugar boost. Cake and honey tea, anybody? You

26

can let go now, Beth."

Beth released her cramped fingers and headed for the kitchen. First, she washed, and then while Carl and Jemma also removed the blood, she heated the kettle and made tea sweetened with honey and cut huge slices of cake, weeping a few tears more as her practical side assessed that Seb wouldn't be eating his ration so it could be shared between the three of them. Sometimes she hated that practical streak. So callous, so unemotional, but in the end, it was what kept them safe, overriding decisions based on emotion not common sense.

They changed their clothes, leaving the stains to soak out in salt water, and ate in the hall, Carl monitoring Seb's pulse and adding an extra log to the fire to keep the room warm overnight.

"Best make Seb a bed here, I think," Carl suggested as they licked up the last crumbs.

Beth nodded and they, all three, went to collect mattress and bedding, Jemma bringing the pillows and blankets rolled into a ball. Seb slept as they rolled him onto the mattress close to the wood burner. There was the faintest hint of colour returning to his face as Beth, Carl and Jemma drank soup and chewed large hunks of bread and butter.

"I forgot to feed the animals," Jemma suddenly remembered, leaping to her feet.

"I'll help you, tonight," Carl said, laying aside his bowl and spoon, "While Beth sorts that delicious pie I can smell burning...."

Beth threw a cushion at him as she hurried to the kitchen and Carl and Jemma put on anoraks and boots to cross the dark yard, just the glow of the dynamo torch to keep

27

them on the raised path. Jemma could hear water from the overflowing moat lapping against the boards.

The animals greeted them with grunts, baas and clucks and the stamping of hooves and tucked in eagerly to the food as it was distributed. Jemma rested her forehead against Aldebaran's nose, gaining strength from the horse's solid steadiness. She raised her arms, caressed the fine coat and gave her a light hug. The horse stood patiently, perhaps sensing Jemma's need for comfort and chewing steadily at a mouth full of hay. Carl gave his daughter's shoulder a squeeze. "I'm proud of you," he said in a rare show of honesty.
Normally, he hid his feelings in teasing remarks, the pride only showing in his quiet eyes. Jemma, now almost as tall as her Dad, reached up and hugged him too. "Will Uncle Seb really be OK?" she asked.
Carl nodded. "Give him a week or two, yes he will. You and Beth saved him, between you."
Jemma expelled her breath in a relieved sigh and they walked carefully back to the house, the wind still trying to push them off the rain soaked board walk, which still, just now, sat solid on the raised dyke protecting the house from the moat, only lifting and floating as gusts of wind sent a flurry of ripples against the boards.

It was bed-time. Carl decided he would sleep in the hall, adding wood to the wood-burner to keep the room warm for Seb during the night. He gathered more blankets and slept on the settee.

Chapter 3

When he opened his eyes in the morning, he found Seb watching him from his mattress. They exchanged smiles. "My God, Seb. Don't ever test us like that again. I thought we were going to lose you.....and we've burned an extra day's ration of wood, keeping you warm overnight."

"Sorry," Seb apologised. "Can I have my arm back now? It's gone all pins and needles."

Carl rolled out of his blankets and checked pulse and blood pressure before removing the drip and untying the frame.

"I'll go fetch some tea and set some breakfast cooking," he said. "I expect the emotional trauma of last night will have Beth and Jemma oversleeping this morning."

Seb looked grim. "The rainfall's the worst it's ever been. I'm not sure the sluices and dams will hold it. Can you go round and shore everything up with timbers? After breakfast, of course."

Carl nodded. " I heard on the radio that Worcester's gone under, except for Fernhill, and Tewkesbury has been washed away completely, poor buggers. Bewdley has water belting through the houses on the High Street and the Upton people are living on the Malvern Hills. What a mess. I still think sometimes I'm dreaming a nightmare and I'll wake up to find it's only 2034 and the government is doing the right thing. I kind of can't believe they just sat there talking and implementing nothing while the country just fell apart."

 Seb sighed. "I know what you mean, but that's what politicians are, Carl. Good talkers. We knew back in 2024 that they hadn't done enough."

He gave a sudden grin. "That's why we're here. Self

sufficient in food and power and my heart aches for all those innocent people drowned or starved but we shouted as loud as we could, offered advice and aid for as many as we could and with luck, enough people will get through on their tiny islands, to restart the world when the population has shrunk enough to stop impacting on the climate and maybe things will get back to some kind of balance. We just have to hang on in there."

Carl put his head on one side and considered his friend, "I think that cut on your arm has turned you into a politician. All talk and no action....."

He hurried off to the kitchen while Seb spluttered for a reply, and found a sleepy eyed Beth adding kindling to the wood stove. He filled the kettle from the gravity fed tap and put it on the hob, then hacked at the loaf of bread making slices to toast. He gave Beth a hug as she stood from the fire door and she turned in his arms to hug him back. The near death of Seb made her say, "I love you, Carl Martins, for all your many faults."

Carl squeezed her tighter and replied, "Yes, well. I love me too, but I love you more. Let's get this breakfast sorted. Seb's awake and hungry."

They worked quietly as a team. Many years of practice making the routine smooth. The routine created a pool of calmness and happiness between them. A strengthening of loving bonds that had stood the test of time, the strain of disease and the disintegration of the world around them.

With apple juice, toast, bacon and eggs assembled, they returned to find Seb sitting up and leaning his head back against the base of an armchair, blankets still across his legs. He gave Beth a welcoming smile and sniffed happily at the breakfast smells.

"Can you manage?" Beth asked, placing a plate on Seb's knees.

He bridled, "Of course I can. You just watch how it's done," he said indignantly.

He picked up his fork and shovelled the egg onto the toast, then added the bacon and folded the toast over, picking it all up with his good arm and taking a bite, chewing carefully so as to enjoy the flavours as they mixed on his tongue. "There's nothing like a near death experience to make breakfast taste a hundred times better," he commented.

"Seb! How can you joke?" Beth cried.

Seb grinned. "I'm still here aren't I ? And the arm will mend."

Beth shook her head and concentrated on cutting up her toast, blotting out her feelings.The door opened and Jemma scuffled in, "Uncle Seb! You're alright!!" she said delightedly and ran to give him a hug from a kneeling position.

Seb reached to steady his mug. "I told you it'd be OK, didn't I?" he said. "Now, I am glad to see you care, but you need to get some breakfast in you because while I'm out of action, you are chief engineer, with Carl as back up and me as advisor. We need to find a way to operate those sluice gates without getting as close as I did, and with the water pressure increasing, they need strengthening. You can work out the stress figures with me and then implement them. Yes?"

Jemma nodded and Beth added, "Your breakfast is keeping hot in the stove. Just got to make your tea."

Jemma hurried off, gulping a little at the increased responsibility she was shouldering. Chief engineer!

The rain was still pelting. Even understanding that the

icebergs had all melted, evaporated into the air and that this rain was the icebergs condensing out as they met the cooler land temperatures it was hard to believe that the rain could just keep falling and falling. It was habit now to don waders and waterproofs and add buoyancy aids and a lifeline when going to check the dykes, pools, sluice gates and reservoirs. Just ten years ago this would have seemed ridiculous, even in the wet winters, but now the water had serious power. Swirling currents and a dyke giving way could easily sweep one of them away. Eventually they would ground somewhere on the marsh but even then there was the danger of getting stuck in the deep, sucking mud and, if not found, dying of hypothermia. Tying on to the various life hooks was another thing that had become a habit after a few close shaves when these new conditions were unexpected and had caught them unawares. Jemma remembered her Dad sitting, concussed, his face a mass of colours as the bruising came out. A dyke had given way beneath him as they had stood gazing out over flooded fields and the rushing water had taken him into the sweeping branches of a willow tree, pounding him against the thick wood as the water eddied and his clothes caught on the twigs so that rescue was almost impossible. Seb had acted quickly, sprinting for a rope, tying himself on and letting the current sweep him into the tree where he could grab Carl, keeping his lolling head clear of the water and shouting to Jemma to use the sluice winch to pull them back to safety. Until then, the self-sufficiency had seemed like a challenging game. There were still shops out there in nearby Redditch, Alcester and Droitwich where you could buy food, although the choices were becoming less and less as other countries either flooded or burned or decided to use their own food to feed their own people.

In the UK, people began to panic as food supplies dwindled and Carl and his family felt safer growing their own food, knowing that fights were now breaking out as town residents started to see their families starving with winter coming to an end and stored food running out. They hadn't, until the water became fierce and wild, considered that they might find themselves in danger. They still thought, somehow, the government would come to its senses, employ experts and create a country that could survive. Instead, even as the towns flooded and people died of waterborne diseases, or hypothermia when their houses were swept away and there was no place left to shelter, or simply drowned as barriers failed and the water came rushing through in an unstoppable torrent, the government still talked of the economy and the need for foreign trade, ignored the pleas for dams around towns and energy systems that were independent of a national grid.

More and more people joined the climate change movements and the anger and desperation exploded into angry riots as the towns, isolated by floods began to starve, waiting for helicopters to land supplies or the water to become navigable so that supplies could be landed by boats.

Now, pockets of the practical and tough survived, creating their own electricity on the higher land away from the rivers. London was almost gone and with it, all confidence in national government. The monetary system ceased to exist as computers failed and bank funds became inaccessible. The survivors created their own system of keeping tabs on who deserved supplies by pulling their weight and who needed help simply through age or sickness. The high land of Birmingham struggled to house refugees from the lower land and provide food for the desperate population but at least their manufacturing strength and engineering knowledge gave them a bartering tool. The growers of food needed new tools that were not power driven and these tools could be used in negotiation for food.

A new type of economy was emerging but, in amongst the team players, swapping one need for another were the new form of marauders and pirates, using small solar powered engines and paddles to drive shallow bottomed boats into the areas where food was grown and stored. Some had even become boat dwellers, surviving completely on food raids.

Feckenham was a peninsular on the edge of the Redditch highland – a long thin ridge with sides too steep to grow crops easily. Seb and Carl quietly created siege weapons hoping they would never have to use them but realising attack was becoming more likely as the land and food supplies dwindled. February would be the worst month.

Gradually, values changed. The pen pushers and money men found their skills useless. Some managed to offer skills in logistics to help the producers work as a team providing a network of what was needed and getting it to the right places. These were the people who could "think outside of the box". But the rich were sneered at as they offered money which they promised would be paid when they could access it. Sportsmen now abandoned their sport and applied their muscles to farming. Of the non producers, the only survivors were doctors, nurses, vets, transport drivers, plumbers and electricians and the like – people who used their hands as well as their brains. Teachers found work passing on skills more than knowledge. Funnily, entertainers who could release stress through comedy or music, also survived but they were still expected to pull their weight in the essential factories and fields between the festivities. Comedy was a luxury enjoyed only when the tasks were done. They came into their own at the times of celebration, Midwinter, as the shortest day passed and plays were read out over the radio in the dark evenings with people sitting in their candle lit homes. Harvest festival was a happy time– the day when the last of the crops were taken in and, tired out, the whole village celebrated together with trestle tables right down the High Street and actors, singers, musicians and comedians occupied the village green, making people laugh long into the night.

There was another feast around Easter as the floodwater finally drained away, leaving the land free to plant food. It was a feast of thanksgiving for those who had survived another Winter. In July and August, as the outside temperatures became unbearable, the actors were paid for their short films, watched by millions sheltering underground from the burning sun with little else to do. Any work would be done outside at dawn and dusk and even during the night, so the day was free to watch films while solar panels produced a glut of energy. Only the fire watchers took short shifts in the sweltering above surface air, sealed in their refrigerated suits and ready to release the underground reservoirs of water to protect the towns and villages if a fire ignited, threatening homes, crops or the carefully separated woodland areas, where the earth below was kept scoured of any dry, dead wood that could so easily ignite.

Seb's ability to invent and understand so many laws of physics kept them comfortable at Shurnock, under the

Summer sun. The underground reservoir tanks around the cellar room absorbed the heat, and the perspex panels allowed shimmering light to dance across the walls, refracted into colours by the moving water. It was restful, calming, perfect for meditation. Beth often sat, cross- legged, hands clasped and back straight, concentrating on her breathing and the well-being of the moment, erasing her anguish over the deaths caused by the politicians' refusal to listen to, and act on, the scientists' advice, even when they were predicting millions of deaths. She sometimes felt selfish, thinking only of herself and her family, but almost ten years ago had almost suffered a meltdown, in Carl's words, "Trying to save the whole world."

She had cried and cried, with Carl holding her tight as islands submerged and whole nations drowned. She had sprinted hard across the fields, climbing desperately away from her emotions to stand on the top of Clee Hill and shout and scream as news of famine in the cities arrived, the infirm and children trampled underfoot in the surge of people trying to grab the last crumbs of food. Slumping onto a rocky outcrop, she had laid her head in her hands and cried herself dry, but eventually raising her head, she had watched the sun set and the moon rise as if in a personal message of hope and returned home only with a determination to survive with as many of the Feckenham villagers as she could help, and here, almost ten years on, the villagers had learned, and working as a team they mostly still lived, dirtier, thinner, but stronger in both muscles and community spirit. Beth had learned to live in the moment, watching her daughter grow and teaching her everything she could about climate change, growing food and survival. Stuffing the knowledge in, almost in a frenzy as soon as Jemma could walk and talk just in case some freak event would separate them.

And so, here was Jemma standing on a dyke, lugging a trolley of timber and metal sheeting, her head filled with figures and diagrams recently calculated with Seb, her Dad following quietly behind, ready to take orders and apply muscle where it was needed.

Jemma parked her trolley and unloaded her tools, quickly taking measurements of the damaged sluice, the water now gone except for a layer of soft, sludgy mud exploding into circles each time a raindrop landed.

"So what do you want me to do?" Carl asked as he arrived beside her. Jemma studied the waterproofed plans carefully before answering, trying to ignore the hammering rain that blurred the figures and made even thinking difficult. Gradually, the plan of action fell into place in her mind and she nodded to herself. "We'll start with the broken sluice and put in the machinery to raise it and lower it and open the fins first, and then put in the sluice gate and join them up. That way, we won't have to deal with so much water pressure while we're working and then we can let some of the upstream water into this sluice pool and ease that pressure while we strengthen the other sluices."

Jemma pointed to the top sheet of metal. "That's the replacement sluice gate," she explained. "Can you reach and fit it in the sliders if I guide it from the other side?"

"I should think so," Carl said, testing the weight.

"We'll do that after we've set up the lifting mechanism, OK?" Jemma said.

Carl nodded. "Sounds good to me," he agreed.

"You take the extra cog wheels up the west side and I'll do the east," Jemma said, handing him the carefully marked machinery and taking her own load.

They worked silently, except for the odd grunt and curse

as holes refused to line up neatly and fastenings dropped from rain soaked gloved hands to hide in the shallow mud at their feet. Jemma was glad to have had such perfectionist mentors. The cogs fitted neatly and father and daughter shared an ecstatic grin as the sluice was dropped into place and raised and lowered using both sets of wheels. They exchanged a high five, the water flicking into their faces from their wet fists, and moved upstream. The water was bending the metal of the next sluice up, threatening to break loose as the gate below had done. Carl was worried, frightened that one of them would be harmed as Seb had been, but he looked to his daughter, trusting her mechanical knowledge.

"What do you think?" he asked.

"We 'd best open just one fin to start," she said, "and ease the pressure a bit. Then, when the sluice gate isn't bending so much against its fixings we can open a lower fin and eventually the sluice itself. Gosh, Dad. No wonder it nearly took Seb out."

She moved forward positively and tried to crank the fin open but the water pressure was so great it wouldn't move. She stood back to think.

 "Shall I try?" Carl asked.

Jemma shook her head. "If I can't shift it, it'll break if we use too much muscle. Let me think a mo."

She cast her eye over the supplies and tools.

 "We only need to reduce the pressure for a couple of seconds," she said. "How about, you use one of the shoring planks to divert the water? Just shove it in across the corner. Mind it doesn't knock you off balance and try not to let it push down against the fin until I've cranked it."

Carl nodded and selected a timber from the trolley. He balanced carefully above the sluice and looked at Jemma.

"Ready?" he asked.

"Ready," she confirmed.

They were so used to working together that they acted almost simultaneously and a split second before the timber tore itself free of Carl's hands, Jemma had the fin open and the water sprayed through. The wood thumped hard against the sluice but its length spread the impact and in fact reduced the bend of the sluice gate as it took some of the immense pressure, spraying water squeezed between the two into a metre high fountain, pushing Carl away from his precarious position.

Twisting, Carl managed to leap back to the bank, landing heavily and slipping but avoiding the gushing water now rushing into the pool below. A little winded, he sat up carefully, grateful for no broken bones.

"OK?" Jemma called across.

Carl gave her a thumbs up, still too winded to speak, and slowly struggled to his feet. Jemma was opening another fin now and the water whirled and swirled, exuberant in its freedom as it began to fill the pool below. Once more, they acted as a team, fitting the extra cogs and adding a second metal plate to reinforce the bending gate. Jemma shut off the water flow as the water returned to a safe level.

Later, this flow would be used to turn the waterwheels and hydro plant. It couldn't be wasted. Now they knew what to do, they worked quickly, strengthening the other gates, only their ebbing strength making the work harder. They missed Seb's cheerful comments and his odd unmusical song as they worked, so important in boosting their morale. The high fives were mechanical, lacking emotion as they finished the second to last sluice. Carl checked his watch. They'd been working four hours without a break. He fished in his jacket and produced an energy bar and a drink squirt for each of them, nudging Jemma's elbow to attract her attention. Jemma hadn't realised how much time had gone by, only knowing she was getting fatigued. She took the snacks gratefully, pulling the release tops off with her teeth, drinking thirstily and nibbling eagerly, feeling the energy flow through her tired body and mind. They worked more easily on the last gate and Jemma gave a leap of victory as they finished, her fist rising high in the air in triumph. Her Dad's teeth shone through his waterproof helmet in a grin and he thumped Jemma proudly on the shoulder and gave her a hug before they walked home, every step taken carefully on the slippery ground.

The warm air of the porch greeted them as they opened the door and took off their wet waders and waterproofs, shaking out the worst of the wet before opening the inner door to the great hall. Beth had been hard at work while they had been out and the hall glittered and glinted with sparkling stars and tinsel. There were scents of apple and rosemary and cherrywood vying with those of soup, cinnamon, red wine, rum and rich fruit sponge. Around the walls, huge candles spread flickers of light and shadow creating a feeling of well-being, an instinct developed over a thousand years ago and handed down from century to century. Seb was wearing a silly hat, his arm now in a sling and an empty glass in his good hand. He waved it at them as, blinking in surprise, they entered the room.

"Happy Mid Winter," he exclaimed.

Jemma looked blank. The emergency work and Seb's injury had made her forget it had been Midwinter's Eve the night before. Normally, they would have celebrated but the trauma had washed the thought from their minds and now Beth and Seb had decided to make up for it. Beth was stirring a warming saucepan of steaming liquid on the wood-burner. Another saucepan stood on the hearth, steaming gently and emanating the aroma of vegetable soup.

"Hurry up and get changed," she said, "Or me and Seb will have drunk all the punch."

Carl chuckled. "What a way to celebrate," he muttered, thinking of their struggles on the dams and dykes. "Give us five minutes. Come on Jem."

They dashed from the room and clattered upstairs, still feeling chilled but eager to change into festive, warm clothes. The waterproofs had kept them dry but in the saturated conditions, it was impossible not to become bathed in cold droplets of sweat and Jemma shivered as she rubbed herself down with a harsh grained towel to get her circulation moving and then dressed quickly in woollen clothes, mostly in festive reds, browns and oranges. Warm colours, to warm the heart and mind. She hurried downstairs again, just beating Carl in the punch queue as he jostled her from behind, trying to reach round her with his glass. Beth slapped his arm away.

"Wait your turn!" she scolded, and he hung his head like a young lad in trouble at school.

Jemma laughed as her glass was filled and she sipped the hot amber liquid, feeling the heat slide to her stomach and a warm glow reach out through her whole body. Mince pies were also warming on the stove and soon they were all sprawled in armchairs, smiling silly grins from the touch of alcohol that none of them were used to on a stomach only partially filled with mince pies. The saucepan of soup had replaced the punch and was making gentle bubbling noises. Dishes warmed on a metal shelf above the stove. Beth pushed herself up from her relaxed sprawl and started to fill the bowls. Carl stepped forward automatically in his traditional role as meal server and took a bowl to Jemma and then Seb, laying a bowl next to Beth's chair and returning for his own then handing round sticks of bread made especially for soup dunking.

Once upon a time, Christmas dinner was a formal kitchen meal with shining cutlery and a table laden with serving dishes of meats, potatoes, vegetables, gravy and cranberry sauce, but as life got harder and food became more difficult to obtain, Christmas had been gradually replaced by a celebration that the shortest day had passed and Spring was on its way. The need to reduce energy use made it more sensible to stay closer to one source of heating and cooking and the Martins' celebration had become an informal affair of sitting round the hearth in comfortable sagging armchairs lit by the flickering flames. Soup dishes were wiped clean with the last of the bread and Jemma headed for the kitchen with Carl looking over his shoulder as he went and commenting,

"Just this once, Seb Fielder, I will cover for you in your duties, but don't expect me to do this next year."

Seb waved a languorous arm. "This is how traditions begin," he suggested hopefully.

Beth laughed. "Not a chance," she said. "I suspect you will be left in charge of the washing up all by yourself, this year, if you aren't careful,"

There were clattering noises from the kitchen and Jemma and Carl returned quickly with hot casserole dishes kept warm in the dying embers of the kitchen stove from breakfast. They ate quietly, enjoying the flavours and smells and restoring the energy burned in the morning's harsh labours. They finished with a glass of Beth's home-made wine, fruity with the mix of elderberry, grape and blackberry. Carl sniffed it carefully, took a sip and rolled it around on his tongue, before swallowing and looking contemplative.

"Definitely an improvement on the wine of 2034," he said in the voice of an expert wine-taster.

Beth threw a cushion at him. "Thanks for nothing," she retorted.

Jemma looked mystified. "What was bad about that?" she asked. "Wasn't it a compliment?"

Seb laughed. "The wine of 2034 either exploded or came out of the bottle as froth and hit the ceiling," he chuckled. "We never really got to the taste bit."

Beth nodded with a smile. "My first attempt at wine making. Well! Everyone has to learn."

Jemma bounced to her feet. "We haven't given out

presents," she said.

She hurried from the room and was soon back with an armful of gifts wrapped in brightly coloured cloth and ribbons. Seb stood carefully, and swayed a bit, putting his good arm out to save his balance. "Still a good strength of alcohol," he muttered with a wide grin and exaggeratedly wobbled out of the door, returning with a sack of bulging items.

 Sighing, Carl cleared the dishes and dumped them in the sink. There would be a grand dishwashing session once more water had been heated. For now, he just gave the pans a quick scrub with rosemary leaves and cold water to stop everything sticking to the surfaces. He too gathered parcels and found Beth doing the same.

Carl still found it a jolt that gifts now were all made by the family. No wrapping paper and cellotape. No plastic toys needing batteries, but gifts of wooden sculptures or new tools, some made by Seb, and now Jemma, on their own lathes. Beth had even tried pottery baked in a kiln with heat provided by the Summer sun. He thought back to his childhood when the list of "I want...." was ridiculously expensive, mainly status symbol toys and games and realised he preferred a celebration where personal effort in the creating replaced the scramble for money. He looked around at his small family group and felt immense happiness swelling from his heart as he watched their pleasure in the small gifts given. It was as if the effort used in creation filled the gift with love.

 This year, for the first time, they did not indulge in silly games, not actually admitting that the injury and hard work of the morning had exhausted them but instead quietly enjoying the flickering patterns created by wood burning and candle light in a room darkened by the

43

persistent rain clouds drowning the world outside.

"Tell us a story, Dad," Jemma suggested.

Carl roused himself from his relaxed position. "What about?" he asked, giving himself time to think.

"From when you were small," Jemma said.

Carl paused, thinking back to times when the whole world had seemed a carefree, happy place. Sure, there were things going on in the adult world that were not so good, but at fourteen, Carl was tasting freedom for the first time. His face crinkled into laughter remembering his first go at hiking and camping with his venture scout patrol. He began the story.

"When I was fourteen, I moved up from scouts to venture scouts and our leader challenged us to try a hiking holiday, carrying our own equipment and cooking our own food. We had to plan where we would go and everything. We thought it was great – real Ray Mears survival stuff. The only difference was, our scout leader was going to go over our plans before we set out to make sure we would actually survive and even was happy to drive us to the start of the trek and pick us up at the end." Carl paused and licked his lips. "How about a drink for the story teller?" he suggested.

Beth smiled and poured everyone more wine, handing round mince pies at the same time. Carl continued.

"We made lists and tried to convince the grown ups to take us to America for the trek, but they said the UK was a better idea, so we settled for Devon. None of us could cook so we wanted to live on baked beans and chocolate and coke. We didn't know why everyone smiled at that until we tried to lift the load. Gee, those tins and bottles were heavy. I couldn't even lift my rucksack off the floor. We agreed we had best take a pot and matches and dehydrated meals instead, and bacon for the first night. We were going to be all macho and sleep under the stars, but the grown ups said take a tent. Dead boring, we thought. We were only going away for a couple of days." He grinned, thinking ahead. "What a useless bunch we were. We had just twenty miles to walk across the moors. Even had a couple of tors marked on the map to keep us right and we still got lost. Dirk fell in a stream with the matches in his pocket so we couldn't light the fire the first night, when we'd only just started out. Luckily, Ken, our patrol leader had some money with him and was pretty fit so he sprinted off back to the place we started and bought some more from the local shop, but then he couldn't find us in the dark coming back and spent about an hour startling the local ponies and sheep calling to us until he eventually heard Matt playing his mouth organ. It was Ken who really knew how to put the tent up, but he'd left that to us while he went for the matches and we didn't put the pegs in right. It looked fine. It just wasn't. So, anyway, we had managed to collect water and lay a fire and with a lot of blowing and re-laying of the twigs we got the fire going and heated the water and cooked our meal in the frying pan. We were very hungry and in the end ate it only half rehydrated while the bacon burnt and stuck to the pan. Matt was the biggest eater and got really annoyed about the bacon. The rest of us thought it was hysterical. Anyway, we rolled into our tent, probably about midnight after all our struggles to cook and Dirk knocked into the poles by mistake and the whole thing fell down on us. Four lumps of heads poked up into the canvas, struggling to find the way out to re-pitch it with Ken telling us how useless we all were and me crying with laughter. He tried to show us how to put the pegs in with a mallet in the dark and hit his thumb instead of the peg which made us all laugh more and so we couldn't hold the torch steady for him to use the mallet and after hitting his thumb a few more times he said if we moved the torch one more time, he'd hit us instead. About two o' clock we got back into the tent and slept and woke in the morning to find it had fallen on top of us again and we'd been so tired we just slept through it. Anyway, we managed breakfast and set out, taking it in turns to use the compass and the map and managed somehow to walk around in a circle and end up back at the camping place, finding our fireplace and a couple of tent pegs we'd missed when we packed up, so I suppose that was lucky. Ken said we couldn't have lunch 'til we got to our intended lunch place so we concentrated harder on our direction, using landmarks more carefully and did get to our lunch spot – one of those trig points so we knew we were right. The wind was really blowing and we used about ten matches starting a fire to boil water, but we felt well chuffed when we had boiled water we'd carried from the stream and laid a fire with sticks we'd collected ourselves. After that, it was easier as we only had to follow the coast, but we'd lost about three hours walking in circles and had to pitch the tent in the dark and find more wood and lay the fire in the dark too, after running about ten miles. Being fourteen year old boys, we all thought it was funny, even not being able to work out which end of the match we had to strike and we had brought chocolate so didn't starve even though we gave up cooking that night, just had a drink and went to sleep. When we arrived at our rendez vous the next day, our scout leader said,

 "What did you learn?" and we all looked at one another and said all together,
"What not to do."
He didn't look too surprised.
 "Well, that will be a help next time you go camping, then," he said."
"And was it?" Seb asked.

Carl took a bite of mince pie and considered.

"I seem to remember Matt left scouts quite soon after that and we never put Dirk in charge of the matches again, so I guess the answer is yes. I mean, the next time I went camping, I practised putting the tent up first and just made different mistakes the next time."

The afternoon had passed and everyone busied themselves with the tasks of farm life in midwinter, feeding the animals and sorting their straw bedding. Seb went for a secretive check on Jemma and Carl's work in the dusk light, carrying his powerful wind up battery torch, while Beth cooked more soup and small pies with jacket potatoes for their evening meal. The candles were well burned down as they ate, drank a final toast to a happy new year and went to bed.

Jemma lay tucked under the warm blankets and quilts and tried to imagine life back when you could drive from one end of England to another and waste time hiking, learning the sort of survival skills they now used on a daily basis. Fancy being fourteen and not knowing how to light a fire. She couldn't believe her capable dad had been so hopeless. She thought of other stories he had told of going to football matches with his Dad and thousands of people all standing and chanting together, the most important thing in life being that their team put the ball in the net more than the other team did. The euphoria of winning, he said, would make him dance and leap in a sea of red scarves on the way home from the match, the voices all raised in jubilant song. It was hard to imagine.

Carl also spent some time lying awake and thinking of the past. Having been raised as a city lad, he hadn't thought much about the world outside of Liverpool until 1998 when suddenly he was old enough to take note of the news and saw people dying in ice storms in Canada, the great Chinese rivers flooding and an incredibly powerful hurricane destroying parts of America. He remembered his Dad arguing with one of his friends as they watched the rivers flood on television, Dad saying it was a one off and his friend telling him this was the hottest year on record and using the new computer they had bought to show him pictures and facts backing up what he said that global warming could change our way of life forever.

Since that hike across Devon, Carl and Ken had spent more time walking the coast around The Wirral, where they lived, watching the sea birds pecking along the tideline, and listening to their calls, enjoying the rush and crash of waves on the shore. Sorting out their feelings. People were starting to ask serious questions about what they were going to do with their lives and they didn't know the answers. The argument between his dad and his friend had been heated and afterwards, his dad had been thoughtful. Dad was good at numbers, a high powered accountant but he didn't just use numbers in his job, applying them to his reasoning in arguments about everything from probabilities of Liverpool winning the football league to solving starvation in third world countries. When Carl came home from his patrol of the coast that evening, he found his dad scribbling notes from his new computer and from that day on, life in the Martin household changed.

Instead of the football, they went to forests and beaches and hills by bicycle and his academic father started to teach him the practicalities of survival, buying hens for eggs and starting to grow his own vegetables and fruit.

Gradually the lawn area reduced until there was just enough grass to support a couple of sheep. He smiled, remembering Bessie the goat who didn't stay long on account of her tendency to eat clothes hung on the washing line. Carl had asked, hopefully for a horse but was told they weren't useful. Only animals that pulled their weight were permitted in the Martin's smallholding. At school, he was teased about "The Good Life" and his friends called his parents Tom and Barbara, but he didn't mind, proud, in fact of his Dad's reasoning and reactions to what he thought the future held.

"Dad," Carl asked. "If we can't have a horse, please can we have a cat. They are good for stopping mice eating the chicken's food, and Joe, at school has some kittens that need a home."

"Good argument," his dad had said. "We'll have a male, though. I'm not going to act as nursemaid to a bunch of kittens within a year."

Carl eagerly called Joe and soon a long furred black kitten joined the team.

"Name?" his dad demanded.

Carl looked at the long fur almost drowning the small body. "Mammoth," he said.

His parents exchanged looks, a mixture of amusement and incomprehension followed by resignment.

"Mammoth, he is," they agreed.

Carl found himself soon in charge of the animals. Milking the ewe, organising shearing, collecting eggs and cleaning and feeding. Mammoth was a friendly and curious kitten that attached himself almost permanently to Carl's heels, only jumping onto hay bales and fence posts to avoid peckings and kickings from the other animals. It changed Carl's thinking on jobs.

He knew he would never make a farmer having to sell

his animals for slaughter, but he found his jumbled hormones would find some kind of order as he patted his sheep and talked to Mammoth, calming the seething whirlpool of confusion, anger and uncertainty that often filled his mind. He came in to the house one day and said," Can I be a vet, Dad?"

His dad looked up from his paper and gave him a considering look. "Your brain is good enough," he commented, "But are you tough enough? You won't always save a life, you know."

That was Dad, straight talking as they came. Carl stood in thought, weighing up lives he might save against those he would not and decided it would be OK. He stood straighter, pushing his shoulders back, "I think so," he said.

His dad nodded, "Best get your head in those books then," he advised. "You'll need top grades."

Carl snuggled deeper into the blankets, feeling a sudden rush of gratitude to his straight talking father and wishing he was still around to thank. "Thanks, Dad," he thought as his eyes closed and he slept, Beth already sleeping beside him.

Chapter 4

It was such a relief having the hydro power as back up. Wind power was all very well but if the wind was too strong or not strong enough, the sails wouldn't work effectively and after a few days, the batteries used to fail. Knowing they could raise a sluice gate and create enough power for the hydro units to recharge and give them eight hours power had changed their lives. Jemma could stay in touch with Sonya and two other old classmates in a zoom meeting so long as the web connection and her friends' electricity lasted each Monday night. The whole family could also listen to local radio two nights a week and check for emergency news each morning. The world news might be bad, with fires raging in the Southern hemisphere and tornados, hurricanes and flooding causing massive destruction in the north but it seemed to be an inbuilt instinct in humans to need to know how people were coping. Knowing that the areas of Redditch and Birmingham were still operating successfully was comforting.

In the middle of January, the snow came, temperatures dropped to minus 15 and the hydro gear was oiled,insulated and covered as the reservoirs froze. On the last days of temperatures above freezing, Seb and Jemma had charged all the batteries to their maximum capacity, draining the water from one pool to another to achieve maximum power, trying to get through the next month and a half to the anticipated thaw in March. The rooms appeared to have shrunk as false walls and multiple layers of curtaining trapped layers of air for insulation, keeping the cold out and the warm in. This was the toughest time of the year with food supplies carefully monitored but dwindling, lights used with care and the continuing darkness and gloom threatening to drag them down into the depths of depression. Jemma, used to the pattern and not remembering anything different, tended to take it in her stride and Seb immersed himself in invention, seeing the harsh cycle of the seasons as a challenge to his ingenuity. Carl cursed more and removed himself to the barn when his mood darkened. It was Beth who struggled most, unable to block the awareness that out there beyond their safe haven, people were dying of starvation, hypothermia and exposure caused by governments who, in the past, knew what they should do but over and over and over passed the buck to the government that would follow theirs, until it was too late to break the spiral leading into climate chaos. Even knowing that her own family had called out again and again and had even worked with the local schools to teach the upcoming generation what to do and how to cope, she felt she could perhaps have done a little bit more and saved just a few more lives. Perhaps she should have joined the more violent, most desperate protestors that stormed the political meetings calling angrily for change, aggressively trying to make people understand the necessity for positive action, and the futility and helplessness reduced her to angry tears or fits of violent rage which had to be expended in physical labour until she was forced to stop, sobbing with exhaustion. Provided she and Carl suffered emotionally at different times, they could support and strengthen each other and so far they had always come through.

Checking the food stores again as January neared its end, Beth reckoned they would have about three week's food left when the thaw came and they could start growing in the greenhouses placed against the southern walls, where the strongest sun would shine first and get the first crops growing. A few seeds were beginning to germinate by the warmth of the stoves but they would need the natural light to develop into a meal worth having. In the cellar's dry room, seed of rice, oats and other grains (developed to grow in wet soil in March as the land dried out, or for sowing for quick growing crops from April to June) waited for their moment to be released into the fields.

"Come on sun," Beth urged, gazing out at the snowy scene from the kitchen windows, the snow still falling from a dark grey sky.

It was almost as if the sun had heard her. The next day dawned overcast, but the snow had stopped, and a pink line appeared on the horizon as the sun climbed above the distant hills. Slowly, the meagre heat burned away the cloud and the brightness of blue sky and white snow was dazzling, blinding to eyes adapted to the blackness of Winter. Like small children, the whole family, donned skis and went out to dance in the snow, creating patterns and words of gratitude in the snow above the ice lakes that covered the fields. They threw snow balls and built a snowman, glad there was no one outside the family to witness their childish glee, and just like children, they returned to the house blowing on fingers that burned and stung as circulation was restored and stamping out the pain in frozen toes, tingling as the blood began to flow. They warmed themselves with mulled wine, drunk in celebration of another winter of darkness coming to its end.

In celebration, with the snow storm ended, and the sun shining brilliantly, but the ground still hard from weeks of low temperatures, the villagers organised a snow party, everyone donning skis or skates and making for the village shop, built on high ground and now cleared of snow. It was like a holiday. So many smiling faces, pinched from cold and hunger but now stretched wide in smiles of relief. They were not alone and the hardest part of the year was behind them. They swapped stories of their winter isolation and offered solutions to unsolved problems. The nearest villagers had brought fire bowls and wood, whilst those with excess stores brought food and they stood close to the flames and shared their food and laughter. Parting was hard, but at least there would now be solar power to help them keep in touch, and until the temperatures rose, the fittest could visit on skis and skates with sledges of supplies or just to socialise again. They hugged and kissed, relishing human touch beyond their closest kin and people joked about wife and husband swapping after a winter of too much proximity. With difficulty, driven eventually by the cold wind, people said goodbye and departed, knowing the importance of return to their homes before the light faded. Jemma and Beth turned and waved furiously as they reached the bend in the track. Seb and Carl were pulling the sledge home, having delivered a supply of excess nuts. Seb's arm was still infuriatingly weak so that Carl reduced his power to match. Seb glared at him, angry at this show of sympathy for his weakness. "What?" Carl said defensively. "I can't help it you aren't pulling straight. If I pull harder, we'll go in circles."

"Damn you, Carl Martin and your practical mind," Seb growled, "Why didn't you fix my arm better with your sewing?"

Carl's face creased in a frown. "Why weren't YOU more careful with the sluice gate?" he yelled back,"Then I wouldn't have had to do any sewing."

54

Beth put her hands over ears in an exaggerated movement.

"I don't like it when my boys quarrel," she said in a singsong voice, and the two men looked away and down at their skis realising it was the anguish of parting from the village support that had set the conflict off but both too proud to apologise.

Jemma quietly took up another rope and started to pull to support Seb's weaker push with his ski pole. She gazed at each man, daring them to comment aggressively and the argument abated so that by the time they were home it was if the ill feeling had fallen off the sledge and slid away downhill.

It was two days later that the trouble came. Three ice-rafts full of men to the fore. Two further rafts at the rear. Only Jemma, returning to the house from the barn saw them coming across the fields in their flat bottomed boats on runners, metalwork gleaming in the sun. She squinted, trying to work out what they were carrying and if they were people she knew. As they drew nearer, she saw they were gaunt. Hollowed cheeks shadowed against skeleton faces and she realised the reflecting light was glinting off weapons. Her lips formed the words Oh God silently and she sprinted to the house.
"Dad! Seb! The marauders are coming."
Thundering feet came from cellar and upper floors as Carl and Seb converged on the porch.
"You know what to do," Carl said. "You and Beth get the horses and get out of here. We'll try to see them off with the siege weapons and if we can't we'll get away on skis. Where's Beth?"
"She might be in the greenhouses," Jemma said hoarsely. "I'll go and look."

"Hurry!" Carl said almost angrily that their getaway plan was not working exactly as it should.

Jemma turned and sprinted round the house in her shin high boots, perfect for work in the areas of slushy mud around the house.

"Mum!" she cried, "Where are you? We have to leave, quickly."

Beth heard the voice but not the words, recognising the urgency but not knowing why. She opened the greenhouse door and called out. "What's the matter?"

Jemma skidded into sight. "It's the boat people. Raiding us, I think. Dad says we've got to get the horses and go."

Beth's eyes widened in alarm. "I need warmer clothes," she said practically, " And we'll need some food. You get the horses out and I'll meet you by the barn."

Beth hurried towards the kitchen door as Jemma sprinted for the barn, passing Seb and Carl setting up something that looked a little like a cannon but with batteries instead of a lighting fuse.

 "Where's Beth?" Carl asked again, seeing Jemma alone.

"She's coming," Jemma tried to reassure him.

Seb called to Carl, "They know what to do. I need you here."

Carl swung back to Seb and they quickly connected circuits.

"OK, fire it," Seb said. "This is a warning shot, right."

Carl pressed a button and a lick of bright light flickered out in the direction of the oncoming men, fierce and hot as flame.

Seb called out. "Don't come any nearer and we won't hurt you. Please tell us what you want and we might be able to help."

The men paused in their advance and heads huddled in discussion. Jemma saw no more as she rounded the house and headed for the barn but she heard a thud and a crackle of high voltage electricity. Focussing her mind on what she must do, she grabbed saddles and threw them onto the backs of Aldebaran and Cassie, trying to control shaking fingers as she fastened the buckles and then grabbed the tack, fitting the leather straps over ears and under chins while the two horses stood quietly, sensing but not understanding her urgency. She clicked her tongue encouragingly and led Aldebaran first out of the barn, tying her loosely and dashing back for Cassie. She could hear the crackle of electricity and the thud of ammunition from the other side of the house as she now held both horses ready.

"Come on, Mum," she said fretfully. "What are you doing?"

There was a yell of triumph from beyond the house and she heard her dad's voice high in frustration.

"For god's sake, Seb. Press the button."

and Seb's voice cried out in return. " I can't dammit. They're children! Look at them," His voice cracked with emotion. "Look at them. I can't shoot children. We'll have to run. Come on. "

Jemma could hear Carl shouting back as their voices receded. "You're too soft you bloody great lemming...."

Beth was still not in sight as three men, long hair and shaggy beards unkempt, appeared running towards her where she stood by the horses. With a gasp and a sob, Jemma leapt onto the mounting block and rolled across Cassie's broad back. The men had seen her and were almost at the bridle. She kicked at Cassie's side in her urgency and pulled her horse's head round to swing around and away from the grasping hands of the leading man. Cassie took a slithering step in the mud, skidding around, her haunches bunching to leap, Jemma felt the reaching hand brush her ankle as the horse took off and in mid stride the land turned from squelching brown mud to dry earth and someone right in front of them leapt sideways with a yell, falling away with his arms across his head. Cassie, once started was a hard horse to stop and Jemma held on as the frightened animal galloped across an icy expanse and over a plank bridge, a drive opening up in front of them that gave direction to Cassie's flight. Jemma concentrated only on balance and forcing her mind to calmness, knowing Cassie would react eventually to her rider's emotions. The drive reached a road of sorts and the horse skidded right and thudded on, eyes rolling in panic. Jemma tried to send messages of restraint and ease through her hands on the reins, and called now in a soothing voice. "It's OK Cassie. Whoa now. Slow down," Still Cassie flew on and Jemma repeated her words until, eventually, the actions and words finally got through and Cassie slowed to a hesitant and shambling walk and then halted.

Chapter 5

It was a long way down from the shire horse's back. Jemma considered what to do. Once down it would be hard to remount. Best to stay up here while she thought. Who had she almost run down in her panicked flight? It hadn't been Dad or Seb or Mum and she didn't see how any of the marauders could have got round in front of her without her seeing them. Whoever it was would not have been happy about it, but if she had hurt them, should she go back to help? She looked uncertainly over her shoulder and around at the trees, bare except for a covering of ice crystals. Perhaps it was best to go to the village and get help. The snow looked quite deep, but powdery. Not ice. Easy enough for Cassie to manage. The only trouble was, she would have to pass the gate to Shurnock Court and be in sight of the person she had nearly trampled. She looked the other way, but except for Sonya, now living on the ridge, she didn't know anyone who could help her in that direction. Biting her lip indecisively she wheeled Cassie around and encouraged her to walk along the snow covered road. Glancing towards Shurnock as she passed, she saw a band of men with horses standing in front of the house apparently arguing amongst themselves. They carried swords and seemed to be wearing some kind of uniform. Luckily no one was looking her way, engrossed as they were in their discussion. There was such a mixture of emotions in Jemma's head that it was hard to sort them out. She felt almost numb from too much conflicting information. She had lost the marauders. That was good, No one was chasing her. That was good too, but what about Mum? Why hadn't she come out of the house and joined her?

And how could she find Dad and Seb if they had been going to get away on skis? Suddenly, she found her teeth were chattering as a suspicion of the reality around her crept into her mind and she realised the dykes and dams of her time were missing. A ramshackle cottage came into view that shouldn't have existed and, peering ahead she realised buildings of her time had vanished. Her hand went automatically to her waist where the survival kit still hung, updated through the last decade as Uncle Seb offered her new items with a smile and a chuckle and she accepted them, in what had become a long standing joke with just an underlying atom of seriousness. "What if I take it off and then I really fall through time?" she had asked herself and superstitiously kept it on.

"I've done it," she thought as Cassie clopped trustfully on beneath her. "I've gone into another time."

She looked around her more carefully, gradually accepting that there would be no one in the village she knew. No one she could ask for help.

"So, what time am I in?" she asked herself.

What would the people of this time think of a girl entering their village on horseback? She glanced down at her clothes. She had been wearing her sheepskin jacket against the cold wind when she went to the barn to muck out, and under that, her close weave hoodie over layers designed to keep out the cold. The sheepskin might be alright in a lot of different times, she supposed, her brain concentrating on practicalities to blot out the rising sense of panic and nausea.

Cassie had reached the top of the hill and set off down the other side so that now, Jemma could see thatched roofs ahead and below her stretching into the distance. There were smells reaching her of pig and manure and smoke overlaying the stench of too many unwashed humans. Her nose wrinkled involuntarily. The unwelcome thoughts were permeating her mind. She really was here, in a time not her own, and like that other lady who left the note, she was going to have to find a way to survive, and a way to return to her own time.

At least I know it is possible," she said to herself. " The newspaper said she got back. Just got to work out how." She reached out and patted Cassie. "At least I'm not completely alone," she said. "At least I've got you to work things out with."

Cassie plodded on in the steadfast way typical of shire horses, not thinking too hard about what is to come, simply happy that the here and now are fine. Jemma found it difficult to not wonder what would happen when she reached the bottom of the hill and came to the turning into the village. She could hear the ring of hammer on metal ahead of her and see another horse tethered to a rail. There were more smells, of metal heated and tempered and she realised she was approaching a smithy. Clenching her jaw to stop the chattering of her teeth, she fought the desire to swing round and return to Shurnock. Some time, she was going to have to meet the villagers. It might as well be now.

The other horse was a bay with a white blaze down its nose. It had spotted Cassie, and raising its head, it let out a whinny of greeting. Cassie harrumphed in reply, and continued with her plod. The other horse pawed the ground a couple of times and shook its head. Jemma reached forward again to reassure Cassie and encourage her to move on. Cassie gave an acknowledging shake of her head. A man had appeared next to the horse and watched them come, his face inscrutable, straight mouthed neither smiling nor frowning, waiting, perhaps, for Jemma to indicate the manner of their meeting. Jemma raised a hand and half saluted a greeting, as if doffing a non existent hat. The man turned his head and called to the smith. Jemma saw the smith dip what might have been a horseshoe in a bucket of sand and come to the boundary of his workplace. His lips puckered to form a silent whistle and Jemma realised they were admiring Cassie. She felt pride fill her at the strength and beauty of her companion. As they came level, the man stepped forward and reached up to the horse's nose, smiling and stroking the well brushed coat. The man spoke admiringly, his eyes questioning, but Jemma couldn't get the hang of the words. She tried a smile and the man smiled back. He spoke again, voice rising in a question. Jemma frowned and shook her head. "I'm sorry," she said. "I don't understand," and almost laughed, thinking how typically English she was, unable to speak the tongue of the native people and hoping they would understand her if she spoke loudly and clearly. The smith still watched with interest. The man turned to him and indicated his horse. The gestures seemed to suggest he was going to leave his horse with the smith while he took Cassie and Jemma somewhere. But where?

The smith nodded and waved him away and the man turned back to Cassie and took hold of one of the reins. He looked over his shoulder up at Jemma and waved towards the village, talking, perhaps explaining what he wanted her to do. Jemma felt she had no choice. How quickly she had made contact. What would happen? Would she find everyone's language incomprehensible or was she being taken to someone she would be able to understand? As the man led her towards the village, she studied his clothes. Her mind seemed to have chosen to shy away from panic and concentrate on the details around her. She felt insulated and shielded from the terror that could quite easily invade her mind if she thought too hard. He wore a sort of close fitting hood of leather, reaching over his ears, and below that, a leather jerkin. His trousers were short and tapered in at the knee with long socks covering his lower legs. She guessed from his slightly stilted walk that he was wearing boots designed for horse riding, a little too narrow in the toes for walking long distances.

They had rounded the corner from the main road into the village high street and Jemma gulped a bit at the familiarity of some of the houses that still stood in her time, with timber dwellings filling some of the gaps that in her time were town houses of a newer age. If only the door would open and someone she knew step out. If only this was a dream that any moment now she would wake from and find the land just beginning to thaw as the days lengthened and the melt water flooded, but she knew, as she smelt the village smells and felt the gentle breeze, this was real. Whatever century she was in, it was not her own. The man, led her to a horse trough beside the village pump on the green, and she saw there was a mounting block there too. The man tied the horse to a rail by the trough and indicated she should dismount. Jemma felt safe on Cassie's back and didn't want to climb down to earth where she would feel exposed in full to the man's gaze. A few people were appearing from the houses around the green to look at her, making her feel vulnerable. Their curiosity wasn't malevolent, but their faces were shuttered., neither friendly nor unfriendly. It was as if they knew that giving away their emotions was something to be wary of. Now, feeling conspicuous on horse back whilst all the villagers were at ground level, she slid off Cassie's back and half hid behind the sturdy legs. She noted that all the women, stood in their doorways, wore long skirts, almost to their ankles. She glanced down at her baggy trousers with their elasticated bottoms, comfortable wear for mucking out the horses and wondered what the villagers were making of her visible legs. If only she had a skirt so that she would blend in more. The man strode over to a small cottage and knocked on the door, pushing it open without waiting for a response and sticking his head in. Jemma could hear his deep voice and a querying higher voice in response. She still stood part hidden, wanting to run, but knowing there was nowhere safe to run to. A lady dressed all in black opened the door wider and stepped out, gazing over to where Jemma stood. She looked, at first shocked, and shaking her head, retreated into her home, but was back in seconds, carrying a cane in one hand and some bunched material in the other. Arriving at Jemma's side, she said in a clear voice, "Clothe yourself, child," and held out the material. Jemma took it, with a mixture of gratitude and embarrassment. It was almost like sacking, but was clearly a wrap around skirt with a tie waist. Hastily, she covered her legs and the lady's sharp blue eyes gazed into Jemma's and she gave a sharp nod of approval.

"Edward wishes to know if you have brought the horse to help with the ploughing," the lady said, her diction less guttural, vowels and consonants soft like French, but the words mostly the English Jemma spoke as a native of Feckenham, learned as protective camouflage rather than the Scouse of her Liverpudlian father or the Oxford accents of her uncle and mother. Unable to think of a better reply, Jemma nodded. The man had understood, but had further questions. He spoke rapidly to the lady, who listened carefully and then tuned back to Jemma. "Edward asks, where are you from and where is your permit?"

Jemma shook her head, unable to answer. Was it best to say Shurnock, or did it belong to someone else so that she would be called a liar. Where else could she say? And what permit did she need? She fumbled hopefully in her sheepskin pockets and found she had a small piece of card left there from the previous Autumn when she had found one of her Mum's old membership cards for an organisation called Organic Gardening Association. She couldn't now remember why she had pocketed it but now she wondered if these people could read or whether its official appearance would be enough. She held it up and the man took it and gazed at it, scratching his head, then thrust it back at her. "I'm living just east of here," Jemma said, waving in the general direction of Shurnock Court. A story was coming into her head, close to the truth. "My family are all gone. Killed maybe," and the possible truth reduced her voice to a sob, her eyes filling with tears as the wall against emotion that had kept her steady crumbled and collapsed, letting her understand that the invaders were after taking Shurnock in her time and would have intended to kill them all so that they could take all the remaining supplies for their starving children and perhaps use the building overnight for shelter and warmth before fleeing back in their boats to the lands that flooded along the Avon, carrying some of the seed that Beth had harvested the year before. If only she could know her family had escaped and found shelter with one of the other Feckenham families. If only her mum had managed to get to Aldebran and fled inland. "I should have fought that man," she thought. "I could have kicked him or hit him with something if only I had thought of it." The tears, now released, ran down her face and she wiped them away with her sleeve, trying to pull herself together. She tried taking a deep breath but remembered

Seb's voice crying out that he couldn't hurt the children. That innate kindness that always shone through, that might have led to his and her dad's death. Inside her, a flame of anger kindled and burned against the unfairness of life. Why should evil and selfishness have victory over such goodness? How dare it? The flame burned stronger and although a part of her shuddered and strained to be able to smash the faces of the marauders and bring everything back to the happiness of the last midwinter celebration, she found a stubbornness growing within to not be extinguished herself. Her breath juddered as she again heaved air in and wiped a sleeve across her eyes once more, but she found the tears had ceased and that the lady was reaching an arm out to steady her while she spoke to Edward. Edward seemed unsure of his ground, scratching his head, looking at Cassie, and Jemma and the lady in turn. The lady seemed to have more of a grasp of things than Edward and eventually Edward shrugged and appeared to be agreeing to something, stepping back from the door and then walking off along the street. The lady gave Jemma a compassionate look and, pointing to herself, said,

"I am Margery. What is your name?"

Clearing her throat and sniffing, Jemma replied, "Jemma,"

Margery smiled and said, "Would you wish to come in and sit a while? Ned has gone to tell the fieldworkers they have a horse but no plough. The law is that unless you have a permit, you must have your own plough, but you have a permit, so all is well, eh?"

Jemma nodded hardly believing that her mum's membership card had done the trick. Perhaps no one had ever actually had to show a permit before so no one knew what one looked like. Perhaps they were so desperate for help that they chose not to question too closely.

"It is unusual for a young lady to be in charge of such a

handsome great horse," Margery said carefully.

Jemma fought to keep her voice steady.

"Bandits came and attacked our home," she said and felt her eyes filling, "My family shouted to me to take the horse and get away..." her throat seemed to fill with a lump, taking her voice away. She swallowed hard, blinking away the tears.

"I did what I was told and when I went back, there was no one there."

Margery reached out and took her in her arms, rocking her like a small child, the fabric against Jemma's face was warm but coarse. Jemma longed to be completely honest with this comforting lady and ask her advice but how could she? She wanted to ask what date, what century she was living in, but was frightened of what might then happen. It was enough that she had made contact and at least for now had someone giving her support and kindness. Jemma pulled back. "Thank you," she said.

A question burned. "Why can I understand you, but not Edward?" she asked, and then immediately wondered if that was a mistake.

Margery smiled. "I once belonged with the high classes of this land. The wife of a son of a catholic family with many lands. But under the queen, his family lost favour and with it, much of their land so when my husband died, I found myself, like you without a home, unless I flung myself on the charity of my brothers-in-law or my grandson. I have too much pride and prefer my own company. So. I teach the small children of the village their numbers and letters and receive a small payment and a roof over my head for my services and as a result speak two forms of English. I assume you must be of yeoman stock, perhaps with some landed background. Yes?"

Jemma nodded slowly, thinking it was a fair description of

her family background. Her brain was beginning to unfreeze from its rabbit instincts and consider what she had to do. With luck, she might be able to earn money hiring Cassie out and ….. could she insist on leading the horse? That might lead to more fieldwork which she was more than capable of. She still needed shelter and more than anything, she needed to get home and find out if her family were alright. That meant she had to go back to Shurnock Court, but what about the men she had nearly mown down? Did they live there? How could she find a way back, a way to keep visiting if they were always there?

While she had been thinking, Margery had led her into the cottage and sat her on a bed covered with woollen blankets. Margery sat on a wooden chair and was slowly weaving a garment, obviously considering the tale of her unexpected guest. Her eyes slid occasionally in Jemma's direction, almost as punctuation to her thoughts.

Jemma looked around her, at the sparse belongings and wooden walls with the thatched roof above. How did she cook in such an inflammable space? Looking more carefully, she saw that the corner of the tiny cottage was made of stones, and a small fireplace with a chimney took up the corner, a cauldron hanging above the dead ashes in the grate. Close by, there was a wooden dish, with a spoon sitting in it and a fiercely sharp knife hung from a hook in the stonework. Nails banged into the wooden walls acted as hooks on which hung a shawl and other garments that Jemma couldn't identify. "No proper windows," thought Jemma. "Just one opening with shutters, No glass." Jemma thought furiously. When was glass first put in windows? She must have read about that somewhere but for now the date eluded her.

68

There was the sound of scuffling footsteps from beyond the door and Margery got to her feet, smiling at Jemma, "Let us see what they have decided to do," she invited. Her smile widened. "You have timed your visit just about right. One of the oxen has recently died and the horse they were going to use has gone lame due to a faulty shoe. The ground is claggy and all attempts to haul the plough so far have failed. It is almost as if you were sent by God, although it may be blasphemous to say so."

Two men now stood at the door. "We've come for the horse," one of them explained, glancing over his shoulder at Cassie who was patiently nibbling the blades of grass showing through the snow on the village green.
Jemma leapt defensively to her feet ready to refuse unless she was allowed to go too but Margery waved a calming hand.
"Tis a big strong horse, Hugh. I think 'tis best if you allow her mistress to order her or you may find the horse running off and you paying for its loss. Reckon Jemma will offer you a fair rate for her labour."
Hugh had removed his hat and was turning it awkwardly between his fingers. "Master said 'tis not a woman's job," he mumbled .
"Nonsense!" Margery replied crisply. "Always, it is the owner of the horse who has its control. I grant you, that is normally a man, but Jemma has the permit and has inherited the horse so this time it is a woman who will lead. Come Jemma," she beckoned Jemma forward. "I will come with you to make sure the law is upheld this first time."
Jemma moved hesitantly from the bed to the door, shy in the presence of the men who couldn't help but stare at this tall, upright woman, in her strange clothes. It was odd

to see a woman in a sheepskin jacket and such baggy leggings under her skirt, but things had changed under the queen and perhaps this was a new fashion. Hugh replaced his hat as Jemma hurried over to Cassie and untied her. She clicked her tongue familiarly and gave her a rub around her strong shoulders. "You have work to do, girl," she said. "Come, now."

Cassie obediently turned and followed Jemma with her shambling gait. Margery had put on her shawl and, using her cane for support, led the way, northwards out of the village. Jemma was struck again by the familiar houses with their wooden beams, but looking more closely she realised the brickwork was missing. Instead, there were the wattle and daub panels of Tudor times. There were a few windows with glass in the biggest houses, tiny panes held together with thick lead and a few using bricks much smaller than the houses of her time. People came to doorways to gaze as Cassie clip clopped over the cobble strewn street, her head level with Jemma's ear, almost as if she wanted to whisper encouragement to her young rider.

Eventually, they swung left into a vast field, where a plough sat amongst the part ploughed ridges and furrows, leaning erratically, half buried. Jemma led Cassie forward, grateful for her waterproof boots with their grip-soles. Grateful, too for that other lady's note which had given her an interest in old styles of farming. Jemma had used a plough with Cassie and Aldebaran pulling, creating drills for Beth to seed, but it had been of Seb's design with a sharp cutting blade and wheels designed to spread the load. After Jemma had read about Tudor and Victorian farming, Seb had shown her how he had started with their designs and then improved them using the workable materials of the

21st century.

The men stood unhelpfully around as she worked out the best way to strap Cassie to the plough which had been altered from being pushed by one man to being pulled by two oxen and then altered again for a horse much smaller than Cassie. "Thanks, Uncle Seb," she murmured, grateful for his alterations to the basic saddle so that hooks on ropes could be extended to various lengths to fit different machinery from carts to ploughs to seed feeders and even a very basic kind of combine harvester. Taking the metal strengthened cords, she fastened them to the almost capsized plough and returned to Cassie's lead rein. Once more she clicked her tongue and walked forward. Cassie, used to the routine, stepped after her and the plough pulled free of the mud and followed them unsteadily. The group of men were standing straighter, impressed by her quiet efficiency and Cassie's strength. Margery was nodding approvingly. Pride showing in her stance.

"I'll need someone to steady the plough," Jemma told her.

Margery looked along the group of men and pointed at Ned, issuing instructions in a brisk voice. He clumped across the field and took the handles, nodding at Jemma who set off across the field, using the trees that marked the boundary line to keep her furrow straight. The sun was high overhead, just a little short of its zenith, about 11 o'clock, Jemma thought.

"Lucky we ate a decent breakfast, hey Cassie," she said, "This might be a long day ahead of us."

There had been years in the past, before Beth had become so expert at growing the best crops for the changing climate and rationing their supplies, when they had gone hungry in March. In some years, lunch had become a luxury meal enjoyed only every other day so she knew that she could cope with hard work and no food, but would she be able to drink? Even though Cassie was doing most of the strenuous work, the lumpy soil with its covering of snow made walking difficult and Jemma could feel sweat forming as she tried to maintain a steady pace.

They reached the edge of the field and swung round to create the next pattern of ridge and furrow. She wondered if they would be expected to cross plough to reduce the clumps. It seemed, through time that the argument raged, Was it best to break up the soil, turning the subsoil over and reducing the tilth, or was it best to just add organic matter and avoid damage to the subsoil structure below? Beth held to the latter view, but Jemma wasn't ready to argue with men who would have been taught by their fathers and grandfathers the best way to work, even if they had been able to understand what she was saying. Normally, her family would not have ploughed snow covered land, but she knew crops had changed over time and perhaps these crops needed below zero temperatures to germinate. Fixing her eyes on the entrance to the field, straight ahead of her, she saw the men were distributing canisters of seed and working down her original drill, while another two men followed them, turning the soil back into the groove with half moon shovels. Another group of men, at the far end of the field, were loading some kind of vegetable into a cart, harvesting and clearing the land she would soon plough.
 "Thank goodness for that," she thought. "We might just finish this field today."
She tucked her head down determinedly and strode on.

The pattern was soothing. Gradually, her mind that had

seemed to freeze all emotion, as she and Cassie had bounded into this time of the past, freed itself. She began to think and plan. In her survival kit were six meals. All she needed was a quiet place with no one watching where she could put water in her cup and gather wood to make a fire. She had the solar batteries. Right now they held almost no power after the long sunless winter, but here, in this time, the sun shone bright and if only she could feel safely hidden she could set them up to charge. She still needed food for Cassie and a place for both of them to shelter. How much would she earn for this day's work and where could she buy food? Was there an inn and how much would a room be? She felt a sense of urgency to get this ploughing done so that she could find the answers to the questions fizzing through her mind, but knew Cassie's pace could not be hurried. The horse's ears flickered as if sensing Jemma's thoughts and Jemma gave her a reassuring stroke, and was filled with a desire to hug her patient companion. Turning automatically as each strip was completed, Jemma realised they had completed half the field as she had thought through her options. As she approached the gate end of the field, one of the men gave a sharp whistle through his teeth and waved towards the gate. The men started heading in that direction and Jemma realised it was time for a break, but what could she eat? Uncertainly, she released Cassie from the plough straps and led her out onto the track, looking for a ditch from which she could drink and perhaps find some grass to snack on. There was a stream running into the adjoining wood. Cassie clomped over and slurped thirstily. Jemma looked doubtfully at the running water with its small puddles of ice. She was awfully thirsty, but was it safe to drink? She remembered her dad saying,"Always boil water or use sterilising capsules before you drink. You never know who or what has been using the water before it reaches you."

She had capsules in her kit but should she save them for later? What if someone saw what she was doing? How could she explain? Cassie had drunk her fill and Jemma now led her back to a patch of long grass to pull at, tying her loosely to a handy branch. One of the men, she thought he might be Hugh, was watching her from the gateway and now he walked forward holding a jug in one hand and a wooden mug in the other. He offered them to her. "Thirsty?" he asked,

Jemma took them gratefully, and as he filled the mug, she hoped he was not carrying any infectious diseases. She sipped cautiously and found it was some kind of cider, spicy with the kick and sting of alcohol and the sweetness of apple. She hoped she wouldn't end up drunk and couldn't help smiling at the thought of ploughing wavering lines while she gradually sobered up through the long afternoon. As she finished the drink, Hugh took her arm and led her to the group of workers. Margery had long gone, seeing the men accept Jemma as a valuable member of the team. Hugh had created a dry space for Jemma to sit and pushed her towards it with a small smile and a crinkling of the eyes. Shyly, she joined the men, some of them eating what looked like pasties, others just drinking and resting. One of the other men, who she thought might be the leader, gave her a welcoming nod and pointed at himself, "Will, " he said. Then he went round the group, pointing,

" Ned, you know already. Then John and Simon, That's another John. We call 'im Jos and Stephen. Then Richard and another Richard, but we call 'im Dicken. And Hugh you already met."

 He paused, swigged from his mug and added,
"You'm good with yon horse."

Jemma flashed him a smile, unsure what to say.

"My dad trained her well," she tried.

Will frowned. "Say again," he replied.

Jemma tried to work out how she should speak differently. The language had a great deal of the country burr of her time, but also an underlying softness of French combined with parts that were guttural, like German. She tried again.

"My dad taught her well."

She pointed at Cassie as she spoke, using body language as best she could and Will smiled sympathetically now but said no more, perhaps sensing Jemma's grief which she did her best to stifle. She knew later, on her own, she would let the tears come but if she let go now she might not be able to stop and there was still half a field to plough.

Will stood smoothly, fit and muscular.

"Time to move on," he instructed and Jemma almost laughed to see the various reactions, from eagerness, through matter of factness to unwillingness from the motley crew.

She went to fetch Cassie who nuzzled her shoulder as they set off back to the plough. One of the Johns followed her and took up station on the plough handles as she attached the straps and clicked Cassie on. She couldn't remember if this was Jos or John, but it didn't matter just now. Her thoughts wandered off on a track of their own. If Mum and Dad and Seb got away, she thought, they'll be wondering where I've gone. They'll have the whole village out looking for me. The conversation, so long ago, about leaving a note behind the skirting board whispered through her mind and tears welled again but she wiped them away angrily and forced her thoughts back to the ploughing. As she reached the wood end of the field, she suddenly became aware of bird song. More birds than she had ever heard before. So many different voices. It filled her with a kind of joy overlaying the inner sadness. As she swung around for the next strip, she could see the fluttering of wings amongst the snow coated branches. They must be looking for food, she thought, her mind filled with delight, or were they nest building? Her mum and dad had told her that once there had been hundreds of species in the Worcestershire countryside and she had seen pictures in books but she had never expected to see and hear them. The volume of noise was amazing and she promised she would give herself time to come back here and watch and listen, just to see if she could identify the birds now extinct in her time. There might be sparrows and robins and starlings. How great if she could actually see and hear an owl or, she hesitated trying to think of the names, or a woodpecker. A picture came to mind of a green bird with red on its head, and then a question mark. Was that right, or was it a red and black and white bird? How frustrating that now she could maybe really see them, she didn't have a book to identify them with. Each time, now, she reached the wood, she let the birdsong lift her spirits and tried to hold the different songs in her head.

The sun was now low in the sky, glinting behind the highest branches of the trees, but she was on the last leg, finally admitting to tiredness and suddenly feeling vulnerable again. Where could she sleep? The village people thought she had a home somewhere east of the village. She would have to head out that way as if she knew where she was going and then make herself some kind of shelter for the night. She was at the end of the field now and led Cassie back to the gateway before releasing her from the plough. John leaned on the shafts, his shoulders slumped forward, fatigued from holding the plough upright as Cassie hauled it along. The seed-men came next, the cannisters now empty, patting her on the shoulder as they passed and while she didn't understand the words,she knew they were pleased with her efforts. The harvesters with the cart had already gone. Finally, came Richard and Dicken, shovels resting on their shoulders, patting each other on the back. They walked back towards the village and waved each other off as they departed for their homes. Will was distributing coins as they left until there was only the two of them left, standing once more by the pump and trough. Jemma worked the pump and Cassie drank as the water flowed, slurping noisily in appreciation. Jemma saw Margery watching from the door, as if to check Jemma was not short changed and it was obvious Will knew he was under observation. He rubbed his chin thoughtfully and then handed Jemma some coins. Margery called out questioningly and he replied gruffly, holding up three fingers. Margery seemed to approve, giving a small nod, and Jemma looked at the three coins in her hand. Her first day, ever, of paid wages. At home, she thought, everyone just worked as a team and no one bothered about money. The payment came in food on the table and a nice soft bed at night with walls and a roof for protection from nature..... and mankind too.

Speaking slowly and as clearly as possible, Will said, "We have another field tomorrow. You can help, yes?" Jemma nodded, relief singing in her mind. Will grinned.

"Meet here an hour after sunrise," he said.

"OK," Jemma replied and watched the incomprehension. She smiled and nodded, thinking. "I've just used American slang and I don't know if America has even been discovered yet."

Will waved and headed off across the green.

Jemma felt stiff and tired but clambered onto the mounting block by the trough and swung onto Cassie's back, turning her to head out of the village, back towards Shurnock Court.

"If only," she thought, "I could turn back through the gates and fall back into 2046, just before the marauders came and warn everyone so we could all escape before they arrive. We'd lose the food but we could have got to the village and been safe until others could help drive the invaders out, or at least get them to agree to live and work alongside us."

It was getting dark now, the hill beyond the village was behind them and blocking the rays of the setting sun. She encouraged Cassie to plod a little faster. They had yet to make a shelter for the night and the temperature was dropping fast. Jemma began to wonder if she should try to get back to her time. Would it be safe? Supposing she went straight back into the invaders' hands? Would they kill her or just chase her away? She had heard they sometimes took hostages but at this time of year there would be no point. There was almost no food left to bargain with and she would just be another mouth to feed. She shivered. How did the time shift work, anyway? Could you manipulate it to choose when you returned to? Clopping down the hill, she decided she would take a chance and enter Shurnock's gates, but should she stay mounted with Cassie's hooves echoing on the hard ground or should she leave Cassie in the road? But then, if she did that, and changed times, Cassie would be left behind. Cassie had maybe saved their lives today. No way could Jemma leave Cassie behind. Besides, if anyone came out at Shurnock, Jemma could get away faster on Cassie than running. She would stay mounted,

Even with the decision made, Jemma hesitated at the junction. The sky was clear above them, the tiniest pink rim showed to the west as the sun set. Stars were pricking into existence as the sky darkened to the east. Jemma took a couple of deep breaths and nudged Cassie with her knees, shaking the reins gently. Feeling a slight cool breeze caress her fingers as they moved slowly forwards. Jemma felt her jaw clenching and her breath came in unsteady huffs of the cooling air. She was shivering again, though not from cold. Adrenalin made her heart pump faster and she could hear the throb of the circulating blood loud in her ears. How stupid. She needed to be able to hear if there was any noise from the house and she was being deafened by her own reverberating pulse. She strained her eyes, peering into the deep shadows and watched Cassie's ears twitching as if she too was listening for danger.

Several metres from the house, she stopped. The moat was still before them but now she must cross the plank bridge. The hollow thud of hooves would wake anyone sleeping in the darkened house.

For minutes that felt like hours, she and Cassie remained still, straining their senses for danger. No light showed, the night was quiet as even the birds settled to sleep. There were no scents, no smells. Jemma took a final deep breath and nudged Cassie forwards. Obediently, the shire stepped out and clomped over the bridge, the noise thunderingly loud in the quiet night. As they reached the other side, Jemma hesitated again, waiting for men to explode out of the door. Nothing happened, except that her teeth began to chatter again uncontrollably with uncertainty and fear. She wanted to swing round and flee, but at the same time, she wanted to step into this place that would one day be her home, and bar the door behind her. It was time to dismount.

Stiffly, she swung her leg clear of the saddle and slid down, feeling for the ground with her toes before releasing her grip on the saddle. Looking around, she saw that there was a barn where their barn would stand, with huge timbered gates. She led Cassie towards it, looking around for anyone disturbed by the clicking hooves, Still no one appeared, but Jemma felt so tense that her muscles seemed to be being stretched on an invisible rack, wanting to freeze her into invisibility. She tugged at one of the doors and heaved it open, peering inside and finding the barn empty except for four bales of hay and wisps of more hay in a manger. There was the smell of horse droppings but no horses. Jemma frowned trying to make sense of these clues but could not put a sensible meaning to them. She led Cassie forward to the manger and added more hay from the bales. Cassie nuzzled her neck in gratitude and started to eat. Jemma removed her saddle and tack, gave her a stroke and apologised for not being able to brush her down. Then she left the barn to go to the house, but, returning to the deep night, she found her legs refused to move to the house. It could easily be full of sleeping men. She had probably frightened them as much as they had frightened her, suddenly appearing right on top of them, but if they thought she was a witch........

No. It was not safe to enter the house. No way would she be able to outrun anyone who chased her, not knowing the lay of the land in this past time, when they might know every inch. She glanced back to the barn and decided she would sleep tonight with Cassie, on a bed made with hay bales. Her stomach rumbled. Yes, she was hungry. She went into the barn, and pulling the door closed, took off her survival pack, pulling out the kit she had designed specifically for this event. Had she got it right? Cup, matches, dehydrated food. Was it safe to light a small fire in the barn? When it was full of bales, no, but with the floor bare of everything except four bales, she would risk it. She even had the heating funnel that allowed water to boil more quickly so the fire would not have to burn for long. She took the cup to the moat and scooped water, returning as quickly as she could without spilling the precious liquid. She laid it on the floor and looked around for wood to burn. There was none, but using her tiny wind up torch, she found the dried remnants of old horse dung and setting up the cup, with the food pack emptied into it, and the water heater, she gathered a handful of hay and the dung and struck a match. The flame caught easily and leapt up, heating the water rapidly. It reminded her of her dad's story of his scout camp. Thank goodness, he had learned the correct way of doing things after that first disastrous attempt and passed the learning onto her. The granules of food swelled and took on the smells of a delicious meal combining with the odd smell of burning manure and hay. Jemma sniffed hungrily, stirring the mixture with her spoon. As it filled the cup, she began to scoop the mixture up, chewing and swallowing eagerly, then dowsing the fire, quickly. The flames had been comforting, a link to the wood-burner fires of her time, but the smell of smoke might alarm someone sleeping in the house. They may even see the glow of light through the wooden barn walls. She drank the last of the juice,pulled a couple of hay bales over to be near Cassie and lay on them, pushing more hay into her survival bag to use as a pillow, and curling up like a baby in a womb, seeking comfort and warmth as she hugged her knees to her chest. For a few seconds, she thought of her family and wondered if they were safe, wondered if they were looking for her, but exhaustion swamping her, she slept.

She woke to the sound of Cassie's hooves as the horse changed her stance. Where was she? What was she doing sleeping in the barn? She lay still for a moment while her brain took in the scene and remembered. There were motes of dust dancing in lines of sunshine penetrating the knots and cracks in the timbered walls. The light was almost horizontal. It must be close to dawn. She eased her legs straight and sat up, rubbing her eyes, itchy with stable dust. She felt empty of emotion. Dazed and disbelieving. How could what had happened, have happened? She thought of her Dad's words in years when harvests had failed and life was tough. "It's no use thinking of what if. Just accept the now and work out what to do with it. Move on."
She gazed at the contents of her survival kit laid out on the floor. She had food and could make safe drinks, Her hand felt for the coins she had earned. She had money to buy more food. The next thing was to find out if her home was a safe haven or occupied. Even before she ate, she must know if she had the place to herself. She stood up and crept to the door, peeping out through a crack, looking for any kind of movement. Nothing.

Pushing the door open, she scuttled across to the corner of the house, trying to stay out of the line of sight of windows and doors. She felt like someone in a detective drama, and almost felt silly. Creeping along the wall, she saw that the window openings were shuttered, and trying to peer through the shutters, there were curtains or drapes on the inside. She paused at the door but was not yet brave enough to try to open it. She thought of banging on it and then running away to watch and see if anyone opened it, but why alert anyone inside to her presence? She carried on round the house and was surprised to find a whole two wings missing. The house had shrunk, or rather, it had not yet grown to its final size. Standing back to look up, she saw that the higgledy piggledy roofline of her time was now just two straight lines. Even the fancy chimneys had vanished "No", she thought again. "What I mean is, they have not yet been built." It was a difficult concept to accept.

The natural world was waking up. She could hear ducks quacking to each other on the moat and the volume of bird song was rising in the nearby trees. Somewhere, not so far away a cock crowed. Worrying that the noise would wake any sleepers, she quickened her pace, rounding the far side of the house and seeing glass in some of the windows. Holding her breath, she peered through the tiny panes, the glass thick, distorting and darkening the inner rooms. There was no one peering out at her. The rooms she could see were empty. Still she hesitated. The men could be upstairs. Well, she would light another fire in the barn, eat, drink and take Cassie back to the village. Maybe she could find a way to ask about Shurnock during the day's work.

She felt easier in her mind with the decision made and the exploring of the house postponed. Her instinct said it was empty but why take a risk when she had no need? She gathered water, and used another match to light another fire. She must set up the solar battery so as not to waste matches. They would be needed when the sun did not shine. Glancing at her watch, she wondered how

83

accurate her agreed meeting time was. An hour after dawn was when? She hadn't looked at her watch as the sun rose. It must be nearly time to leave. Where could she put the solar charger? Dragging over a hay bale, she stood on it and reached high to hang it from the top of the barn door, facing south and not obvious to anyone who had never seen a solar panel before. It even blended nicely with the colour of the wood. Once again, she drank and ate fast. Cassie had already finished her meal and Jemma did not dare let her stand and drink at the moat exposed to watchers from the house. They would use the village trough again. As fast as she could, Jemma saddled up and led Cassie to a tree trunk, polished with the feet of horse-riders using it to mount and dismount through the ages and clambered onto Cassie's broad back. Cassie needed little prompting to trot off and seemed to know they were headed back to the village. It was as if she was keen to pull her weight and look after Jemma, as she had done almost throughout Jemma's life, since at four, Carl had held her in front of him on the saddle as they rode to the village for supplies, the adventure of self sufficiency only just beginning.

Jemma looked about her as they walked, taking in details of the tiny cottage as they passed, and sniffing the smoke of the Smithy forge, just being pumped into life by a small boy, his face blackened by smoke as he grinned at her passing. The horse of yesterday had gone. Was that the horse that had been going to do the ploughing, she wondered. It hadn't Cassie's muscles and powerful build. More a cross-breed between pony and horse, shaggy and broad but without height. It would have been a good puller for its size. Jemma wondered if it was sad or relieved to be not doing the work, and then, in her considerate way, she worried someone was not now

84

earning the money she was taking to feed that horse. She would have to try to find a way to share the work, if she could.

She turned into the High Street and saw Will standing by the trough with two of the men from yesterday. Will raised a hand and gave a shout of greeting. Jemma thought if he had been a modern day foreman, he might have checked his watch to see if she was on time or perhaps a tiny bit late, but he only glanced at the shadows and seemed happy she was there. Jemma let Cassie lead her to the trough and let her drink without dismounting. Another man was approaching, carrying a spade and then a fifth man approached on a rattling cart, the horse of yesterday pulling it, with the cart filled with sacks of seed and more tools. Will walked forward to meet him and wave him on, also indicating to the other men that they should follow the cart. Will then turned back to Cassie and indicated that she should follow him back to the field of yesterday. It seemed they were going to collect the plough and Cassie would pull it to the next field. Jemma climbed down to lead her while there was a mounting block to hand. Riding in the skirt she had been given was a lot more awkward than in her trousers, despite its loose folds. She supposed she should be riding side saddle, but had not got the right type of saddle and anyway didn't know how to do it. They walked briskly, without talking. Fastening the plough and with Will taking the balancing shafts so that it didn't sag and slide around on the muddy, rutted road surface, Jemma led the way back through the village which was gradually coming to life. Girls were lining up with buckets to use the pump and the odd hen pecked for grain in the street. They turned right onto The Saltway and then slewed left into another vast field. The day was a mirror image of the day before.

Jemma listened carefully to the banter at break times as the men ate and drank, sharing the flagon of cider with her as before. Slowly, she found herself able to make out the words and smiled, realising the youngest members were being teased about their clumsiness in sowing seed and one of the youngest, Richard, she thought, was standing up for himself and boasting that even if he didn't throw quite evenly, he was twice as fast as the older men. Stephen, she thought, reacted to the insult, betting that he could easily outrun the younger man and challenging him to a race at the end of the day. "Nay," Will interrupted."If you have that challenge hanging over you, neither of you will work this after noon, trying to save your energy. I'll not have that. You have your race tomorrow, on market day."

The two antagonists glared challengingly at each other. Then Stephen spat into the dust. "Nay, 'tis not worth the effort. I'll show'm this a'rternoon that I'm just as fast wi' the seed'n."

Jemma could remember competitions like that between Seb and Carl with Beth remonstrating that the race was fine but they'd both be disqualified if they didn't sow evenly and in straight lines, and within five minutes claiming they were both disqualified and now could they just get on with the job properly. The happy memory made Jemma smile but with a quake of sadness swelling from her belly. "I must get back," she thought, "I must know they are safe and see them again. I want their arms around me and to see their smiles." She tried to swallow the expanding grief and desperation, stuff her feelings back into a box within her mind.

The older men were pushing themselves back to their feet. The young men leaping up agilely as if to prove themselves equal to those of more experience. Once again, Cassie was led to her yoke and trundled alongside Jemma as she led the way. A flock of birds flew over, wheeled round, circled and came into land on the field and the men waved their arms angrily, chasing the birds away as Jemma realised they were after the new sown seeds. Will called to the men with spades to hurry up and get the seed covered and they picked up speed. It began to rain as they finished for the day. Just a sprinkling, rather than a heavy downpour, somewhere between snow and rain, and the men welcomed it, knowing it would help the seed to burrow in and germinate. Will handed her three more coins as they reached the village.

"Thank ee for thy help," he said. "I reckon you saved us a day's labour with yon horse. Where can I find you if'n we need you again?" Jemma didn't know what to say. How could she explain she had no home? She looked down at the floor, thinking desperately.

"Um, I might be moving around," she said, "With my mother and father gone, I don't know if I might have to go somewhere else. To live with someone else. I like being here but I might not be allowed." It was as close to the truth as she could get. If only she knew more about who owned Shurnock. It seemed odd that the barn had had hay but no horses, and the house had felt deserted. Thinking back to that morning, she realised there was another oddity. No hens, no crops growing, no vegetables planted. Surely there should have been a pig or two. Could she ask Will? Was it safe to ask? She looked into his face, he looked back, sympathy showing in his eyes, but not offering advice or asking questions. Once more she longed to burst out the unbelievable truth and say, "Help me. Please, help me," but she still dare not.

"As soon as I know, I'll come and tell Margery, and she can tell you how to find me," she said instead.

He nodded and turned to follow the rest of the men into

87

the village.

Unable to easily mount Cassie without a mounting block, Jemma set off back along The Saltway towards Shurnock walking, promising herself that she would, this time be brave enough to inspect her home properly. She realised in the full daylight that there were, in fact, two ways to approach Shurnock, just as there had been before the floods in her own time. Here, there was a track that used to lead across the fields, where the moat might also be crossed. The difference was, that now, the track led through a forest of willow and alder, preventing anyone at Shurnock spotting her approach. The trouble was, that Cassie was too big and bulky and would be seen before they reached the moat, never mind the house. Jemma led her as close as she dared and then took her in amongst the trees, tying her to a branch and stroking her nose. "I'll be right back," she promised, "But I have to check the house by myself. OK?"
Cassie harrumphed in apparent agreement and Jemma slipped off through the towering trees, keeping now in the shadow of the giant trunks, spreading long in the setting sun. Once again, she stood still and careful, watching the house for movement, for the sun glinting off metalwork that moved, using her ears and nose to detect any signs of human presence. Still, there was nothing. She moved forwards, trying to breath evenly and keep her heartbeat under control. How oddly the human body acted under stress. She felt small as she approached the house, insignificant against its aeons of history. There were doors on both sides of the house. Facing her were the old doors of pre-Tudor times, accessed through a garden wild with overgrown herbs. On the other side, was the porch and front door that she had approached before. With no signs of life, she approached the old doors and

found one was unlatched and creaking gently on its hinges in the smallest of puffs of wind as they filtered around the house. Jemma found she was holding her breath as she slowly pushed the door wider and knew that if she saw anyone now she would be unable to prevent a shriek expelling itself from her stilled, air filled lungs. The room was empty. Should she call out, ready to run if anyone answered or she heard a sound, or should she creep in, retaining the advantage of surprise if she encountered anyone inside the house? She thought she would call but then found her throat so constricted with fear that she couldn't make a sound. She stepped forwards slowly and eased her way towards the fireplace. There were ashes in it, but putting her hand down, she could feel no heat. Looking around the room, it felt recently abandoned. Chairs were pushed back from an empty table as if left in a hurry. There were no furnishings other than the drapes on the shuttered windows, hanging dirty and dusty with age, but once of bright colours as of woven tapestries. Jemma moved across the room, opened the latched door, her breath hissing between her teeth as the metal latch clanked and the noise reverberated up the spiral stairs. There was no response, no scuffling of feet on the stone stairs. No exclamation of anger. There was another room across the tiny hallway. This was the empty room she had peered into from outside. There was a candle stub lying on the floor and a feather and, was that an ink holder of some sort beside them? There was straw on the floor as if someone might have slept here, but no covers. Jemma retraced her steps and finding her feet reluctant, pulled herself up the spiral stairs. The only room up here was empty, except for two more straw pallets, and one abandoned cloak. Who did it belong to? Would they be coming back for it soon? Jemma walked over to the window and found she was looking out eastward over the moat, when she wanted to be looking north to the road. She felt jumpy up here where if anyone came in downstairs unseen she would be trapped, but she wanted to inspect the cloak more carefully, hoping it would give her some clue as to the date she had returned to. She gathered it up and took it back down stairs, How odd it was to have her bedroom missing from the upstairs space, and no bathroom either. It was disorientating but also unnerving. Almost a feeling that she didn't exist but was some sort of out of time ghost, destined to walk forever in a timeless no man's land. "I'm not going to think of that," she told herself. "One moment at a time, Jemma."

As she reached the bottom of the stairs, she peeped cautiously out of the front door. No one in sight and then checked the back. Still no one. Tucking the cloak in a corner, she slipped out and still looking carefully about her, returned to the woods where Cassie greeted her with a loud neigh. Jemma hurried forward, shushing her urgently. Cassie nuzzled into her shoulder as if relieved she hadn't been forgotten.

 "Come on, then girl. You can have another night in the barn with all that lovely hay to eat,"

She led Cassie over the bridge and unsaddled her in the barn, doing her best to brush her down and massage her muscles with her arms and hands. Cassie leaned into her, enjoying the caress. Eventually, Jemma left her and returned to the house, feeling familiarity as she opened the front door and turned into the hall, wishing she would hear her mother and uncle arguing like children over some insignificant point, but still somehow feeling nearer them by being in the space that one day would be theirs.

She looked at the empty grate and decided she had best collect some wood so she could make a meal and a hot drink before the darkness descended. There had been plenty of dead wood in the trees where Cassie had waited. Jemma hurried out again and realised she had nothing to put the wood in. Sighing she gathered together the biggest armful she could manage, laying the sticks and branches carefully parallel so that they lay in a tight bundle. There was one branch so big she would have to drag it on its own but that would give her a whole night's fuel. She strode back to the house with her bundle and then returned, sprinting, for the branch. The sun was almost gone. As she dragged her prize through the herb garden alongside the hall, she remembered the solar battery hung, still, on the barn door. Her heart lifted as she realised she would be able to use it to cut the branches and could even attach the burner to heat the water more quickly without wasting wood. Leaving the branch outside the door, she hurried around the house and over to the barn, feeling more confident, now, that no one would come with the darkness descending. With no street lights or battery torches, few people would venture out at night, except perhaps for illegal poaching.

In the end, she used her battery burner to light the fire, more for comfort than warmth and sat staring into the flames as she slowly ate her meal, chewing carefully to enjoy every morsel of taste and convince herself that the meal was filling. That was the trouble with survival pack food. It gave all the nutrients but none of the satisfaction of a real food meal. The flames made pictures in orange, red, yellow and black. Faces and animals, flickering one to another so fast that a shape was barely established before the next replaced it but it was absorbing, washing away the tensions and fears of the day. Jemma sipped from her cup, water flavoured by herbs from the garden.

The eating time had been a holiday from planning and thinking, but now she must decide where to sleep. She glanced towards the stairs. No, not up there where she might be trapped. She could sleep here, in the hall where she felt closest to her family. There were doors both sides where she might escape if discovered, but the floor was flagstone, cold and uncomfortable. How she wished for a soft mattress, or even her favourite armchair. The straw bales upstairs were too big to lug around. There was the straw in the other downstairs room, but no way out except through the front door. She found herself dozing, chin sinking to her chest as she sat cross-legged in front of the fire. She hadn't looked at the cloak yet. Rolling lazily onto her knees, she crawled across the room and gathered up the cloak, spreading it wide in front of the light from the fire. It was a heavy weave, red wool inside and black cotton outside. She fingered it consideringly. Expensive? Probably. It was mud splashed, a corner ripped, a tear in the fabric, and was that blood around the gash? She sat back on her ankles and then went to check in the room where she had found the cloak. No blood on the floor or in the straw, but now she was worried again. Even if the owner of the cloak didn't return, what about people who were looking for him? She remembered that time when she had almost stepped into the time of a yard full of wounded soldiers. Had that already happened? Or was it about to happen? Suddenly, she felt herself threatened, overwhelmed by fear. Like a tide of blackness rushing in. Leaping to her feet, she doused the fire, collected her belongings and the cloak and fled to the barn. Cassie looked up, startled by her entrance. Jemma dropped her things by the hay bale and, with eyes gradually acclimatising to the dark, felt her way to Cassie's nose, giving her a clumsy hug, she said, "I've come to sleep with you again. I kind of like your company."

The horse watched her quietly as she spread the cloak over the bale and wriggled under it, once more using her kit bag as a pillow. It was comforting having Cassie there to watch over her. A link to the future and a companion in the past. Jermma slept, once more, exhausted and without dreams.

Chapter 6

She woke again to glinting sunlight and Cassie watching her. Yawning and stretching, she looked at her dwindling food supplies. There didn't seem to be any shops in Feckenham, unless you counted the Smithy. Where did people get food? Surely they didn't all just manage on what they grew. She had earned money, but where could she spend it? She needed to save those survival meals for emergencies if she could. Today she would glean her breakfast. She set out confidently, collecting blades of grass and bark of silver birch, adding a few leaves of mint and dandelion, If only it was autumn instead of the end of winter, she thought, I could collect mushrooms and blackberries. On the way back to the barn, she saw a cherry tree tucked at the back of the yard area, still sleeping its winter sleep but a promise of beauty and fruit in its fat buds, and there, next to it was a grape vine. There were a couple of things to look forward to, she thought. Cherries and grapes. She still felt frighteningly ignorant. Still no idea of the year. Nor even what day it was. There was no work to do today as she had no seeds to plant or even crops to tend and Will had offered nothing in the village. She couldn't actually remember when she had ever had nothing to do. Always there had been the animals to feed, plants to water and things around the house to fix, even before she had finished school. She pushed open the barn door, reattached the solar batteries to charge in the sun and took Cassie out to graze on the long grass within the moat, kicking away the snow with her boots. Looking around she noticed for the first time the apple trees, gnarled, hollowed and ancient in 2046, here they were in their youth, a little tousled and tangled, but showing the fat buds soon to be blossom. They needed a prune, but would have to wait now until there was no frost. Beyond the trees was an area of earth, weedy and bedraggled, with furrows full of snow but showing signs of once being managed on the brown topped ridges. Again, she kicked away the snow and found in fact that there were pea plants sprouting. Sticks lay at rakish angles but the tendrils were clinging on and scrambling upwards as best they could. Jemma knelt and pulled away nettles and vetch, ignoring her stinging fingers in her excitement. Was there anything else in this abandoned plot? Now, with a more positive frame of mind, she saw turnip tops and carrots, and yelled with delight. She would be alright. Her folding knife would work as a trowel for now. She ran to fetch it and dug eagerly, until she had enough for two days of thick vegetable soup. If only there were also potatoes, she thought and looked around hopefully. There was a sort of ridge over there. Digging gently, scooping the soil away she sat back, incredulous. Potatoes. She threw one in the air exuberantly and caught it neatly as it fell. Then, gathered up her treasures and carried them to the house. There, her smile drooped. How could she cook these things without a saucepan? Her cup was ridiculously small. The potato could have been cooked in foil if only foil existed. Could she cook it directly in the ashes of the fire? Could you roast it on the end of a knife. Raw turnip was edible but she had so wanted soup. She kicked the turnip in frustration and watched it fly across the room and bounce off the wall. Wanted to kick the rest all over the room, too but she stopped mid strike. Paused. Thought. Hadn't Will said today was market day? She looked at her watch. Nine thirty. By the time she'd saddled Cassie and reached Feckenham it would be 10 o'clock. With luck, she could buy a saucepan there.

Maybe even find where she could buy oats for Cassie. Once more, she collected everything together, put the cloak back where she had found it and headed for the village.

The green seemed full of carts and people. Cassie's ears flicked in nervous enquiry. She had probably never seen so much activity in her life. Jemma slid down and led her reassuringly, her smile growing wider as she saw copper pans, tools, even eggs, meat, bread, flour, butter and cheese. She clutched her coins, trying to work out what they were worth and what they would buy. Some of the traders were waving items around and calling out prices. Others stood quietly waiting for offers to be made. The pan man was a shouter. Jemma watched carefully and saw that there was a fair amount of negotiating taking place. She sidled nearer and tried to get the hang of a fair price. She was pretty certain her coins were shillings, but what was a pan worth? The pan man caught her eye and waved a pan, too big for what she wanted, "Shilling," he offered. Jemma shook her head because she didn't want that pan, but he misunderstood and offered her a lower price. She couldn't help smiling as she stepped forward and picked up a pan and kettle, repeating the price he had just offered for the one pan. He looked a little taken aback, but shrugged reluctantly and gave her change for her shilling coin. She gave him a dazzling smile and tucked her purchases quickly into Cassie's saddlebags. Exuberantly, she walked on, spending with what felt like wild abandon on oats, cheese, bread, eggs and seed. She even bought a flagon of cider before running out of space to tie things onto Cassie's saddle. She realised that some people were trading from their houses around the green, one a carpenter, another, a tanner, a man and lady selling bread. Her last purchase was a trowel to save her knife blade for serious cutting. She still had three shillings as she set off home. Yes, she thought, home. Maybe I'm in the wrong century, but I'm in the right place.

"We're going to be alright, Cassie," she said. "You and me, together. We'll be OK."

Cassie seemed happy – grass to munch under the sun, water and oats and a warm barn. She would have welcomed a rug and a good grooming session but she was sure Jemma would sort that just as soon as she could. If Jemma was happy, then so was Cassie. Back at Shurnock, Jemma again tied Cassie to a branch and crept cautiously up to the house but it was empty as before and no one seemed to have visited while they were away.

She was soon letting Cassie free to nibble at the fresh grass and settling to eat a real cheese sandwich which tasted fantastic. Happily she chopped her harvested vegetables and made a fire and set the soup to cook during the afternoon while she used her trowel to collect soil from the growing area to make an indoor flower bed to germinate her new seed. She suddenly thought of that other lady fallen back in time and wondered if it was her that had planted the turnips, carrots, potatoes and peas, and then she thought of the note tucked behind the skirting board. Would it be there now? She bounced upright and ran to the house, only pausing as she reached the great hall and wiped her hands nervously on her recently acquired skirt. Kneeling, she tried to peer behind the skirting board, but the crack was too small to focus on. Frustrated, she went to fetch her knife and slipped it into the tiny gap, trying to lever the timber away from the wall. There was a sliver of white paper but as she levered, the paper slipped lower and no matter what she did, it was impossible to reach. If only she could have got hold of it, she could have used the quill pen and the ink to add to the note, but then, she thought, she had seen the note in her own time of the future and knew she had not written on it. With a slight thud of adrenalin, she realised they had also not found a note from her to say she had gone back in time so that meant she had never written one, unless someone else found the note and took it before, she told herself. Anyway, she couldn't write one now because she had no paper and that other note was unreachable, but it was there, telling her it was just as possible to go forward in time as back. All she had to do was work out how it was done. She thought back to all those other moments when times had met or shifted. Was there anything in common? She shook her head, unable to spot a connection. She glanced at the skirting board and wondered if that Margot was here in this time of now or had she already returned to 2020? Was the cloak hers? No, she thought. It's too big. That's the cloak of a tall man. Her brain raced round in circles searching for more clues, more information and at last came up with an idea. The churchyard would have gravestones and on them would be dates. Just look for a new grave and she would know the year. Could she do it now? Yes. It was only 3 o' clock. Cassie was fine where she was. Jemma would walk to the village and take a stroll round the churchyard. She hesitated briefly. Cassie would be in full sight of anyone approaching Shurnock across the front bridge. Would anyone come? She was still bothered by that group of men she had barged through when she first slipped through time. If only she knew who they were and why they had been here. She made a decision, and led Cassie round to the apple tree pasture, giving her a long rope to graze off. Only people rounding the house or looking out of the windows would see her there, and

Jemma didn't intend to be away long.

"Back soon. I'm just going to the village to look at something," she told the horse.

Cassie gave her a brief glance of acknowledgement and bent her head back to the grass.

Jemma set out at a run. That was one great thing about living and working on a farm with almost no machinery. It kept you really fit, she thought. Running to the village in Autumn and Spring had been just something she did so as not to waste any time she might have been able to spend with her friends. It seemed that every second with them was more precious than a trunk full of jewels. Computer meetings were OK but you missed out on the body language and the sense of touch, inter-reacting with a high five or a playful smack at a terrible joke or something. Those brief hugs in welcome or to say goodbye. She shook her head angrily at the ache of loss invading her heart.

 "You're doing fine, Jemma Martins. Just you keep your head in the now," she scolded herself. "Look at the birds, or something."

She ran on, turning her head from side to side, her feet dealing easily with the rutted track,even in the snow, and made herself concentrate on the tiny things. Even this early in the year, there were flowers on the tracksides, and there was a rabbit hopping amongst the colourful blooms. Jemma had probably only seen rabbits for the first eleven years of her life, before the floods got so bad. It had become a thing her mother called her excitedly to watch as it danced across the fields drying slowly to drought when, once it would have been a pest to grumble about as it munched its way through the vegetable patch. There were more birds than she had thought, peering at her from their twiggy camouflage. Blackbirds seemed obvious, and that must be a robin, with its red breast and cheerful song. There was another cheerful songster with a speckled chest, singing from high up in a hazel tree, but she didn't know its name. Looking back, she realised she was only attracted to the brightly coloured birds, kestrels, kingfishers, those woodpeckers and the cuckoo that Mum said sang its name when she looked through the books of birds once common in England. She was running downhill now and slowed to a walk, thinking it less likely to attract attention.

The market traders were packing up. Trestle tables were returned to houses or stacked on the back of carts, with mules or donkeys standing patiently between the shafts. Jemma walked casually across the green and through the arched entrance to the churchyard. She was unprepared for the familiarity of the church. Even more than Shurnock, it stood as it would so many centuries later. There were fewer gravestones in tall grass, and more wild areas but she felt that if she opened the door, the church would be filled with people she knew, celebrating a wedding or perhaps a christening. She knew it could as easily be a death but shied away from the thought. While part of her mind urged her to look, to check, the hard, practical part told her not to be so stupid. At this time of the day, the church would be empty, and that was that. It was much more important to work out what century this was. She walked around the church yard, finding a stone for a John Throckmorton, rather a grand affair, date of death 1580. A much smaller grave nearby showed fresher soil. Mary, it read, died 1601. As she walked, she realised there were clumps of many deaths all at one time, and then a gap. She felt her heart lurch, realising these were probably plague deaths and 1599 seemed a bad year. No one she had seen here had seemed bothered. Thinking of the faces, there were many scarred as if from blistering or marked like chicken pox but hidden beneath the dirt of rarely washed faces, she had thought little of it. Now, she looked around uneasily for rats, those carriers of the fleas that carried plague, and jumped as she saw scurrying brown fur near the small brook that ran along the back edge of the church yard, but then the animal came briefly into view and she saw it was an otter, and stood for a moment transfixed by another animal she had never before seen in real life.

"You're beautiful," she told it quietly.

The otter was only interested in fish and paid her not the slightest bit of attention. Jemma brought her mind back to the question of what year. So, maybe 1601, she thought. Was that Queen Elizabeth or King James? Her attention suddenly focussed on the fact that church attendance was non-negotiable in both of these reigns. She needed to know what day it was. They had worked two days and now this was a market day so none of those days was a Sunday. That made today either Wednesday, Thursday, Friday or Saturday.

Hopefully, she went to look inside the church for any kind of calender or diary or a duty list. Anything. The church was without decoration. Plain glass in the windows, no tapestries. The pews were simple benches. Jemma had rarely been in the church at Feckenham. Sometimes her family had gone for a Christmas service, more as a social meeting than in praise of God. Their view was that any God would be pretty mad at the human race and what they had done to their home planet and it was better to show action rather than words in gratitude of what they had and look after it, much better than sitting in church, but they were happy for others to do what they thought right and never argued religion with their friends and neighbours. However, Jemma connected the services with candles, gold fabrics and greenery and shivered a little at this sparseness.

Despite her background, she slipped onto a bench and let the centuries enfold her. All the people that had sat here and prayed, for love, health, help for others, a happy marriage, an end to suffering. It always seemed to Jemma that the walls of the church absorbed the prayers and emotions and then let them seep back into the atmosphere as the centuries passed. In a way, it was comforting to be part of that river of time. One day, in the future, her parents would sit right where she was sitting now. She knew it because she had sat there with them in a time yet to come. Pulling herself out of her reverie, she looked around for a book, but there was nothing to help her and she left the church, her emotions tumbling one over the other like water over a weir. All she could do, was return here tomorrow and loiter until she was sure it was not Sunday, and then keep doing it until Sunday actually arrived. She wondered for the first time how the villagers who could not read and had no paper to write on kept track of the days. Perhaps it was acceptable to ask those more knowledgeable what day it was after all. Well, if tomorrow turned out not to be Sunday, maybe she would ask Will or Margery then.

With the decision made, she headed home, running again once she was clear of the village and reflecting that it had been good to have a day off. Her first ever proper day's holiday, if you didn't count putting Cassie out to graze and buying shopping as work. It was becoming a fixed routine to sidle through the trees and watch Shurnock carefully from afar. Still there was no sign of occupancy, and Cassie was grazing undisturbed as Jemma came round the house and greeted her.

As Jemma worked through the evening chores, she searched through her mind for what she knew about the 1600's. Before the gunpowder plot, but after the discovery of America. Somewhere just down the road, Shakespeare was writing plays, and the Throckmorton family were fighting amongst themselves about the rights and wrongs of catholic versus protestant. She frowned. Had Mary Queen of Scots been executed yet? Jemma wasn't sure. If Elizabeth died in 1601 (That sounded right, or was it 1603), then probably Mary was already dead. Anyway, whether it was James or Elizabeth, Jemma reckoned it was best to announce she was a Church of England supporter if asked. Even if she was asked by Catholics, they weren't likely to announce the fact to her, and would likely just leave her alone, unless, they saw her as a threat to any plots they were planning. Returning to thoughts of the men she had almost run down, she wondered if they were plotters. In that briefest of times, she had had an impression of furtiveness. They had been shocked by discovery as much as the suddenness of her appearance, and had appeared to be fleeing in all directions as she'd burst through their midst.
Perhaps that was why they had disappeared in such a hurry, leaving the cloak behind, because they thought they had been found out. Would they return when there was no further retaliation? Jemma rubbed a hand over her face, feeling overstrung with the uncertainty of her position. She would have loved to make a bed of straw upstairs and sleep undisturbed there, but she knew she would be woken by even the tiniest creakings of the timbers and could never sleep the night through in the house. Sighing, she went to join Cassie for another night in the barn.

Even as she approached the High Street the next morning, she knew it had to be Sunday. The smithy was quiet and people walked sedately and without exuberance in clothes brushed down and cleaned of muck. Close to the church, carriages were stationed and ladies and gents stood talking politely in garments richer than anything Jemma had seen the villagers wearing, but still the colours were subdued. Groups of villagers hovered beyond the churchyard wall and Jemma saw Margery talking to a tall lad with a family resemblance. Too shy to join any of the other groups, Jemma walked slowly towards the pair. Margery looked up, saw her and beckoned.

"This is my grandson, John," Margery introduced him. "John, this is Jemma, who has the horse I was telling you of."

John gave her a sweeping bow, part mocking, part hiding his own shyness.

"John Throckmorton, at your service," he announced. Jemma had no idea how to respond other than to offer a quiet smile and her thanks and was quite relieved to see that a clergyman in black and white, looking rather like a magpie was ushering the aristocrats into the church. The villagers filed in behind. Jemma was shocked to find that the richer classes were seated on the pews in an obvious show of superiority. The most powerful at the very front and Margery and John in the furthest back of the pews. It seemed the rest of the village were expected to stand, when they were not kneeling in prayer.

The vicar was a short, dark haired man who mumbled his way through the service with minimal eye contact and no attempt to generate enthusiasm in his congregation. Jemma supposed it was unnecessary in a society where high fines were issued to non church goers. Even worse, they could be imprisoned . No wonder the church was filled to capacity. The final prayer before the Lord's Prayer gave Jemma the clue she needed as the vicar intoned a request for God to give our queen good health and longevity. "Elizabeth," she said to herself. "It must be Elizabeth."

Slipping out with the village groups, Jemma quickly escaped back to The Saltway, not wanting any of the carriage travellers to notice her and ask questions. She was sure that already, questions would be flying from villager to villager about the girl with the horse. As she marched briskly down the hill, she heard one of the carriages rattling along the track from behind her. Maybe she should have stayed hidden until the carriages were gone, but it was too late to do anything different and the track was in a gully, the banks too steep to climb. She would just put her head down and try to be as unnoticeable as possible. She need not have worried. The carriage rattled past without slowing, a pale face showing briefly at the window, and then it was gone. She walked on, her mind on the pew dwellers. Some must live in the biggest two houses in the village, but there had been three carriages. Looking back, as she reached the top of the hill, she could see one heading west, away from her along The Saltway, the main road to Droitwich, but with turnings off to many tiny villages, like Norwood, Bradley Green, Hanbury and Himbleton. Hanbury had its own church, so those people at Feckenham's church most likely lived south of the main road. She wondered where the carriage was going that had passed her. Cookhill, or Edgiock? Not Coughton. They had their own church, she thought. She turned automatically onto the track for Shurnock, deciding that, although the sabbath was supposed to be a day of rest, she must try to give Cassie a good rub down. She wished she had been able to buy a brush at the market, but hadn't seen anyone selling them. No matter how hard she thought, she couldn't think how she could make one, needing bristles from a pig or something similar.

She ate, first, enjoying again the luxury of cheese and bread and promising herself an egg for her evening meal. Then she stuffed hay into the cloak, winding it tight and used the twisted corners to create a strap to put her hand in. Cassie got a good polishing, rather than a brushing but seemed to enjoy it and her coat shone glossily in the afternoon sun. Jemma even teased the mud out of the tussocks of hair on Cassie's fetlocks before standing back to admire her friend.
"Good enough for a show, hey, Cassie." she said.

It was odd having nothing to do. No one to converse with, not even a book to read. She sat for a while, watching Cassie munch the grass, thinking vague thoughts about things she knew of Elizabeth I. Church services in English, and Protestant. Witches being burned or hung. Lord Cecil leading the government and all those people vying for favour, like Walter Raleigh and the Earl of Essex. Loads of them getting it wrong and being locked up in the Tower of London, or even executed. Better to be a simple peasant, and keep her head down. It was odd to think that Shakespeare's mum and dad, and maybe his wife were living just ten miles or so away in Stratford. She was tempted to saddle Cassie and go to explore Alcester and Stratford, but then thought that maybe on the Sabbath horse-riding might be against the law. It was better to stay here, at Shurnock, out of sight. It was not really warm enough to just sit out here, even with her many layers of cold resistant clothing and the intermittent blasts of sunshine. She decided to have another search of the house for any clues to the identity of those men, or even anyone else that had lived in the house. Even anything that Margot might have left behind as a clue to how to travel in time. She began in the room with glass windows, pushing the straw around and trying to look behind more of the skirting board panels. Nothing. She started thinking about priest holes. After all, Warwickshire and Worcestershire were the home of the Throckmorton family, who were mostly Catholic and famous for hiding priests. Trouble was, there was no panelling to hide things behind. Like in the films she had seen before they gave up the television, she hopefully tapped at the walls enclosing the spiral staircase. Well, yes, they were hollow, but there didn't seem to be a way to get in. She wandered back into the main hall, and tried again to retrieve that paper, but it eluded her, the wood stiff and resistant to leverage. She crawled into the fireplace and stood, looking up the chimney to the tiny speck of light high above her, but decided not to feel the walls because she would end up covered in soot, and surely, anything hidden here would just burn and be destroyed. She ducked back into the room and looked at the drapes. They were no good as a hiding place because anyone wanting to open the shutters would have to also open the drapes.

It suddenly occurred to her that she hadn't checked the cellar. Glancing out of the door and into the herb garden, she could see steps leading down to a thick oak door, just as they did centuries later, although Carl and Seb had added an inner staircase, too, which they used more often. She meandered through the herb garden, and leapt from top to bottom step in one giant jump, hearing in her head, Beth's voice urging her to be careful. The door opened easily, not even a creak and she peered in. There were cobwebs and long shadows. Jemma automatically felt for the light switch and then laughed at herself. "No electricity, dumbo," she said and returned for her torch, winding the dynamo and being grateful it didn't need shop bought batteries. She shone it around from the door and saw barrels and a wooden box. Lifting the lids of the barrels, she found, to her surprise there were nuts and apples and flour and cider. Someone had intended living here recently, so where were they? She couldn't help returning to the steps up to ground level and peeping out, just to check no one was in sight. All was still. She returned to her exploration. The box was square about 30 centimetres long, and 30 centimetres high and held shut with a tiny metal hook through a loop of leather. Jemma eased the hook open and gently lifted the lid. There were rolls of paper inside. A thrill of excitement rushed through her body. Whatever this was, it must be of some use to her but it was too dark in the cellar to read the papers here. Shutting the box and reattaching the hook, she carefully lifted the box and carried it to the house. She put the box on the door step and went to fetch the cloak to sit on. This was the place with most light, but the step would still be cold. Opening the box again, she lifted the first roll that came to hand. How brittle would it be? How long had it been in the cellar waiting for discovery? It was difficult to unroll, still flexible but wanting to curl up as soon as she let go of a corner. She hurried to collect stones from the garden and place them on the corners, laying it out on the ground. The writing was strong and elegant and incredibly difficult for Jemma to read. It seemed that some Tudor letters had changed their sound or appearance over time with F and S looking the same to her and so many extra curls and flourishes, and blots, too. It seemed to be a diary, or was it a letter? There was a date at the top of the page, 26th March 1565. Jemma's eyes ran over the text, uncomprehendingly, trying to pick out words she could understand so that she could figure out the letters. She was only used to proper typing. No one hand wrote anything any more, except her mum with her seed labels. Even in school, most children typed, having simply changed from computer keyboards back to manual typewriters when mains electricity failed. Seb wrote on his diagrams, but more numbers than letters so that hardly counted, and Jemma had seen her dad's notes from University, totally illegible in a hurried scrawl and almost in code, he said because the lecturers always spoke too fast to write full words neatly. It seemed everything reminded her of her family and made her head hot with caged emotions fighting to burst out and drown her in tears. She shook her head angrily. Falling to pieces was not going to help. She put her head down to the writing. There were occasional capital letters so were those names? Starting with an N, ending with an f or an s. Couldn't be an f. Might be Nicholas, she thought. Then, taking those letters, she started to track back through the writing, marking the matching letters. Here was another name. Could be Marco. Her eyes ached with the effort to decipher, but gradually, she began to make out words. Something about keeping the garden for Marco, in case he returned and Nicholas saying he was a demon he had seen vanish right in front of the villagers who, led by the clergymen from Worcester, had come to drive him out. "But I am sure he is of good heart and not a demon," Jemma read, her finger tracing each letter of the words. "I wish that I could have gone with him to his other time." Jemma gasped. Keeping her finger on the words, she paused, looking into space. Was this another time traveller? How many people were there wandering around in a time not their own?

"N says I should stay away from here, but here I find peace amongst the vegetables he planted and away from the religious squabblings and plottings of my kin. If only we could live in peace."

The writing finished and Jemma allowed the paper to roll closed. It was getting dark again and Jemma cursed the short days of January, and then wondered if it was actually now February. She realised. now she wasn't concentrating that she was extremely cold and also that Cassie was still out, eating the grass. She jumped up and sprinted around the house, apologising to the horse as she led her back into the barn. She felt guilty about not having a rug for Cassie's back. The night was cold. The best she could do was to give Cassie the cloak and sleep in the house herself with the fire to warm her. No one was going to come in the night, especially on the Sabbath. She sorted oats and water, added the cloak and gave Cassie a hug goodnight before running to the house and using the solar power to light the fire, so much quicker than matches. In no time, she had soup cooked and knelt in front of the flames, warming herself from both inside and out. She looked wistfully at the box sitting just inside the door but knew it was impossible to read any more by torch, candle or fire flame. Hoping the straw was insect free, she pushed it together, curled into a ball and eased into dreams of trying to decipher codes to save the world or even buy an ice cream and woke, tired and confused, not sure where she was with the distorted gloom of a cloudy day filtering through the thick glass of the other room. She felt stiff and unwell and desperately wanted to curl up in a proper bed with sheets and blankets on a soft mattress with a proper pillow, and hear grown up voices talking calmly from another room. She had never been alone before, isolated and without support.

"I do have Cassie," she thought and went quickly to the stable to talk to her horse. Cassie was a good listener.

"It's Monday, today," Jemma said. "What do you think I should do?"

Cassie made no comment, encouraging Jemma to make her own decisions.

"I was thinking, maybe I should go to Alcester and see if I can buy you a rug and a brush, or do you think I should save the money for food? I mean, I don't know how often I can get work with you, at least until the snow is properly gone, and I haven't even got hens to lay eggs."

Cassie took some hay from her manger and chewed thoughtfully.

"Perhaps we should go and check things out and make a decision about buying stuff when we get there?" Cassie, listening to the tone of voice, sensed a decision had been made and seemed to give her approval.

"OK," said Jemma. "I'll just make myself some breakfast and then we'll go."

Chapter 7

The track was empty. No one walking. No one on horseback. It was still cold and Jemma was glad of the gloves she wore when mucking out to keep her hands warm. What luck she had been wearing them. With the sheepskin jacket, skirt over trousers and her hood up, only her nose and cheeks felt cold, but Cassie's breath steamed with every breath and there was occasional ice beneath the top layer of snow. The land, going east, had hardly changed. Perhaps a few more trees and a few less hedges, but it felt so odd to know that although the landscape was the same, the people were all different. She kept having stray thoughts about going to visit Sonya, or asking Seb to invent a hook to make it easier to cook on the fireplace using the saucepan. She realised, now that she should have bought a cauldron that could be hung rather than a pan that needed a flat base so she was having to wedge it in amongst the flames and build the fire around it.

There were men working in one of the fields and sheep baaing in another as she passed. No one paid her any attention and she wondered if she and Cassie were invisible or whether it was just safer not to pay attention to other people. Cassie's gait always appeared slow but the strides were deceptively long and soon they were climbing the ridge, south of Astwood Bank. The road gradually bent south east and became busier with more carts led by donkeys and mules and then, people on foot. How great it is, thought Jemma, not to have to keep looking out for fast cars and vans and places to pull in, in case one came whizzing around a corner. Of course, most people in the 2040's travelled on foot, or by horse, the roads too rutted for bicycles, but still some things were delivered or collected by cars and vans and with the roads empty of competition, speed limits seemed no longer to apply. One had to listen all the time for an approaching motor, but now there were only other horses and carts to avoid and

Jemma found she was almost the fastest traveller, dodging the heavily laden carts.

Alcester was a metropolis. There were real shops with glass windows. Not the huge expanse of supermarket plate glass, but real windows letting in light through the tiny panels and produce laid out with the happy knowledge that it would stay dry and be secure from snatch thieves who would have taken their chance with barrows once left in the street. Jemma found herself floating in that unreality where the two sets of time ran in parallel. The High Street looked almost the same with its wide market area and black and white frontages. The only difference was the clop of horse hooves and rattle of cart wheels replacing the hum and buzz of car engines, mostly electric, with the odd occasional roar of an antique petrol or diesel model, out for a spin using carefully rationed and dwindling supplies of the ancient fuel.

 Most people seemed to be tying their horses to rails and leaving them in the care of small boys. Jemma, afraid of losing Cassie and not knowing who she could trust, dismounted and led Cassie along the single street of shops, wishing she could use a padlock as she would have done with a bicycle. She was very aware of eyes watching and admiring Cassie, the odd frown suggesting suspicion of her female owner. The shops seemed to be selling mostly food and clothes. Just one, right past the church, and tucked up a side street looked like a hardware shop with planks of timber and nails, mallets, axes and saws. No one seemed to have prices written up. There were fewer people here in the side street. Jemma decided to hobble Cassie and keep a sharp eye out for would be horse snatchers as she entered the shop, leaving the door open for a better view. There was just the one shopkeeper, who inspected her carefully and raised his eyebrows when she asked for a sweat blanket. He shrugged, not understanding, so Jemma asked about brushes instead. He still looked bewildered, so she led him outside and made brushing movements along Cassie's coat. He smiled and nodded vigorously, now leading her back into the shop and pointing to exactly what she required. "How much?" she asked, holding up one of the coins she had as change from the market day, and not having any idea what it represented. The shop keeper first paled and then flushed and he shook his head emphatically. Jemma shrugged and jingled the coins she held.

"How many?"

He put his head on one side, considering and then made her an offer, poking around at the coins she held. Jemma felt she was getting the hang of this bartering and shook her head in turn, closing her fist on the coins. The man shrugged in turn and made another offer which Jemma agreed to, taking the brush from him and proffering one of the shillings for change. She led him back to Cassie and demonstrated a rug but he shook his head and pointed back up the High Street and then poked his fingers to the left. Somewhere up there, then, was a seller of horse rugs. Jemma found there were two more turnings leading to back street shops and one sold all manner of horse equipment. This had to be a shop for aristocracy with carefully written labels on products. Jemma bought more oats and a sack type blanket and found there was very little money remaining. One more week of food at the most. If only she had her own animals she would be fine but how much would hens, pigs and sheep, a cow or a goat cost? Lots more than the money she now held.

Tomorrow she would have to tell Margery she was living at Shurnock Court and Margery would tell Will and perhaps soon after that she would be driven out of the village as an imposter or a wanderer. It all depended on who knew what about who owned what and how quickly information spread around the area, but Jemma had to find work or pretty soon she would starve and Will was the only contact she had. Was there a way of saying Will could leave messages at Shurnock, without her saying she was living there? Jemma frowned. She would

have to keep working on that. As she reached the end of Alcester's main street, heading home, she inhaled the smell of baking pies and bread and her mouth watered. It was lunch time and there was the baker's shop wafting glorious scents in her direction. With almost no hesitation she blew another penny on a hot pie and two bread rolls and ate the pie one handed as she led Cassie out of town. It was wonderful to eat proper baked hot food. Poor Cassie had to make do with an apple from the barrels in the cellar. Jemma found a mounting block outside an inn and scrambled back into Cassie's saddle, reflecting that her Mum would be furious at her riding so much without a helmet, but they just didn't exist and in the rush of escape, she hadn't had a chance to grab her own. She would just have to be more careful and more alert, she thought, and after all, in fifteen years, Cassie had never thrown her. They would be OK. Despite promising herself she would be alert, she found her mind kept going off at angles on the ride home, thinking about ways to hide where she was staying, trying to make sense of the letters or diary she was reading. Who had written it? Who was Nicholas? And where did Marco fit in, and suddenly she realised how close Marco and Margot were in sound. In this age where very little was written, a mistake in name was easy. Whoever wrote the diary had known Margot in the past. If only Jemma could find them, they knew about the time travel. If only they had worked out how it happened. Jemma spent some time thinking about Nicholas and the churchmen. If they had wanted to drive Margot out as a demon, what would they try to do with Jemma if they discovered her? She swallowed fearfully. "I need to get home, " she thought. "I'm not cut out for adventuring."
Even without believing in a god, she found herself looking up at the grey sky and praying.
"Please let me go home. I just want to be back safe with my mum and my dad and Uncle Seb. Please."

Her eyes flicked back to the track ahead and found it blurring with tears, which ran, hot down her cheeks, and dripped onto the sheepskin. She let them flow, shoulders slumped, wanting to just give up, wanting all of this to be over one way or another. She felt.....broken and... and unmendable.

She saw that Cassie's head had dropped, sensing her despair and perhaps feeling helpless. She reached out and patted her mane.
"Sorry Cassie. Just give me a moment and I'll be OK. It's just that I have to let the hurting out, and all the fear and everything and then I can be strong again. It's just that I'm very frightened and not used to being in charge and I don't think nineteen year olds are supposed to be able to deal with this kind of thing. Leastways, I haven't been taught how to deal with it, and I don't think I'm quite tough enough and I so want to be able to ask someone to help but there isn't anyone, except you."
Talking to Cassie was helping. Jemma gave her another pat and continued. "I was thinking maybe I could ask Margery for advice, if I can think how to say it without mentioning travelling in time. What do you think?"
Cassie shook her head emphatically, but that might have been simply because, while Jemma had been deep in thought, the rain had begun, and now it was pouring down, melting the snow underfoot and turning the track to a quagmire. Cassie was suddenly slipping in mud and Jemma took a tighter grip on the reins and clenched her legs against Cassie's saddle, no longer thinking about anything but balance. The return journey seemed longer than the journey out and it was with relief that Jemma turned Cassie in at the entrance to Shurnock, glancing quickly to make sure there was no smoke from the chimneys and all was quiet.

Dismounting, Jemma led Cassie quickly into the barn and rubbed her down, first with a fistful of hay and then giving her a good brush, before adding the rug and feeling much happier in herself now she was looking after her horse properly again. The brushing had warmed her, but her clothes were still wet from the rain, even her hair was wet under the saturated hoodie.

"I'll have to go get dry and warm," she told Cassie, "OK?" Cassie whiffled down her nose and Jemma gave her a fond final pat of gratitude before jogging for the house.

The solar battery hadn't recharged under the cloud and rain. Cursing, and mentally apologising to her mum, who didn't like swearing, Jemma laid the fire more carefully and lit it using a match, building in twigs and then thicker wood. Tomorrow she would have to use her folding knife to cut more logs. She was nearly out of wood but tonight she must get warm. That slight feeling of illness from this morning was growing into aching joints and a shivery feverishness. No swellings, she thought. Probably just a cold because I'm not immune to Elizabethan illnesses and I haven't been eating properly, and I'm mentally run down., Not plague, anyway. Thank goodness Cassie doesn't need that cloak tonight. She stripped off the wettest layers – the skirt which had kept her trousers dry, her sheepskin and her hoodie and hung them on her survival kit string, with a smile of self congratulation for bringing it with her, and then stood near the fire, letting the heat steam dry her remaining layers while the soup boiled in the kettle. It was dark outside with the pelting rain, now changing again to snow. Jemma decided the best thing was to dismantle straw from the upstairs bales and bring it to the fire. She piled it as high as she could and then wrapped herself completely in the cloak, sitting on the straw to eat and then curling up on her side to watch the flames and add wood as necessary until she slept.

She slept all afternoon and all night and on into the next morning while her body tried to fight the illness within. She woke sweating and shivering, her throat sore and her head aching as if cold ball bearings were bouncing and sliding within her skull and saw the fire was out. At first, she just lay, feeling the aches in her joints anchoring her to the ground and looked at the black ashes in the grate, but eventually she accepted that she must get wood and relight the fire and dig up more vegetables for soup or she would just get more and more ill and no one even knew she was here. She rolled out from under the cloak, groaning and shivering more as she slowly struggled into the skirt, hoodie and sheepskin, and put on her boots, using fingers that seemed to belong to someone else.

Opening the door, she found snow piled high in a drift. The brightness hurt her eyes but there was no alternative. There was no one who would fetch wood for her and relight the fire. No one even to give her a hug and words of encouragement. She stepped out, feeling weak and light headed and struggled to lift her feet clear of the snow as she walked towards the woods with her knife and the string in her pockets. It was no real distance to the trees but it felt like miles and it was if the distance shimmered, first near, then far and then near again. Finally, she reached the trees and stood looking helplessly at the snow covered ground, the fallen branches and twigs buried and lost under the wide white expanse. The feverish part of her mind said,
"Just give up Jem. You can't do this. Just lie down in the snow and let the end come."
But as she went to comply, she thought of Cassie in the barn, relying on her for food and release and knew she couldn't just leave Cassie there to die. The villagers would have taken her and looked after her but no one except Jemma knew where she was. Fighting the apathy in her mind and the messages of pain from her nerve endings, Jemma stumbled into the trees and felt around in the snow, moaning at the cold stinging her fingers, as her gloves became wet and useless. She stood and kicked the snow away, each kick sending shooting pains through her joints and muscles, and finally found branches and twigs, making a bundle within the string, tying it tight and, with effort, ignoring the aches, she rolled it onto her back. Taking the end of another fallen branch, she groaned again

as the effort released lactic acid into her muscles so that her body felt on fire while her mind felt like ice. Several times, she stopped to rest, once kneeling in the snow, her head resting on her arms to ease the aches and throbs, but she held onto the thought of Cassie and crept on until at last the house loomed large in front of her and she hauled her load over the threshold. She tucked her hands under her armpits, trying to create warmth to override the stinging pain in her fingers. Took them out and blew on them, pathetic breaths from lungs that refused to function properly. The wood was wet and the solar battery flat. How could she light the fire? She stamped round the room, angry at her feebleness and inability to think, her throat like sandpaper obstructing her mind. "Cassie," she thought and fled to the barn, still stumbling on legs that refused to function properly, rubber instead of muscle. Jelly instead of bones.

Cassie could immediately sense the distress and swung her head in Jemma's direction. Jemma collapsed onto a hay bale. "Oh God, Cassie. I feel so ill. Listen. I'll leave the barn door unlatched and then you can leave if you have to, to get help."
 The useless feverish tears fell as her voice cracked.
 "I don't want you to go, but you must if you're hungry. Here, I'll fill your manger now, but if I don't come out tomorrow, go to the village, OK?"
While she spoke, she added hay to the manger and undid Cassie's tethering rope, before hugging her and stumbling back to the house, tears again falling, brought on by the fever in her mind. Holding onto the walls as the world spun and bucked, she felt her way back to the door. Was this plague after all? She felt under her armpits. No swelling. That was a good sign, but it was so difficult to move, to think, to deal with the loneliness. "Pull yourself together, Jem," she said in her head What else must she do? She had to sort the fire. Thoughts were disjointed, lost in cotton wool, buried in sawdust, sliding like water droplets over a waterfall. Fiercely, she held on to one priority at a time. Use the knife to cut into

the wood to find dry wood shavings under the wet. Shave them into the grate. No, she chided herself as apathy suggested she had done enough. You need way more than that. No point lighting the match until there's enough wood to burn hot and dry the other wood. Just keep going, Jemma. The pile of shavings grew at the same speed as the lump in her throat making swallowing difficult, making her breath wheeze, but at last there was enough and with trembling fingers and chattering teeth, Jemma lit her match and the shavings caught. Trying not to knock the glowing heap with her shivering muscles distorting co-ordination she added the driest twigs she could find, coughing as the smoke rose, making her eyes sting and water, but the warmth grew. Stubbornly, she stood and fetched her trowel and took the kettle. That snivelling corner of her mind urged her to just sit and watch the flames but she had to have food and water to survive. Each step was pain. Her breath wheezed and she wondered if she would be able to eat at all with the swelling of her throat. Defiantly she knelt and dug where potatoes, carrots and onions should be, attacking the near frozen ground with anger until it gave up its treasures, putting them in the kettle and adding water after bashing a hole through the ice with the kettle. She was crawling by the time she reached the door, unable to balance on her feet, and dragged herself over to the fire just in time to feed it more wood that hissed and steamed as fire and water battled for supremacy. She hung the kettle, rattling from its hook and slumped onto the straw. Had she ever felt this ill before? No. But she knew that she must drink, and eat when she could and try to stay warm and wait. How many days? she wondered.

No one came. Days blurred and she lay sleeping for much of the time, using her watch as an alarm to stir her into wakefulness every two hours to add wood to the fire. She hung the solar batteries hopefully on the window shutters and greeted the sun when it shone with an exhausted delight, knowing that now, if the fire went out, she could light it more easily using the battery, even cut the logs without causing pain to her muscles.

Maybe that was what saved her. That tiny boost to her morale, that saving of energy to fight the illness within her. She lost count of the days when searing pain flooded through her kidneys any time she moved and she drank and drank trying to wash the bugs from her system and then she woke one morning to sun shining in through cracks in the shutters and knew she was over the worst. She was shuddery with weakness but the thudding in her head was gone and she could swallow with only an echo of the previous agony. She cautiously moved arms and legs and stretched her back and felt the tiny stabs of pain as a luxury of movement. Unsteadily, she pulled herself clear of the cloak, and hung onto a chair to stand upright. The room swam and then steadied and she focussed with a sort of delight. "Cassie," she thought and an emotional lump rose from her chest to her throat, Would she be gone? It was a struggle to get her boots on, muscles not working together as they should, but it was as if the thought of Cassie burned like a flame, a focus point beyond anything else that mattered and Jemma moved forward as if in a dream until she found herself standing at the barn door, expecting emptiness, but hoping. Hoping.

The door had been pushed wide and the barn was empty. Jemma leaned on the doorpost, bereft. Her best friend, her much loved companion had gone.
"Cassie, what will I do without you?" she thought, tears springing again to her eyes.
She, turned and started back to the house, feeling hollow inside. At least Cassie would be alive somewhere and safe, Jemma told herself. Cassie had done what Jemma had told her to do.

Half way back to the house, she saw a movement on the edge of her vision, and glancing towards the apple trees beyond the corner of the house, there was a splash of white, a flick of a tail, and Cassie was wheeling and trotting towards her, still munching a mouthful of grass. The meeting was not as romantic as a Bronte novel but the love and relief was there on both sides. Jemma felt her legs fold with relief and Cassie bent her neck to nuzzle Jemma's ears and neck, while Jemma reached to fondle the pricked ears above her. "You stayed!" Jemma said. "And you looked after yourself, you great old girl. Well done Cassie. Well done."

It was enough. Jemma spent that day quietly, drinking and building her strength, eating biscuits like ships biscuits made from the flour from the cellar and water, and drinking potato and turnip broth and stewed apples, foods designed to replace vitamins lost in vanquishing her illness. She still felt shaken, a little wobbly and thought she would spend one more day doing nothing but rest. The weather was grey and sulky. No one would be doing much in the fields and Jemma had no other skills to offer. However the next day, she promised herself, she would return to the village. This last day of rest, she would wrestle with those letters in the box.

She ate eggs for breakfast and then carried the box upstairs to sit cross-legged on the wooden floor, using the light from the glass windows as best she could. It was another grey day of temperatures lurking around freezing. Cassie was fine in the sheltered barn with her rug and hay. The continuous burning of the fire had made even this high room warm enough to sit still in, wrapped in the cloak, using her brain rather than her muscles.

She took another paper roll from the box and this time used her knife and cup as paper weights, Again there was a date 25th June 1565. Was it coincidence that they were written around the solstices, Jemma wondered. Maybe they were holidays when people could escape their normal routine.

"The garden has needed some work today. I hope Marco would be pleased with my efforts. I think I must ask William for some help if he has time to spare. I walked today all around the herb garden, hoping I would find myself on the edge of Marco's time as before and wondering if I would be brave enough to step through into the future, but to no avail. I did meet the cat that Marco said followed him often and we made friends. I am thinking that the wise woman at Himbleton may have helped Marco escape. Perhaps I may visit her again for advice. I really should destroy these thinkings, but they do ease my mind and somehow give me peace..."

It took Jemma several hours to decipher those words, skipping from sentence to sentence and back again as a new word was deciphered and other words guessed, in context. With most of the words made clear, she read the whole thing again, and then sat back to think. Whoever wrote these words definitely knew about the time-slips. It seemed that although she didn't know how they worked, another woman, possibly a witch did know, ,,,,if she could help Margot back to her time. Was it possible for Jemma to find the writer of the letters, or the woman at Himbleton? For a few moments, her hopes were raised, but then her eyes rested on the date, 1565. It was now 1601. Thirty six years later. Even if either of them was only, say, twenty in 1565, they would be 56 now and Jemma knew the average life in Tudor times was about forty years. They might be still out there, but it seemed unlikely. There was another name, wasn't there? Jemma checked back. Another William. Couldn't be the Will in the village. In 1565, he would have been only about two years old, if that. It was time to get some more food and relight the fire. Matches again. Then, while the soup was heating, she would get more wood into the house, use the knife to cut the logs, which would make her good and warm, and maybe dig some more potatoes and turnips. The melting snow would turn them to mush if she left them in the ground during a thaw. Better to get them into the cellar.

As she carried the turnips down the cellar steps, she eyed the barrels with their flour and apples. Foods that wouldn't last for very long. Who were they for? Not the person writing those letters. Was it those men she had crashed through and had she frightened them off? Would they be asking questions about her in the village? And would they return if they thought her gone? So many questions with no answers. So much she needed to know to make the right decisions and stay safe. How she wished her parents and Uncle were around to make these decisions for her. Was it always like this, being a grown up? Trying to make decisions and then having to change your mind as new facts were learned, or just ploughing hopefully on, always uncertain if you were doing the right thing. She suddenly recognised the burden of having to make decisions which had to keep your children, your whole family safe, and was glad she only had Cassie to watch out for as well as herself. While she had been thinking, she had worked automatically, carrying the turnips in small batches and stacking them in the cellar, not quite touching to give them ventilation and stop them rotting. She had only dug three or four days worth of potatoes before finding herself exhausted again. It would keep her safe from starvation for a while, anyway. The short days turned to night too quickly. By the time she had eaten, the light was fading, the sun never having shown from behind the clouds, today. Jemma didn't mind. She was still easily tired. Another good night's sleep would do her no harm.

Chapter 8

When she rode to the village, the next day, she found the
illness had swept through the whole village, The smithy fire
burned and she saw the smith working with his boy on what
looked like a spade blade, but when she turned into the High
Street it was eerily quiet, even for another grey skied day with
rain or snow threatening but not falling. No children played in
the street. No one stood on the green. Jemma dismounted
and left Cassie drinking at the trough, heading for Margery's
house. She knocked on the door and waited but there was no
response. Jemma risked a quick look at her watch. Just gone
eight o' clock. Had everyone already gone to work? Which
building was the school? It was barely light. What time would
school start? How many days had she been sick? Was it back
round to Sunday? Should she be in church already? That
couldn't be it. There were no carriages at the gate. Knocking
again, she waited and then eased open the door. Margery lay
on her bed, breath rasping as she slept, face skeletal and
pallid. The room was cold, The fire out. Jemma stepped
briskly across the room and felt Margery's forehead. It was
burning hot, but Jemma could see her body shaking with
uncontrollable shivers. Looking round, she saw she needed
wood and briskly left the cottage, looking around for the
nearest source of timber. There were logs and kindling piled
at the side of the cottage, under the shelter of the thatch and
Jemma quickly carried the wood indoors. She laid the fire but
looking around, could find no matches, just a dead stump of
candle. There was a flint next to the fireplace. Jemma cursed,
wishing she had kept the matches in the kit she still carried
instead of leaving them by her fireplace, or even one of the
solar batteries which were hanging in the window at Shurnock
in the hope of a few sun rays recharging them. Well, in her
studies of history, she had seen how to strike a flint. It was
time to try out her knowledge. She was glad Margery still slept
as she studied the contraption, and experimented, before

getting the knack and creating a spark in the right place. She fed the spreading glow, with the tiniest of twigs blowing gently to feed the fire with more oxygen. With the fire gaining strength, she took the kettle to the pump and filled it, hanging it back over the flames. There was another door at the back of the tiny cottage and outside it was a store of onions and potatoes, peas and apples. Jemma turned cook and set soup to boil in a small cauldron and with all set, she returned to look at Margery, still sleeping. Jemma decided it was best to let her sleep until the kettle was boiled. In the meantime, she would try to find someone else to help her.

Nervously, she knocked on the adjoining door. There were rustling noises and then the door opened to another pale, sweating face, strained with pain and fever. Jemma had been going to ask for help, but instead found herself offering help. "Are you managing? Do you need help? Is everyone ill?" The young lass opened the door wider so that Jemma could see in. Three people huddled in one bed. More feverish faces, a small child whimpering in the arms of her sleeping mother. A young boy, leaning against the wall, knees up supporting his head on his arms, covered in a coarse blanket. The lass at the door looked about ten years old but she had kept the fire alight.
"Good girl," Jemma said. "You must boil water and herbs, make broth if you can and help them all to drink," She looked around the deserted square, thinking, they can't all be ill. There must be someone who can help. The ten year old was wiping a tear from her cheek. "Give me your kettle and your cauldron," Jemma said, pointing at the fireplace where they sat.
 The girl did as she was told, her movements slow revealing the pain she felt. Jemma filled kettle and pan at the pump and took them into the room, hanging them from the bar across the flames.
 "Can you cut onions, and other food?" she asked, The girl nodded and, as at Margery's fetched food from beyond the

shack.

"I'll come back later," Jemma promised. " I have to find out who else is ill."

Jemma found a young man in the next cottage, carpenter's tools arranged in a rack against one wall. He looked at her lethargically, wrapped in a cloak, sitting on his bed, back against the wall, an empty dish beside him and a wooden mug in his hands. He shook his head, not needing help. "Getting better," he croaked and coughed. "Have you wood, and food?" Jemma asked.

He smiled and patted the wall behind him. "Wall's warm," he said hoarsely.

He was obviously too weak to help others. Jemma pulled the door shut and gradually made her way along the five remaining cottages in the row. One empty. One a lady lay dead, looking as if she slept peacefully but no sign of breath, her body cold. No decay in the cold winter temperatures. It was the first dead person Jemma had seen and Jemma found herself shocked and swallowing tears as she realised there was no life, but it was as if a veil slipped over her emotions and made her efficiently practical. There were no police to call. Who did one inform? There must be a doctor somewhere, but where? Only the last house had people not seriously ill. Edward had gone out. His young wife held a baby and looked at her with big eyes.

"Ned is gone to work the fields with Will and Hugh. 'Tis lambing time come. Everyone else is too ill. We din't know what to do. Even the big house is sick," she said.

"Is there a doctor?" Jemma asked.

"He'm died," the young mother replied.

Jemma felt frustrated. She couldn't cope with this all on her own. No phone to ring 999, no computer on which to contact the outside world. She had Cassie to ride for help but where could she ride to?

"Where's Ned working?" she asked and his wife pointed

beyond the big house.

Jemma returned first to Margery. The kettle was steaming, the soup well cooked and Jemma shook Margery awake, helping her first to drink and then sip a little of the soup, before adding wood to the fire and going in search of Ned and Will.

She found them by listening for the baaing of sheep with their lambs. Will and Ned were throwing bales of straw from a cart, while Hugh constructed a rough shelter for the ewes and their new born lambs.

"Tes too cold for 'em. Nivver seed so much snow," Will said in greeting.

"Can I help?" Jemma asked hopefully, and then added,   "
Or should I ride somewhere to get help for the village? Is there another doctor somewhere who can help?"

Hugh spat at the snow.

" Useless. Just bleed people to death. What we need is apothecary, but he dun't come til next market."

"I could ride to Alcester," Jemma suggested.

Will paused and thought. "Might help," he said. "Ask at the big house. But, there'll be no pay for that, I'm thinking. Best you bring more straw from the barn first. And then I can pay you." Much to Jemma's surprise, he winked and she realised he was going to pay her underhandedly to fetch medicines with money meant to pay for minding the sheep. Ned chucked the last straw bale from the cart. "There's two carts," Ned explained. "Follow me."

Cassie good naturedly followed Ned in his cart and before long they arrived at a barn part filled with straw and clucking hens.

"You start loading this cart an' I'll fetch uther'un," he said, leaping down.

Jemma was glad, in this unmechanised world that straw bales were smaller. In her weakened state, shifting full sized bales would have been impossible, but she could manage these stooks and with Ned returning, they worked quickly as a team, two carts loaded and Cassie pulling her weight in straw, back to the sheep with ease. Will and Hugh had just about constructed all the bales they had as Cassie stopped beside them and they hauled the load to the floor, clearing Jemma's load first so she could return her cart to the barn and leave immediately for Alcester. Will handed her another shilling.

"Apothecary shop is next to butchers, down the back alley," he said. "He's a good man. Won't overcharge. Say Will Mogg sent you. Big house might tell you what to get. And pay some."

Jemma rode Cassie back to the village, and feeling nervous, she knocked on the door of the big house overlooking the square, saw they even had a bell handle to pull and could hear the tinging ring inside the house as she pulled on the handle. A maid answered and Jemma stuttered out that she wanted to know if her master and mistress would like her to buy them medicines in Alcester. It was odd and felt wrong talking like the maid was owned but how else did she say it? The maid gave a sort of bob and left Jemma on the doorstep while she went to ask. She came back nodding and handed Jemma a purse.

"They'm all abed," she said. "But mistress said yes, to buy what apothecary say with all the money."

What an odd way to give instructions, Jemma thought, but then, medicines were new and most people didn't read still, so it wasn't like walking into a chemists and asking for cough medicine or paracetamol, was it? Jemma already felt tired, but at least she now felt part of a team, able to discuss things with others, no longer alone.

She mounted Cassie and they set off, concentrating on the most efficient speed, working their way around drifts of snow and the worst of the slushy puddles. Jemma had brought a cup of cider and apples and nuts, so there was no need to stop. Alcester was six miles and Cassie could plod at about 4 miles an hour. Three hours travelling all told. As they rode, Jemma thought about how quickly the illness had spread. She was sure it wasn't plague – not a rat to be seen and no one with swellings and blisters. Was this what they called the sweating sickness? She supposed someone had had it at the market, or else brought it into the church, hoped it wasn't her that had made everyone else ill, but reckoned no, they all got ill together, so she didn't infect anyone else. Dismounting in Alcester, she ate her apples and drank her cider, then found the butchers and the apothecary, a small man with a bustling manner who asked her questions about the number of sick and their symptoms, asking if she herself had been ill, before turning to his multicoloured bottles, clinking them busily as he turned them to the light. Shyly, she mentioned that Will had sent her and that the big house had said she could use all the money in the purse. He took it from her and counted out the coins, his eyebrows rising and shaking his head. He glanced up at her with bright, intelligent eyes, twinkling with inner amusement.

"For this, they must be feeling extremely ill," he said. He looked her up and down and said. "How are you travelling, young miss? Cart?"

"On a horse," Jemma said.

The eyebrows rose again in surprise. "And do you have a carrying pouch of some sort?" he enquired.

"I never thought," Jemma said. "There are bags in the saddles."

The apothecary clicked and clucked his tongue, assembling bottles in rags and placing them in a wooden box.

"Lead the way," he announced, satisfied he had the right medicines. "And is your Doctor Edmunds going to be doling these out?" he asked as Jemma opened the shop door.

"I think he's dead," Jemma said, pointing at Cassie and finding her voice husky, even though she had never met the doctor, and instead picturing the lady apparently sleeping alone in her silent cottage, but never to wake.

The apothecary paused in his packing of Jemma's saddle

bags, his face wiped clean of expression and Jemma wondered what he had thought of the village doctor.

The apothecary finished his careful packing, making sure the bottles couldn't bounce about or clink together and break. He hesitated, then said.
 "Are you good at remembering instructions? I don't suppose you can read?"
Jemma almost bristled with indignation before realising that few adults could read in Elizabethan England.
 "I can read, actually," she said, "And I can mostly remember instructions, too."
"Oh, Well done, Miss," he said, and his praise was genuine, not cynical or sardonic. "Just you wait and I will write you some instructions,"
With horror, Jemma watched the man write with the swirling letters of his time. Why had she assumed she would be reading typewritten text? What an idiot. He stood back, admiring his handiwork, blew on the ink and rolled it up.
 "The medicines are all in different coloured bottles so I have used the bottle colour to write the doses and uses, yes?"
"Yes," Jemma agreed, "Thank you."
He re-opened the purse, removed some coins and returned the purse to Jemma, shaking it so that she could hear it still jingled.
 "I didn't need all that money, even to cure the whole village. Make sure everyone drinks, and boil the water, yes?"
"Yes," Jemma smiled, liking this man with his matter-of-fact manner, honesty and obvious pride in his profession. "Thank you,"

Leading Cassie back to a mounting block, she carefully mounted, avoiding the bulging saddle packs and nudged Cassie with her legs.
 "Back to the village, Cassie, and then home. You're fantastic, girl."
Cassie acknowledged the praise with a nod of her head

against the bridle and they began the long trudge towards home. Jemma knew she was lucky to have such a steady, intelligent mount who needed no guiding to find the safest foot holds. The snow was melting, now, with water trickling through the ruts, and birds sang cheerfully, apparently watching her with curiosity, as she passed. Will and Hugh were sitting perched on the mounting block when she returned to the village and stood to greet her.

"Did you get 'un?" Will asked.

"I did," Jemma replied as she swung down to the ground and struggled to undo the buckles with her chilled fingers. Will came to help, his warm fingers brushing hers as he took hold of the leather straps.

"We'll need some boxes," Will said looking at the rag wrapped bottles.

Hugh nodded and ran across the green towards the inn. Jemma unwrapped the instructions and struggling, managed to work out the swirling words. A colour and a dosage and a word of what it helped with.

"Cough, sweat, throat," she muttered as she worked out the words.

Will looked at her admiringly. "You read?" he asked.

"A bit," Jemma replied, thinking that reading the Tudor script was much more difficult than the letters of 2046. "Let us begin," Will said, and they slowly split up the bottles into five packs, one for the big house and one for each side of the square, adding extra for the houses on the main road and the mill lane. Will called Ned out and, they each took a different box and moved along their row, having already delivered the one pack to the big house with the change clinking in the purse, and Jemma giving the instructions to the maid. Tired as they were, from travelling and fieldwork, they knew that lives could be saved by moving quickly. In each row, they picked the most able to be in charge of helping the others and finally regrouped to exchange tired smiles. Will patted Jemma's arm in gratitude. "A shilling well spent. I think," he said.

132

"Wait to see if it works," Jemma responded.

Will nodded emphatically. "Those medicines", he said, "are good. He saved my dad afore, and other people, too. I seen 'em work."

"Good," Jemma said, and hoped she had got them to the village in time.

She thought that perhaps the apothecary's knowledge of the need to avoid dehydration might be the deciding factor, aided by the herbs he had bottled rather than the other way round. She realised the world had gone full circle by the 2040's with her mum and dad both using the same herbs for healing as the apothecary was using now, in this time 440 years before. She wondered how often that cycle from natural to synthetic and back again had repeated.

She was weary as she returned to Shurnock, realising she had forgotten to tell Will where she was living. He had sniffed at the weather before they parted and said with the thaw coming, they would be muck spreading, using the manure from the inn stables and each villager's animals to feed the fields tomorrow and to bring Cassie the next day to pull a cart. She looked down at her mud splashed jacket and skirt, with bits of straw stuck to the coarse fabric and wished she could have a hot bath. Just soak the aches and fatigue away and feel warm right through. Even a hot shower would be good. She was tired of feeling chilled and her muscles protested about the lack of a soft chair to collapse into. She set the fire and lay on the cloak on the straw, stretching out as best she could, and used water from the cauldron to wipe away the grime. "Be grateful for what you have," she admonished as she sighed over yet another cup of turnip and potato soup, realising how clever her Mum was to use herbs and spices to alter the taste of the day to day meals they enjoyed. So many things taken for granted, so many things now badly missed.

There were more workers the next day. Dicken and Jos were almost recovered and the six of them worked as two teams with the two carts, trundling the manure mix to fields yet to be ploughed and planted in March with spring crops. Jemma had arrived just after dawn, giving herself time to check on Margery and other villagers living alone. Margery's chest was bad, a wheezing cough making it difficult to breath. Jemma propped her more upright and insisted that she sip the soup with herbs she had brought from Shurnock's garden. A few more villagers greeted them from their doors as they finished the day, offering smiles and thanks. It seemed almost miraculous, the eerie silence of the day before now replaced again by sound and movement.

"What day is it?" Jemma asked Will. "I've lost count with being ill."
Will frowned, himself calculating on his fingers, "Friday," he decided and laughed. "I been forgetting to eat the fish," Jemma laughed, too, but had no idea what the joke was. Market day again tomorrow so no work. As she and Cassie clopped home, she did some thinking. Did she have enough money from today to buy hens, she wondered, and would anyone ask questions if she should have already have had hens of her own. She supposed a fox could have taken them, or even the imaginary bandits. She shuddered, thinking of the marauders in that time yet to come, charging at her, almost catching her ankle and once more prayed that her family had escaped. It was good that she had been able to help the villagers so that they looked on her with less suspicion and more favour. Still, though, she wanted to get home to her mum and her dad. It was already getting dark but she would have another go at those scrolls before bed in case there were more clues to be found. She just had to find a way home.

Using the firelight, she found the writing easier to read than before. "Getting used to it," she thought. There were only two more to read.

134

"September 1565
I do not now think Marco will return but I have found a clue to triggering the time slips. I believe that there must be always someone on the same spot at the same time in some other year. The wise woman tells me this and just once I have made it work. Standing on the edge of my time, as I did with Marco, I saw a man run past me in his own time as I walked around the corner of the house and there in front of me was a vast hole with a man digging and a lady talking to him while a small girl looked straight at me and we exchanged a smile so I knew she saw me as I saw her. Their clothes were unimaginably different. Marco's cat was with me and pressed at the front of my legs preventing me stepping forwards into that time. I hesitated, but was not brave enough to step over him and we turned together and remained in our time. If I had stepped, would I have found Marco, or was it some other time before or beyond his time? I know not. I feel sure now that Nicholas was right and that Marco was not killed but changed time as the blow fell so that somewhere in another time he will have continued his life and although I miss him, I am happy that he is safe."

Jemma could hardly believe her eyes. Was this still part of one of her fever dreams? Was she still ill? A hallucination brought on by wishful thinking? She reached for the last scroll, hoping for more clues.

"October 1565
I have come to say goodbye to Marco's garden. It is time to return to my husband, in Malvern. Whatever affair he has had, the woman is now passed away and he asks me to bring up his new daughter as my own. At first I felt to refuse, but I have met his child and she is a sweet thing in need of a mother and my husband asks my forgiveness for his sins. Having already lost two husbands. One to the executioner and one to the plague, I think perhaps I should be grateful for the one now returned to me and no longer rely on the charity of my cousins and brothers-in-law. Especially as my own daughter has now

moved so very far away. So, Goodbye Shurnock Court. William has promised to look after you until a new tenant is found so I will be on my way.

Lady Jane K."

The letters were, Jemma supposed, a sort of diary. Never to be sent to anyone. Just a way of releasing pent up feelings that could not be shared with anyone else, with their hints of witchery or lunacy, not to mention unfaithfulness in her affections for Marco......did she not know that Marco was female?... As well as her husband for some other woman. It read like a romance but it was real life. If Jemma went to Malvern, could she find out more? She was being daft. Malvern was what? Twenty miles away. Too far for Cassie to plod and pretty expensive by coach, even if a horse coach service existed. Scrap that idea. Now, at least she had a clue to how to time travel, but why didn't it happen more often? Surely people must meet on the same spot more often. In every century, people would have walked around this house in day to day habits and she had only nearly time slipped twice before she actually fell into this time. Seb and her dad had never done it, except, she supposed Seb must have nearly done it when he ran past Lady Jane K. and her Mum had only once met someone from another time. Could she return to her own time by just mirroring her Mum's movements and being in the same place that she knew he mum would be? No. She knew immediately this could not work because they had already lived through that time with no duplicate Jemma appearing in their midst. So, she needed, to go to a different time, to work out someone else's likely routine and.... well.... what would the word be?..ambush, that spot. It didn't seem like it could be that easy but she had a fair old grip of Shurnock's past. Tonight, she would try to imagine the patterns of behaviour of those past owners before she slept.

It had been a hard day's work and despite her plan to imagine the steps of those owners before her family, she fell asleep having only established that the many changes to the shape and structure of the house probably meant that in fact, through the centuries, people rarely walked the same path. In the time before this, there had been no upstairs, and now the place was empty and only one upper floor room existed, so not many meetings on the stairs. Then, the added wings would mean, before Tudor times, no one would have occupied the new wing and would walk a different path around the house to her real time. Even her family had added the greenhouse along the southern wall. Then, the barn and the moat had changed. She had seen pictures of the moat filled in with a drive to a front gate by the road and then Carl and Seb had re-dug the moat and put in another bridge to control the flooding. It was amazing, she thought as she drifted into dreams, how many changes Shurnock Court had undergone.

It was market day. No fieldwork to do. She would go early and see if she could buy hens and more bread, eggs and cheese and how great it would be to have some soap. Then she would clear all the remaining snow from the vegetable bed and plant more peas to have a longer cropping season. Day planned, she ate bread and cheese and drank cider so that she didn't need the fire and saddled Cassie.
"You can have a lazy day, today", she told her, warming the horse's muscles with a massage and brush.
"We're just going to the market to buy some hens, in case we're stuck here for a while, and then back here. This afternoon, me and you will walk around the house a few times, just in case we can find a way to slip home. I wonder how much you miss Alder, hey? And the pigs and hens. It'd be good to see them again, hey?" Her voice cracked a bit. She missed Cassie's sister, too. She blanked her mind, deliberately and steadied her emotions, brushing vigorously.

Cassie leaned into her, giving comfort with her calm easy manner.

The village was quieter than the week before. Visiting market traders had heard news of a pestilence and were staying clear, while quite a few villagers were still too weak to leave their homes. Food was becoming scarce and it was harder to rebuild strength with famine threatening. Ned's wife was selling bread from the village oven, and Margery was sat on her stool, offering cheese and eggs. Jemma offered her money and Margery handed over cheese and eggs in return.
"What I really wanted, was hens," Jemma said. "Does anyone have any to sell, do you know?"
Margery thought and then nodded.
"You pass a farm track when you come here, yes?"
Jemma knew there was a track but hadn't known about the farm. She remembered the cock crowing and realised that he would be on that farm. "Yes," she agreed.
"That is the farm of Brian Fermier. He has spare hens," she smiled and waved at the eggs in front of her. "These are his eggs, but he, too, is sick so I watch his stall."
Jemma smiled back. It would be much easier to get the hens home from a neighbouring farm.
" I had better buy some food for hens today, then," she said.
Margery pointed to another stall. "Henry, there, has grain to spare."
Henry saw her pointing and beckoned Jemma with a smile. Jemma had seen him lying, exhausted in his bed just two days before.
"You're better," she said, pleased.
He nodded enthusiastically. "Your medicine," he said. "I thank 'ee."
Jemma shook her head. "No. The apothecary's medicine. I just fetched it."
"No matter," he said. "What would you like?"
"Grain for two hens for a week," Jemma replied.
Henry had leather buckets of grain and handed two over. "No

money," he said.

Jemma didn't know what to do. She had only been a sort of messenger to save his life, not the actual saviour. "Um. How about I pay for one bucket?" she asked. "I did get paid for fetching the medicine," she said honestly, knowing Will had overpaid her for the one cart's worth of straw bales they had shifted.

Henry put his head on one side, considering and then nodded. "3 pence," he said.

She sorted pennies, getting the hang of the various coins she had been given in change and feeling proud of her knowledge. Like, going on holiday to a foreign country and spending money in a shop, she thought.

Her family had only gone once. Across on a ferry to Ireland, using euros instead of pounds when she was about six, Seb showing her the different coins and trying to get her to work out what the price was in pounds and pence from euros and cents, but she couldn't, at six, get the hang of exchange rates and Beth had laughed at him and said he was trying to get Jemma to grow up too fast. Seb had looked at Beth and said, "Our Dad did it OK with us," so that Jemma thought she must be not very clever, and then Beth said,

"Yes, but that exchange rate was 2, so we only had to double the number, or halve it or something, and anyway, things only cost about twenty pence, not £1.75. No wonder she can't work it out."

Seb looked a bit ashamed of himself.

"I forgot that," he said. "Sorry, Jem,"

Seb had given her a hug and given her two euros to spend on a drink of hot chocolate, which had brought back the smiles.

Henry was still talking and Jemma had got lost in her reverie. She tuned back in to find he was advising her about keeping hens. Margery called over.

"She knows, Henry. She's kept hens before,"

Jemma nodded and Henry grinned.

"That is good, then," he said.

"I'll go and see the farmer now," Jemma said. "Thank you for your help."

With Jemma on board, Cassie set off confidently for Shurnock and Jemma had difficulty stopping her short and turning her down the farm track instead, Cassie convinced her rider had forgotten where they lived. She pulled hard against the rein while Jemma explained they had a new place to go. In the end, Jemma slid to the ground and led her, still tossing her head in annoyance. "I know," said Jemma, "You want to eat grass, but we'll only be ten minutes. Come on."

There seemed to be hens running everywhere as they reached a yard area of scratched bare earth, surrounded by open doored hen houses. A dog barked and came bounding towards them so that Cassie pulled back on her reins, but a commanding voice called the dog to heel and it skidded to a halt and swung round obediently.

"Is that you, Hugh?" a voice called.

"No," Jemma called back. "My name is Jemma. I want to buy some hens."

A tousled head peered around the cottage door. A man steadying himself against the door frame.

"I'm sick," he said. "Don't you be coming close."

He began to cough and couldn't stop, bending over to work the muck from his lungs.

Jemma nodded, "I know," she said.

She wondered if the villagers understood about immunity and decided she wouldn't try to explain what with being difficult to understand even talking about simple things.

"Can I just take a couple of your birds and leave you some money?" she asked. "How much do you want?" The man shrugged and looked vaguely at his glut of hens.

"That cockerel is mighty good at making chicks," he said almost as if talking to himself. "Have as many as you like. Can't feed this many so they have to run wild and then I gets more. Say 4 pence each?"

Jemma found herself chuckling inside at his predicament and

wondered why he didn't just remove the cockerel.

"I'll put the money on the coop, shall I?" she asked.

He nodded. "Got anything to put them in?" he asked. Jemma shook her head. He disappeared for a moment and came back with a small wooden cage with a sliding door.

 "It'll go on the horse," he said. "Bring it back next time you're here."

One thing Jemma had learned as a child was how to round up hens and she caught a couple with a handful of grain thrown at her feet, with ease. The man nodded approvingly and without another word, disappeared into the house, the dog sitting in the yard, watching the hens with interest as Jemma strapped the hen cage to her saddle, and led Cassie home. "There you go Cassie," Jemma said, letting the hens go free in the barn. "There's company for you."

"I'll have to make you a coop else you'll be back off to that cockerel next door," she told the hens. "I hope you haven't already been too friendly with him. Come Cassie. You can stay out for a bit and keep me company while I do some building."

With Cassie munching grass, Jemma took her knife to the woods and cut willow and hazel, carrying it back to be near her horse as she worked. Then, weaving them together, she used her string to bind the ends, competent from years of practice, but absorbed in her work. It was one of those jobs that lulled the mind with its rhythm and evolving pattern so that time passed without notice, the only measure being in the completion of each panel. Jemma aimed to create a coop about 2 metres long and wide, and maybe a metre high so that she could enclose the hens in an area where they could peck over the grass or earth without turning it completely to mud in a day and then could be moved to another patch the next day. It would keep the vegetable patch pest free in the areas she had yet to seed and reduce her need to buy grain for feeding the birds. She had forgotten to eat lunch in her enthusiasm to get the coop made and as she stood back to admire her completed creation, she became aware of her hunger. She turned to go to the house and found herself facing a man who was talking to her horse, reaching up and fondling the long mane and twitching, floppy ears. He seemed completely relaxed and not at all interested in Jemma, but who on earth was he and what was he doing here? Jemma stilled an impulse to run, or squeak with alarm. Cassie seemed to be welcoming him as a friend so he was probably harmless. Catching her breath which had escaped her in her shock, she said, "You surprised me. Can I help you?"

It was difficult to know how to approach this dark haired stranger who seemed so at home here. What if he was the owner of Shurnock Court? What would he think of her asking if she could assist him? The man continued to look at Cassie, but said,

"You have a lovely horse. What is her name? I'm sorry I frightened you. You seemed so absorbed in your task that I didn't want to disturb you."

Jemma wasn't quite sure how to react. She started with his question,

"Cassie., short for Cassiopeia. Like the stars," she said and tried to shut herself up, giving away more information than she needed.

The man turned to look at her properly, and Jemma tried to assess him, noticing for the first time, he was carrying a spade and had at some time laid a saw and loppers at his feet. Uncomfortably, she realised that he was doing the same, and assessing her. She thought it unfair that he had crept up and somehow got a head start on her, an unfair advantage. She waved at her work.

"I've just acquired some hens and had to make them some living accommodation."

She needed some clues to who this man was, standing on the land she had begun to think of as hers, without giving her a reason.

"Do you live near here?" she asked, hoping he might have

come from the farm next door.

He could be a son of Brian the farmer, with his broad shoulders and outdoor skin carrying the suggestion of summer tan, paled by winter darkness and roughened by the wind, but his clothes were of a good cut, and his boots were used but not worn. Looking past him, she saw, there was another horse tied to the rail of the moat bridge, all black but for a white blaze on its nose, powerful but far sleeker than Cassie. Built for speed rather than labour.

He shrugged and smiled.

"I live at Coughton Court," he said, " And I see you have been doing my work for me."

Jemma had nothing to say, seeking for meaning in his words. He saw her confusion and added, "I'm a gardener at Coughton, but I made a promise once to keep this garden tidy, too and I come when I can to plant food and keep the weeds down, but I see the weeds are mostly gone."

Jemma felt the world shift around her as the words of Lady Jane K slipped through her mind and without thinking of danger asked, "Are you William?"

The man smiled. A smile of delight, mixed with surprise. His face had been solemn and serious as he stroked Cassie but now he was alight with an inner enthusiasm. "I am," he said, "But I think that only one person knew of my visits and she is dead so, can I ask how you know?"

"Lady Jane?" Jemma asked.

They were fencing with each other. Both aware that they were on the edge of admitting to magic, or witchcraft. Both aware that the other could be setting a trap and if caught they might face death. Both hoping that they had found an ally, someone to confide in and gain support from. William's smile became lopsided as he nodded. "How did you know?"

Jemma's mind was racing. It should be safe to admit to seeing the letters. Was it safe to tell William she was living here? He might have already guessed, but then, she could, like him, have only come to look after the garden, and, like him, come on horseback, although that didn't explain the hens. With hesitancy, she said,

"I found a box, with letters in it. Written by Lady Jane, and she mentioned you looking after the garden. Would you like to see them?"

William laughed. "I can just about read plant names on labels," he said, "Because I already know what they say, but I couldn't read letters. Generally, I don't have to do more than write my name, and I can do that."

Jemma felt awe. Some kind of amazement. William spoke well, sounded educated. She could understand him with ease. How could it be that he couldn't read and write? He was watching her, a smile crinkling his lips and the corner of his eyes and she was aware that she was rudely staring at him. Now she had stopped working, she was beginning to feel cold. She rubbed her hands together and said.

"Would you like to come indoors and have a drink? I can light the fire."

He glanced up at the sky, assessing the light and length of day remaining.

"Aye," he said. "That I would like. Perhaps, while you light the fire, I might prune the apple and pear trees and plant some seeds and clear the snow. I got these seeds from Sir Walter. He brought them from America so I use them to experiment, like the potatoes which everyone grows in Feckenham, now."

Jemma was startled. Here was one of the first men to grow potatoes in England. Just an ordinary man with a calmness and confidence that needed no bragging, happy in himself and what he did and ready to take the world as it came, just a hint of sadness of things lost in the past. She waved him towards the trees and headed towards the house to heat water to make a herbal tea.

She wondered if William had known Margot. They were both gardeners and Lady Jane had known them both. Was it safe to ask? Supposing William knew about the time slips and she missed the opportunity to ask him. She felt as if she was walking along a mountain ridge with precipices on either side and one false step would have her tumbling thousands of metres to her death. All it would take would be one wrong question to one wrong person.

 With the fire burning and the filled kettle heating, the herbs already seeping their scents and flavours into the warming water, she walked through to the other room and looked out through the distorted glass to see William high in the apple tree, cutting confidently, occasionally fingering a branch and running his eye along it, working out the best branches to remove before cutting again. His movements were neat and efficient, reminding her of Uncle Seb, even though their expertise was in different fields. They had the same calm competence. Within half an hour, he had both trees pruned and had dragged the wood nearer the house, chopping it to manageable lengths and stacking them close to the house walls. Almost as if he felt her watching him, he glanced at the window and, seeing her there, waved and smiled. He turned and jogged to the partially cleared vegetables and, using his spade, quickly cleared off the snow and sank the blade into the ground, making a groove in which to place his seed. Gently re-covering the groove, he inserted a marker stick, cleaned his spade and hands with the melting snow and rounded the corner of the house, disappearing from her view. Within seconds she could hear him scuffling his feet in the porch. She went to meet him, feeling suddenly shy. She had never entertained an adult on her own before. Even with her friends, her mum or dad had normally been around somewhere in the background and Jemma had always been the shy one, letting her friends lead the conversation and slotting in a comment whenever she had something useful to add. She wished she had Sonya here, prattling on about some insignificant thing so that the room was never silent. She waved him into the great hall and walked around him to pour the herb tea into the cup and then hesitated, holding the cup made of aluminium. What would he say? Would he notice this strange material and ask about it? She was horrified that

145

she had made such an obvious mistake in her craving for company. It was too late to retract her offer. Swallowing her fear, she turned and offered him the cup.

"What about you?" he asked.

"I only have one cup," she explained. "You drink first and then I'll have a cup later."

He nodded, accepting this as normal in a one person home. Blowing away the steam, he took a careful sip, blew again and took a swig.

"It's thirsty work, pruning those trees," he commented. He lifted the cup a little. "This is good."

He swallowed more, and as it cooled, drained the lot, nodding appreciatively.

"Here, have your cup back. I did bring a bottle with me, knowing I would be thirsty. I'll fetch it."

He turned and left the room and Jemma heard the door open and felt the cold air blast around her feet before he shut the door behind him. She hurriedly turned to the fire and used boiling water to wash the cup out before adding more for herself. It seemed impolite to wash the cup in front of him. He had barely looked at the cup. Perhaps he would say nothing. The door reopened and William came back in, carrying a corked bottle which he opened with a pop and took a quick swig. Jemma sipped her drink, too, hoping William would just chat about Lady Jane or the garden and avoid the more difficult questions. He was swishing the liquid around in his bottle, eyes on the rotating liquid and she realised he was waiting for her to speak.

"Tell me about Lady Jane," she said on impulse. "In the letters, she seemed so sad."

William looked up, surprised.

"Sad?" he questioned.

He thought a bit. "Well, I suppose she was after Marco went, but mostly she was, well, nice. Kind to me. See, I was only a small boy when I first met her. My dad was the farrier, see, and my brother was his apprentice so he had to find another place for me, and they said I'd to be a gardener. Well, the old gardener was getting on a bit, all stiff in his joints and had me running all over doing all the hard work, but I didn't learn nothing because I was always a digging or wheeling barrows and such and being yelled at because I wasn't digging fast enough, and then one day the old man just keeled over and died and I was that frightened it was my fault, I ran away and hid and everyone was ranting about where I'd gone. Anyway, after dark, I sneaked home and my dad was giving me a good cuffing and Lady Jane appeared and asked him all polite and calm to stop and let her talk to me and dad stomped off someplace and I tell her what happened and she say it's fine and to keep working by myself, but I didn't rightly know what to do and then she would slip out and say, "William, why don't you clear the weeds from the raspberries" or some such, and I'd be fine doing what she asked, but sometimes she didn't come and Sir Robert would yell at me instead for being lazy, so I pretty much loved Lady Jane, though I was such a titch. Then, my dad and my brother had an accident with the fire..." William's voice faded away and he swallowed hard, remembering an awful thing, " and, and they died and I was on my own, trying to look after myself for a while, and then Marco came and Lady Jane talked things over with him and then Marco told me what we were to do."

William's face held a nostalgic smile, as he looked Jemma full in the face.

" He was only with me maybe two weeks but he taught me so much. Not just about gardening but about believing in myself and learning everything I could and not being afraid to ask questions to learn more and one day I could be a head gardener, and I loved working with him more than any other person. He took me to Charlecote Manor on a horse once and I'd never been on a horse before and I met their head gardener who also said I should be proud of what I did and always seek perfection and always remember every plant has a life to be valued, he said."

William stopped suddenly, seeming surprised at what he had said.

"I don't normally tell people all that, and I don't even know your name," he said, embarrassed.

Jemma hesitated only for a millisecond before telling him.
 "My name is Jemma."

He seemed so uncomplicated. There could be no danger in him knowing. He gave a small jerk of his head in acknowledgement.

"Well, between them, Lady Jane, Marco and that Charlecote gardener, they made me who I am, and they were right. I am now the head gardener at Coughton and so happy doing it. I used to hear all kinds of shoutings around that place, with Sir Nicholas and Sir Robert going at each other, and then Sir Thomas joining in and sometimes the ladies would step in and tell them to be civil and one day the soldiers came and ransacked the whole house, they say, searching for priests and everyone was frightened what would happen, and not long after that Sir Robert died."

 The smile had gone and William's face reflected remembered shock.

 "Then, a few years later I heard hysterical screaming and then the butler told me Sir Francis from Feckenham, that was Sir Thomas's cousin was executed for treason and not long after that the house was all shut up and all the family went away with just the house-keeper and a few maids and me left to keep it all tidy and Lady Margaret that was Mr Thomas's wife came to me and said she would make sure I could keep living there and keep the garden smart and be paid. She said Lady Jane had told her to always keep me as head gardener because I had been well trained and she would find no one better. No one else had thought about telling us what would happen."

 He paused, thinking about the long ago past.

" A long time before that Lady Jane asked me to just visit Shurnock every now and again to keep it tidy while it was empty, because she was going away, back to live in Malvern, a long way away and she wouldn't be able to visit as she had before." He swigged from his bottle again and was surprised to find the liquid all gone. "So. No one told me you were living here. Are you living here? I mean, permanent? Should I stop coming?"

"Oh, no," Jemma said. "Please keep coming. I don't think I will be here so very long, although I don't quite know how long it will be......It's complicated"

William fixed her with his steady brown eyes and asked his question bluntly.

 "Are you like Marco? A magician who can vanish in time?" Jemma turned away from the eyes which seemed to be searching right inside her head.

 "How can I answer that?" she asked. "I'm not a magician, but yes, I might be like Marco. I don't think either of us wanted to change time but somehow, it just happened to us and somehow Marco managed to find a way back to his time, but I don't know how to, and I think Lady Jane worked it out but you say she is dead so I might be stuck here for always, unless I can work it out for myself."

She turned to face William, afraid of what she might see. Fear of her, judgement, disgust, perhaps even a decision to eradicate evil, but his face was still passive, accepting.

"I heard Lady Jane and Sir Nicholas arguing about him, but I thought I must have not understood. How could anyone travel in time? But then I looked at the tools he had left me and talked to the smith at Coughton who said he had never seen metal like that before, and now I look at your cup and remember Marco had one almost the same, all shiny and smooth and I knew you are like him."

 He glanced down at the floor, and then up again at her face. " I don't know why I'm not frightened. Why do I trust you as I trusted Marco before he near broke my heart, leaving without a word to explain. When I heard Lady Jane and Sir Nicholas shouting, I thought maybe Sir Nicholas drove him away, but I wish he had come to say goodbye and explain."

Even after all these years, Jemma could hear the pain of abandonment in his voice. "Sometimes," she said, "I think things just happen too fast. There's no time to make things right. I'm sure, if he could have made things right for you, he would have. He sounded so kind and, and principled, you know?"

William nodded. "I think you are right, and I think I must go or I will be falling in the ditches in the dark getting back. It has been good to meet you and perhaps we will meet again. Jemma. Be careful, I think sometimes other people meet here, at Shurnock to plan and plot evil things, because it is away from other places, and usually empty. Mind they do not find you here in case they take you for a spy. Always be ready to flee and hide."

He turned to the door and, without fuss, was gone. Jemma watched him untether his horse in the fading light, climb neatly into the saddle and trot away. "I never tried to get home with Cassie," she thought. Should she do it now, before the dark descended? One quick circuit, maybe. Hurriedly, she packed together the whole survival kit and belted it on. Thinking about food, she put nuts and apples in Cassie's saddle bags and brought the rug and cloak out too. Cassie rolled her eyes, expressing her unhappiness in being moved from the grassy pasture and almost looked as if she thought Jemma had gone crazy, leading her round the house with a tight grip on her rein, stopping at the end of one circuit and deciding on one more, following the boundary of an imaginary house of 2046, even leading her through the herb garden and backwards and forwards between the barn and the house, trying to follow the path of the boardwalk. Nothing worked. All the time, she had sweated, afraid that she might change times but not bring Cassie through with her. She had to think of a way to keep Cassie safe if they ever got separated. Perhaps William could take her to Coughton and let her earn her keep there. She felt the tears rise again at the thought of parting from her only companion, her only link to her family.

"I will try to keep us together, Cassie," she said, stroking the long nose. "I really will."

She led Cassie to the barn, and shut her in with the hens who seemed to have taken possession of the hay bales and clucked in annoyance as she plucked some of their bedding free for Cassie's use. "At least you have company tonight, eh, Cassie?"

She left the trio getting to know one another and returned to the house to make toast on the hot flickering flames and eat it with nuts, eggs boiled in the kettle and herb tea. The straw still made a bed by the fire and she rolled into the cloak, keeping her survival kit belted at her waist, William's warning echoing in her mind. She must be ready to leave at any time. She had a night of broken sleep, the creaking of cooling timber waking her to check for intruders, only sleeping deeply in the hours just before dawn, and then waking in a panic, wondering if she was late for church. A check of her watch said she had just twenty minutes to get there. It would be faster to run than saddle Cassie. She grabbed an apple and sloshed out a cup of the cold herbal tea to slurp before she shoved her feet into her boots and sprinted for the church. Thank goodness, she thought, that boot design had improved from the clumpy things she had worn at eight years old. Boots now, were close fitting, still waterproof but flexible, and she could run in them at a good old rate of knots.

She arrived at the church as the villagers were following the gentry in, trying not to puff, but noticing that the volume of coughing and sniffing was easily camouflaging her wheezing breath. There was a different preacher today, explaining that the normal vicar was unwell. This was a man of fire, who berated sinners in a loud voice and the villagers stood open mouthed as he thumped the lectern with his fist and talked of brimstone and fire, the sins of sloth and greed and the requirement to look after our fellow men. Jemma, watching with interest, was sure he was eyeing those in the front pews as he spoke, and asked herself if this was the ancient beginnings of reform, the first stirrings of the Labour Party, not to be formed for more than 250 years. She could have laughed at the shufflings from foot to foot amongst the villagers as he demanded that they repent their sins of theft and the sideways looks at mention of adultery, the preacher's eyes sweeping over his whole congregation. There was almost a sigh of relief as he stepped down from the lectern and released his flock. As the elite followed him to the door, it was interesting to watch the body language. Ladies with straight backs, heads held high, proud of their good works and wise words, some of the men looking at the floor, unable to make eye contact, whilst others obviously felt they had no sins to repent of and walked with confidence. A few, it seemed to Jemma, walked rebelliously, as if rejecting all teachings of the Protestant service, here only to avoid imprisonment or fines. Once again, she tried to stay out of sight, wishing she wasn't so tall, glad of her sheepskin jacket that made her one of the crowd. This time, she held back, waiting for the carriages to depart. A whole family crowded into one carriage which headed north towards Astwood Bank, seven of them squeezing in, the youngest child sitting on his mother's knee. Jemma assumed they must live at Astwood Court. A young family of four set off west towards Droitwich and another group, with about six children, went east. A man she had last seen, feverish and restless, came and took her hand and, to her surprise, kissed it.

"Thank 'ee for your help, lass. My name is Tom and I'm the tanner. If you need fixings to yon bridle and such, you come to me an' I'll be pleasured to help 'ee. I were right ill 'til you came,"he nodded at the man standing next to him, "and John here. He's the thatcher. He don't say much, but he likes to help you, too."

Without another word, the two men walked on, leaving Jemma thankful, but hot with embarrassment.

Young John Throckmorton was remonstrating with Margery, trying to get her to return with him, but she resisted, insisting she had food, warmth and clean water at the pump and was well over the worst of her illness. He looked to Jemma as if asking for help but Jemma lifted her shoulders in a shrug, knowing she would not change the older lady's mind. John visibly sighed and accepted defeat gracefully, giving his grandmother a hug before walking beside Jemma to the main track where he turned right, with a wave.

 The snow was thawing but the dampness in the air made it too cold to stand long and talk and there was mist coming up off the fields, mingling with smoke from the village fires. Jemma felt terribly lonely, walking back to Shurnock. She had a whole afternoon of solitude ahead of her. It almost felt like a sin to try to use the time slips on a Sunday. It was a kind of magic, wasn't it? Should she spend the time, instead on making herself a wooden mug and a proper dish, instead of eating from her cup? If she used the solar battery and laser cutter she would have to be very careful no one saw what she was up to. Witchcraft on the Sabbath. There would be no leniency, but she couldn't otherwise do it without a chisel, which she did not have. She felt almost guilty, firing the laser and watching the small tree drop, neatly cut through. Furtively, she hid her tool, while she pulled the severed wood to the house. She could have used her folding saw but it would have blunted the blade and taken a good half hour instead of 15 seconds. There was a pleasant smell of charring wood as she seared the inside of her soon-to-be mug, leaving a smooth, hardened surface, and she followed this with a dish, happy with the end results, which she placed on the fireplace, ready for use, before hanging the charger up, hopeful of sun to come. She would have to use matches to light tonight's fire, the solar power all spent and not enough sun to recharge it today. She still had not told anyone in the village where she was staying. Was this subconscious caution or just not finding the right time? It was hard to know. She repacked her survival kit, even the discharged solar panel and went to fetch Cassie for another trundle round the house. Sabbath or not, she was going to try Lady Jane's advice and see if she could meet someone from the future on a spot around the house. Cassie, Jemma knew, felt this was a waste of good eating time, refusing to step out and shaking her head against the leading rein, hating the clinging fog. After twenty minutes of walking the whole grounds, Jemma had to admit Cassie was right. There had been no sense of shifting time. No blurring of the land, or feelings of nausea or giddiness as she had felt before when times had met. Jemma left Cassie to graze while she sat amongst the trees, watching the busy birds foraging for food to keep them warm through the cold winter nights. Was Jemma's watch telling her the date right? February 4th. Jemma realised she had missed her birthday while she had been ill. Perhaps that was better than having to celebrate alone as she had never done before. Not even a card or present to open. She smiled. Wanly, thinking that at least, using woodcuts, she knew what her cards would have looked like and could imagine them, but how she missed the hugs and the smiles and laughter. "I'm twenty," she told herself, and felt surprised. In her family unit, she had felt still a child, looked after, protected, and although she had skills and knowledge, there was always someone wiser and more skilled to look to. On her own, with just herself to make decisions, look after herself, she had become an adult, not just in years, but in experience. It was a sobering thought. Average life, here, forty years, she thought. I might be half way through, already. Then she thought of the graveyard and the higgledy piggledy stones, with the tiny graves of so many children and the odd stone showing 80 years and more of age. She was fit and had knowledge of vitamins and what caused disease. She might yet live to eighty. That would be 1660. Could she dodge the plagues, stay out of the way of civil war soldiers fighting their way through Worcestershire? Were they the soldiers she had witnessed riding through their yard on the edge of time? She would have lived through the reigns of James I, and Charles I and possibly seen Charles II reach the throne, if she lived that long. It was hard to accept. Her sense of humour popped up. All that time without a hot power shower. No way! She refocussed on the world around her. She had been so still, as she thought, that the wildlife had accepted her as part of the scenery and returned to their normal pattern of life. Squirrels, small and red, were scurrying around, digging holes, hunting for nuts they had buried in the autumn. Bright coloured birds, that she thought were jays, watched them carefully and occasionally dive bombed the diggers, who scurried away to dig elsewhere, while the jays snatched the newly unearthed bounty. There were large black birds making a terrific racket in the top branches of an oak tree, taking possession and beginning to build dozens of nests. Rooks? Crows? Jackdaws or ravens? She did not know. How wonderful that she had actually seen the birds and animals that she had thought extinct, never to be seen again. She thought back to her mum's books. What would she really love to see? Things that her mum had told her of that were special. Badgers, she thought, with those amazing long black and white noses. A herd of wild deer. Already, she had seen an otter, but how great if she could see a whole family searching the brooks for fish and having time to roll and play. She had seen, in her time, foxes with their ability to change their diet and live on the garbage of human society, but it would be good to see one living in the wild as it was designed to do. She remembered her mum telling her of a wondrous moment, watching a ghost like white owl swooping silently across the fields, wings glowing in early morning light, big eyes seeking out a last meal before bed. Yes, she would like to see a barn owl, but in the meantime, she feasted her eyes on the tiny birds flitting about not so far above her head, mostly brown, but also blue, yellow, green, red and gold. For the moment, she would relish the rainbow kaleidoscope surrounding her and think of nothing else. For an hour, she watched the magic around her, but then the cold drove her indoors. She felt restless, unable to settle, wanting to find company, talk to William of the past and the future, but knew if they were overheard, she could put his life in danger as well as hers. She prowled the house and stopped by the wall under the stairs. Why was this closed in? It would have made a useful cupboard, or, with a chimney on the top, a fireplace that heated the whole house and that upstairs room. She went to check there was no door from either room and rapped her

knuckles against it once more. It really was hollow. She
chuckled at the thought of what she would do if someone
rapped back from the inside. Run a mile. She went upstairs
and looked for a trap door in the planking, trying to get her
folding saw into the cracks between the planks. Her mum
used it as a boot and waterproofs store, next to the
descending cellar stairs, so why now was it closed in? The
only other place you could get at it from, was, in fact, the
cellar. Fetching her wind up torch, she carefully descended
the outdoor steps, opened the cellar door and felt her way
along the stone underground walls. At the end of the cellar
was a wooden wine rack, which stretched from floor to ceiling,
panelled at the back, and now empty of bottles. Jemma tried
to move it but it was too heavy. Shining her torch every which
way, she spotted a wooden hatch just above the rack and her
breath caught in her throat. The wine rack was a ladder and
that was almost certainly a priest's hiding hole. Supposing
those men had been hiding a priest here when she burst
through and he was still there, waiting for her to go, not
knowing when she was here, watching for him, and when she
was away so that he could slip out and escape. Was there
someone still in there now? If there was, how could she
convince him she was no danger? Should she try to undo the
hatch now? She bit her lip indecisively. He might have a
weapon to defend himself and not ask questions first. Best to
leave it and maybe get William to help her. Not the villagers
who might think they must take a priest prisoner or report him
to the authorities, whoever they were. William had survived
working for a family split by religion and would know better
what to do. Tonight, Jemma would sleep with Cassie and the
hens, just in case the priest had heard her exploring and
decided to investigate in the night.
Turning, quickly, Jemma scurried out of the cellar, bumping
against barrels in her haste, stubbing a toe agonisingly and
hopping as she ascended the steps. She gathered her straw
in the cloak, took food but left the kettle and scuttled across to
the barn, making the hens dance about, startled and cackling

as she laid out the straw and the cloak.

"I'm back with you tonight," she informed Cassie. "The house is too scary."

The barn was too dark to do anything, so Jemma wrapped herself in the cloak and spent an hour meditating, sitting straight backed, hands on knees, emptying her mind of all but the present moment where she sat, protected by her horse, warm and dry in her layers of clothes, with food and water to hand, feeling the gratitude for what she had fill her with calmness and acceptance. Finally, having relaxed her mind, she relaxed her body, caressed Cassie's nearest leg, curled herself up like a hedgehog and slept.

Chapter 9

The change of sleeping room had her waking in
confusion again to the sound of a clucking hen. Cassie
clattered a hoof and Jemma focussed, working out she
was in the barn and put the jigsaw together in her mind,
the finding of the priest hole and the fear of someone
lurking in there, waiting for her to sleep. She couldn't
cope with the dangers and conspiracies of this time. Why
couldn't people just learn to live in peace together, she
thought with a spurt of anger, and laughed at herself.
"Live by your own rules, girl," she admonished. She stood
up, brushing straw from her clothes. She reached for
Cassie's headgear.
 "Come on girl. Let's see if anyone in some other time
walks around their house at..." she looked at her
watch.."7 o'clock on a February morning."
 It was another grey, cloudy day, the temperature lurking
around zero and Cassie wasn't keen. She walked half
heartedly, head down, as if she was grumbling in
Jemma's ear, but Jemma had had enough of the fear and
the loneliness. Every opportunity they had, she was going
to walk those paths.

The cellar doors were shut, as she had left them and
Jemma realised she could roll a barrel from the cellar,
outside and wedge it between the doors and the lower
step so that no one could leave the cellar. She could
sleep in the house again tonight.
"What should we do today, Cassie?" she asked. "I had
best go to Feckenham and check if there is any work, and
if not, I thought we might go to look for William."
 Her mind got ahead of her words and her voice wobbled.

"Just in case I go back through time without you, by mistake. I know he'll look after you, and you liked him, didn't you?"

She took a firmer hold of the leading rein and wiped an annoying tear from her eye. She would not cry again. "And he might know of someone else we can help with ploughing and things," she added, forcing her mind from emotional to practical.

Cassie nodded her head, probably just glad to be not walking around the house perimeter again.

"I'll just eat some breakfast, and then we'll go. OK?"

Cassie seemed agreeable, so Jemma hobbled her under the apple trees, ran to put the hens in their new coop and grabbed something to eat, reflecting that she might pinch some of Cassie's oats to make porridge with if it stayed cold much longer. The mist, this morning was even thicker.

There was no work in the village for Cassie. Ned's horse was hitched to a cart but with little food left to harvest and few villagers well enough to help, only one cart was needed to transport the last turnips and the cut kale crops to the village barns. Jemma had to dampen down the feelings of exclusion and resentment. The villagers had paid her fairly and given her labour even when their own horse had been ready for use. They owed her nothing and had to be practical in sharing their food, money and labour fairly amongst themselves, and anyway, she told herself, she needed to see William to ask about Cassie.

They retraced their route, looking in at Shurnock to see all was quiet and strode on towards the ridge and then down the far side to find Coughton Court. A couple of times, Jemma paused, unsure of her route through trees emerging out of the winding, swirling fog which had turned to houses in her time, but once the trees cleared into fields, she could see the towers of Coughton rising up in the distance above the grey blanket and trotted confidently on her way.

As she gazed at the enormous buildings, she found it difficult to believe no one was living here. What a ridiculous waste. The neglect was beginning to show in crumbling brickwork and warped, rotting doors. The property had become too big to be useful. The driveway was weedy and overgrown, used more by horse riders than carriages. Now she was here, she didn't know quite what to do. Could she just leave Cassie in the stable-yard and go to find William somewhere in the vast gardens, or should she knock on the door and announce her presence and intentions? If she had known it was inhabited, she would certainly have knocked and perhaps concocted a reason for seeing William, but to knock now would mean some housekeeper travelling all the way to the front door for little reason. She thought it would be more sensible to search for a tradesman's entrance, which might be off the stable-yard somewhere. She walked Cassie under an arch with a portcullis high above her, hoping it wouldn't break free and drop on her. What a silly thought, she chided.

The stable-yard was deserted, a barn door hanging open, nothing inside but dust and cobwebs, probably a few out of sight spiders. It looked uninviting. There were stable boxes all shut up. No horses heads peering inquisitively out. She left Cassie tied to a rail and looked uncertainly at the closed doors surrounding her. No one was interested, no one watching her, she might as well go straight on and look for William.
"Back soon," she reassured Cassie as she walked

across the yard, footsteps echoing in the encompassing silence.

She smiled at the stray thought that she should leave a note pinned to Cassie saying she was visiting William and please do not wheel clamp her horse for illegal parking.

It was a relief to step into the well-tended gardens and feel she was no longer walking in an empty land haunted by Throckmortons of the past. She still felt adrift in time. The gardens were laid out almost exactly as she had seen them in the future, visiting them in her time when they were open to the public. She must have been about ten. All that was different was the size of the trees and, she supposed, some of the flowers, but at ten years old, she had been more interested in the vast spaces to run about in, the flower beds just being a backdrop of colour to her play. Seb had run around with her playing hide and seek and chase games, while Beth and Carl studied the various herbs and edible flowers and made notes. That lump rose in her throat again. She couldn't help looking longingly at the trees in the ridiculous hope that Seb would pop out from behind one shouting "Boo," or some such word. She did see the shadow of a man beyond the trees, but it turned out to be William. He had a young lad with him and was showing him how to prune the branches back to keep the avenue clear without damage to the trees. He glanced up and saw her approaching and straightened up to greet her.

He gave her a smile. "Have you come to help?" he asked.

Jemma smiled back. "I would be happy to but I didn't bring any tools."

"I can sort those for you," he said, "But unfortunately, I can't pay you as I already have an apprentice."

He put hand on the young lad's shoulder. "This is my grandson, Edward," he said, his mouth lifting at the

corners into a smile of pride. "He will be a better gardener than me, because he also learns to read and so can learn more, reading labels and how to look after the new plants from America. I just have to remember what I am told."
Jemma chuckled and replied, "I think, though that the more one can read, the worse the memory becomes."
She paused, trying to think of the best way to say what she needed to say. She took a deep breath.
"William, I need to ask a favour of you. If I work with you for nothing, would you keep an eye out at Shurnock, and if I disappear, but Cassie is still there, would you look after her? She's a great plough horse. She'll work well for you. I'm asking, just in case, I fall through time without her. I keep leading her round with me, trying to get us both back, but it isn't working. I'm frightened I might slip through when she isn't with me."
She realised she was gabbling, and forced herself to shut up, to give William time to reply.

He was looking at her seriously, with sadness in his eyes. "Do not mistake me," he said. "I am happy here with my wife and my daughter and grandson and this beautiful garden to manage, but I hope you will not vanish too soon, for it seems, every time I meet a special person, someone who cares about the earth, as I do, someone I think I can learn so many things from, they are taken from me again before I have even got to know them. Am I being selfish? Do you think this is such a terrible time to live in? As to your favour, of course I would look after Cassie, although she must earn her keep, as we all do. We are already good friends, as you saw."
Jemma nodded. "That's why I asked you, instead of the people in the village. As to, whether this is a good time to live in...." Jemma paused, thinking. "The time I come from, I think, is the end of the world, or, at least, it is for

162

us, mankind, I mean."

She looked at William with bleak eyes. "My generation, and, more, the one before us, knew there were things they must stop doing, and other things they had to do, but they kept putting it off until it was too late. I expect you can't imagine it, but in my time, all this land floods every year in Winter, and then freezes, and then in Summer, there's no water at all, no rain for months and the sun is so hot, everything burns. So your time is better. You have birds and green grass and crops and animals and there is room to be away from everybody and so many trees."

She waved her arms, spinning around and then she slowed, and stopped and the smile that had filled her from head to toe drained away.

"But, it does not have the people I love, and, well.... I've been thinking that perhaps I won't get back to my time, and if I went further forward, there really would be nothing......but....if I could find a way to get back before I was born and tell all those people who got it wrong what it will be like......"

She looked solemnly at William.

"Maybe, I can change what they do. Get them to change faster."

She looked around and laughed.

"Get them to live more the way you do, using nature and working with animals to help the land grow what we need, instead of using machines for everything. Then, maybe, there won't be fighting and riots and starvation, so many people murdered because other people have no other place to live or eat."

She shrugged. "I have to try. I have to shout and teach and plead and if I do, maybe my mum and dad won't have to fight off the marauders and might stay alive."

She looked at William's face, and then down at the young lad who stood, staring at her open mouthed.

163

"I don't expect that made a lot of sense," she apologised.
William shook his head. He looked around at the flat land
surrounding them and the river in its deep channel
crossing the gardens. "You describe something hard to
believe, but then, this year, the sky has been black as
ash and this last month colder than ever before I
remember, so I understand the weather changes. But
how is it man that causes it and not God?"

Jemma struggled to think of a simple way to explain four
hundred years of development. She shrugged again.
"Not long from now, someone will discover coal under the
ground which can be used to make hotter fires, and gas
which is like air but can be used to make light and heat
houses, and can be pushed through pipes, and then
someone else worked out you can get another liquid out
of the ground called oil which can be used to pull a
plough and make a carriage that doesn't need a horse
and travels much faster, and pushes ships across the
seas and there's another power called electricity which
can turn motors and when all that happens, all the things
we use get hot, and it changes the air high up in the sky
which changes the clouds so that the sun burns more and
that heat......" Jemma paused, realising William would not
know about snow and ice at the poles "....makes all the
snow melt all over the world and it turns into rain so that
the rivers fill up and flood everywhere because they can't
run to the sea. ....Well. That's sort of what happens but I
can't explain the rest. It's too complicated."

William's eyes had stretched wide and then become slits
as he tried to envisage the things Jemma described. He
looked baffled. "Is there really that much snow
somewhere?" he said. "How do you know all this?"

Jemma shook her head and managed a laugh. "William,
we spend eleven years at school learning this stuff, and
even then, there's lots I don't know. I can't explain it in

one afternoon.".

"Is it magic?" William asked, half afraid of the answer.

"Um." Jemma said. "We call it science, but I think science is explaining how magic is done. It's not God or the devil or demons. Just learning how to control things on the earth that are so tiny they seem invisible. Like, how do all the plants grow? Once, a long time ago, taking cuttings and planting seeds would be magic and now, you just do it."

William shook his head again. "God makes the seeds," he said firmly.

"Well, alright, then God made all the other things that people say are magic, too. It's only that we didn't know what he made before, but man took those things God made and perhaps we got lazy and......used them too much, instead of using the muscles God gave us."

She sighed in exasperation. "William, I am not going to get into discussing religion and magic and get us executed, Let's do some work."

Edward nodded and added his child's wisdom. "Gramma says Granpa thinks too much, talks too much and works not enough."

Wiliiam's eyes were full of laughter as he gave Edward a gentle cuff on his ear. "Less cheek from you, young man," he said.

He put his head on one side, considering. "Weeding?" he suggested.

Jemma agreed and William led her to a patch of herb bed struggling against stinging nettles and bittercress.

"Just leave the weeds in a heap on the path and we'll sort them later," William instructed. "Here, there's a use for everything."

He fetched her a fork and spade.

"Just do as much as you like," he smiled. "I need no payment to look after your horse." He looked towards the

165

stable yard. "Is she here?"

"In the yard," Jemma confirmed.

"I will ask Edward to sort her some food and water. He will like to do something a little different to normal."

He strode off and a short while later, Jemma heard the patter of fast running feet pass her and disappear towards the stable, and a short while later, they pattered back.

Jemma glanced at her watch, I'll do a couple of hours and then go home so that I'm home before dark, she decided, and set to, freeing the herbs from the smothering invaders. It was absorbing and fascinating, seeing the herbs that grew best in this Tudor climate. Things that, 400 years ahead, could not withstand the harsh winters and the floods, many sages and thymes that no longer existed except if grown indoors on window ledges or in greenhouses. William returned.

"I think it might be best if you go now," he advised. "The fog is coming down thicker again, You will not want to get lost on the way back. Should I lead you or will you be alright?"

Jemma looked around at the vapour rising and swirling. It was still low. On horseback, she should be high enough to see over it to the ridge and then ride above it to find her way down the far side. "I think if I go now, I'll be fine," she said. "I was wondering if you know of any other villages that might need mine and Cassie's help."

They walked together to the stables as William thought.

"I'll ask around," he promised, "But there's not much to be done until the snow goes and the temperatures rise. Will you have enough food to survive?"

Jemma nodded, thinking she could survive on turnips, nuts, apples and potatoes and the odd egg, even if she had nothing else until March. It was just nice to be able to have something different every now and again.

Cassie was pleased to have company and stretched out to be stroked by William.
"Hey, you're MY horse," Jemma said indignantly, but laughing.
She mounted and looked down at William. "Thank you for helping me," she said, not able to explain how much it meant to share her fears and just have someone to talk to without having to watch her tongue with every word. His calmness neutralised the panic and sadness that occasionally rose to engulf her. She wished she could stay here at Coughton, but goodness knew what his wife would think of her and she was fairly certain there wouldn't be a private spare room to sleep in. They exchanged quiet smiles and Jemma nudged Cassie into movement. "Home, girl," she said.

It was eerie, walking through the fog, just patches of ground appearing like rocks in a grey sea, trees and the odd hedgerow rising like islands to navigate by. Jemma hoped Cassie could sense what was track and what ditch and let her pick her way forward, while Jemma kept her eyes on the ridge, searching for their route upwards and over. There should be a sharp right and then left as two tracks met, somewhere. Would Cassie be able to work it out when they got there? Jemma thought there would be trees straight ahead at the right turn, so they would know when to turn. It was hard to judge distances because they were walking slower than on the outward journey with Coughton's towers to aim for. Jemma thought they should have reached that turn by now, She felt a sinking in her stomach. Had she gone wrong already? Then, suddenly Cassie stopped, ears twitching in enquiry. This was the turn. Jemma nudged her right and breathed a sigh of relief. Now for the left turn. The track they were on was swinging parallel to the ridge, but there had been no sharp turn to the left. Somehow they had got onto the wrong road Jemma tried to envisage the roads of her time and think which would be ancient routes. It was hard with no houses and sign posts to act as landmarks. She must be bending towards Sambourne. They had accidentally gone right at the fork instead of left. She pulled Cassie to a halt, thinking. She was afraid of falling into a ditch on the track side if they tried to turn around. It was so easy for a horse to break a leg if that happened. Then, supposing she missed the turn again and ended up in Alcester? If she went on to Sambourne, there would be more turns up onto the ridge. That might be safer. She nudged Cassie on. The fog was clammy on her face, distracting. It was getting dark. A tree appeared directly ahead of them. Which side was the path? Or was this a fork in the road?

""Try left, Cassie," Jemma said, pulling gently on her left rein.

Cassie clopped on. The world was completely silent apart from the noise of hoof on earth. Jemma wished for tarmac with its distinctive echo and rattle, so easy to know if you had missed the way. Another tree loomed and Jemma had to duck to avoid the swooping branches. Were they still on the main track or were they lost? She could still see the ridge, now over to their left. She needed to find a track going that way. If she dismounted, she would be below the fog level and although she would then be able to see forks in the track, she would no longer be able to see the ridge. Cassie plodded on, waiting trustfully for instructions on when to turn. Jemma could feel uncertainty weaving into her mind with the fog, and felt tired and too young to be out here on her own. Why hadn't she let William guide her on her way? Too much pride. Stupid. Well, now she had to sort herself out. She looked to the ridge, over on her left. Time to dismount and walk Cassie on slowly, looking for a track to their left suitable for a horse and rider. Once they were up on the ridge, they would be able to see more and find a track, either the right one, or another from Astwood Bank.

 It seemed to take hours, stopping occasionally at animal tracks, peering into woods, working out they couldn't go that way and moving on. At last, they came to a road going the right way. Jemma decided to stay at ground level in case there were more forks. It would take longer to walk, but it was better than riding in circles. At one point, she hobbled Cassie and climbed a tree to check they were still heading for the ridge and the world opened out below her, a vast plain of greyness with black trees silhouetted against the moon and stars. She could see their track wriggling and bending as it reached the ridgeside and began to climb. She slid to the floor.
"Its OK, Cass. We're going the right way," she said, and felt relief wash over her. "I'm going to climb aboard." she said. "Wait while I tuck this skirt up."
Hitching it high, she stretched for the stirrup with her foot and pulled herself into the saddle. She clicked her tongue, encouragingly, and Cassie walked on, climbing steadily, the land spread below them, Coughton's dark towers far behind them, the black ridge diminishing ahead.

It was good to reach the top, even though Jemma was not sure exactly where on the ridge she was. She wished she was not so tired and hungry, She wished there were houses and real roads, traffic lights and sign posts. Those things that made navigation so easy, but there was nothing but trees, She seemed to be alone in the world, just her and her horse. So very alone. "Come on, Jemma. You are twenty years old. You are NOT a child. Grow up and make some decisions," she told herself fiercely. Cassie's ears flicked enquiringly. "Think it out", she said firmly. There was a track directly ahead of her but where did it go? "If you are too far north, and you turn right or go straight on, you might end up in Redditch or bending round lanes until you get to Tardebigge or Bentley. If you are somehow too far south, the ridge will drop steeply and you'll know you missed the turn to Shurnock and can turn round and come back."

"Go left, Cassie," she instructed and Cassie swung south. They were above the fog now, and could see for miles across the river plain, but only trees showed above the ground mist layer and there were no landmarks to set Jemma straight. Even the moon had shrunk to a sliver, barely showing above the horizon. It was freezing. She lifted each hand in turn and blew on her gloved fingers, for a morale boost, rather than any physical effect. The material was way too thick for the heat of her breath to reach her fingers, "Daft,you are," she told herself.

There was a dark break in the trees to her right and she pulled Cassie to a halt to study it. It was a track, dropping steeply. It didn't look like the track to Shurnock but it must go towards Feckenham. Should she stay on the ridge and look for the Shurnock road, or try this track she had found.? She shut her eyes and again tried to picture the map. This had to be Church Road or Dark Lane, didn't it? There were no other turnings, unless she was really miles north and this was Dagtail Lane. She couldn't have got that far north, could she? No. If it was Dark Lane, it was going to be steep, she thought. This was the route she took to Sonya's house, though that wouldn't be built yet. How great it would be if she could slip through time here and be able to knock on Sonya's door and ask for help. She decided to dismount, afraid of Cassie stumbling or sliding on the steep icy track, and lead Cassie.

She knew within minutes, she was right. The banks rose steeply above her and the track became pitch black, but it had hardly changed through the centuries and the twists and turns were so familiar that she found herself walking confidently, with Cassie clopping at her shoulder. Reaching the junction at the bottom of the hill, she mounted again, and even in the blackness, felt relief. She knew this road, even if it was little more than a track at this time and could ride it blindfold. She encouraged Cassie into a trot. Bouncing in rhythm, they moved at a fair pace and the activity woke Jemma's mind and warmed her body. There were tracks leading into the trees which might have cut across to Shurnock as she passed Astwood Court, but Jemma had had enough of getting lost and was sticking to the main tracks. If she ended up going through Feckenham, that was better than going in circles again. It was, though, as if an internal clock was ticking, clocking up the miles, and the short cut appeared to her left exactly on time. Cassie knew this route, too and swung left, head up and happy to be nearly home. Jemma wondered what the time was, but would not look while Cassie was trotting. She needed her body straight to retain her balance on the wide back. "Almost home, Cassie," she whispered, feeling jubilant after the near despair of being lost in the fog. One more turn to the left and Cassie increased her pace, looking forward to her hay and drink and the warmth and shelter of the barn. They turned onto the track past the wood and Jemma felt a smile of relief burst across her face. As they reached the moat bridge, she dropped to the floor, easing the stiffness in her legs and allowing Cassie to walk the last yards, to ease her horse's muscles.

"Well done. Cassie," she said. "You're brilliant."

They walked to the barn and Jemma opened the door, leading Cassie in, and stopped dead. There were horses in there. One as black as the barn itself, a grey, and a bay with a white blaze and white socks. They turned their heads and looked at the intruders, half asleep, Jemma thought, or they might have whinnied in fright or surprise. Cassie was making whiffling noises which sounded like enquiry and friendship. There was no doubt, the horses were talking to each other, maybe introducing themselves.

Jemma didn't know what to do. She had been looking forward to going into the house, lighting the fire, cooking food and sleeping in the warmth of the fire on her straw bed. She felt exhausted and cold and didn't think she could survive a night in the open, but how could she go to the village and ask for help when they thought she had the house belonging to her parents to sleep in? She looked at her watch. Just after 7.20. Perhaps whoever was here would not be stopping and she could hide in the woods until they left. If they looked settled in for the night, she would have to go to the village and perhaps she could sleep, secretly, in the village barn if she waited for all the villagers to go to sleep first. She rested her head against Cassie's neck, seeking the strength to keep going. What she most wanted to do, was to curl up beside Cassie and sleep, but if the riders of the horses were going to leave this evening, she could not stay here. Her voice croaked and cracked as she said to Cassie, "Sorry lass. We'll have to go back to the woods, and leave you there a while, and then I'll come back and try to work out what's going on. Come, girl. I'm sorry,"

Cassie pulled back gently against Jemma's insistence,

telling her these horses were friendly and safe, but Jemma kept the pressure on the rein and Cassie gave in with a snort, stepping after Jemma with a resigned air. It was frightening, heading back along the track, and now Jemma was glad of the earthy surface, muffling the noise of Cassie's hoofbeats. Tarmac or gravel would have given them away, instantly. No one shouted or chased them and they made it to the trees safely. Jemma tied Cassie to a tree in the shadows and turned towards the house, finding her feet refusing to carry her back towards danger. She stood and argued with herself. If they stayed in the wood, they would freeze. If they went to the village and admitted they had no home, they would be chased out of town. It was too far to return to Coughton Court and wake William to ask for help. She had to find out who was in the house, how long they might stay and what sort of danger they were. At last, her feet unglued and unwillingly allowed her to creep towards the house. Her heart was thudding again. She stopped by the bridge. She needed a plan. Obviously, she couldn't just go walking in and asking who they were and, from here she could see the flicker of firelight through cracks in the shutters but would she be able to see through those cracks without anyone seeing her? The slits might be too small for a human eye to look through. Would there be anyone in the room with glass windows? If it was lit with a candle, would they be able to see her peering in before she could see them through the distorted glass? She wouldn't risk that. Maybe she could just listen from under the shutters, ready to run if anyone came out of the doors.

This seemed the best plan so, once more she crept forwards, trying to avoid rustling leaves or deadwood sticks that might crack sharply under her feet. She

173

reached the corner of the house and eased to her knees, wincing as the cold bit through her gloves to her hands. Crawling until she was under the shuttered windows, she could make out voices arguing. A light man's voice was saying,

"You are all mad. What is the need to rebel? The queen is old. She cannot last so many more years and when she dies, we shall have James to the throne and he will support us and get rid of Cecil and the queen's government."

"How are you so sure?" Another voice interrupted him. "James is no Catholic. He may be only as bad as the queen, and Cecil is a wily so-and-so. Whose to say he won't wrap James around his finger as Cecil has the queen?"

"Aye," another voice agreed. "If we can convince the queen of Cecil's betrayal and treachery, we can establish a better government and Essex will pay us plenty if we can get his wine licence returned, and if we then have James, without Cecil's influence, he will surely give us Catholics our land back."

The first voice fought back. "Cecil is too clever for you. If you march on London, you will be signing your own death warrants. Let us wait for James and then petition him to support us as we will support him."

Somebody threw something angrily in the room, making Jemma jump."No Robert!" he shouted. "Have you no principles? The queen and her government have murdered our cousin, Francis. We have suffered imprisonment and fines only because we stick to the true faith. Here we are, hiding Father Garnet and Father Gerard and there is Nicholas Owen stashed away at Baddesley only because we stand up for the right. How is it right that I have had to see my father imprisoned leading to his death and see my family impoverished? "

"Robert Catesby," a quieter voice broke in. " You must calm yourself. It is not good to wish for violence. It is not your faith but your rebelliousness that has you fined and imprisoned. Your cousin, Master Wintour is right to wait to negotiate. It is right to stand for your principles, but not to take the lives of others in your quest."

"Father," came the angry voice. "How can you allow so many to lose their lives because of their faith? Lord Essex is right. We must tell the queen of Cecil's greed and treachery. Richard has had the idea that we will ask the Lord Chamberlain's players to act out Richard II in the hopes that the queen will see Cecil for the rogue he is, but if she does not, we have no choice but to find another sovereign."

Another voice joined in." Hush your voice, Robert. Who knows if your cousin Arthur may be spying and listening, ready to report the Catholics he hates to the queen's men. Deposing Cecil is one thing. Removing the queen quite another and I am not in favour of that."

"Henry Cuffe," replied Robert's voice scornfully. "You are such an academic, when I need men of action. Show some backbone, man."

"I agree....,"

"Another voice", Jemma thought. "How many are there?"

"...My father also was imprisoned and fined despite serving the queen faithfully. I am with Robert in this..."

A more practical voice stepped into the fray.

"This is enough talking," he said. "all we need to know is, who is with us tomorrow when we march to meet Essex. Those who will stand for their rights, and fight if they must, will go to Coughton tonight. Any who do not agree can stay with the priests here tonight, or return to their homes, as they wish. I am weary from my ride from Kidderminster and would need some sleep before we march tomorrow."

"You speak wisely Blount," someone said but Jemma had lost track of who was who in the many shouting voices. "I do not wish to fight unless I must but I am with you. Father Garnet will be safe here, and we must ride. So, we have Catesby, Tresham and Wintour. Are you with us Cuffe? Mountjoy? Gaunt?"

The next voice was Henry's. "What of the new things by the fire? And what about your missing cloak? Someone has been here since our last visit and I do not think it safe."

"We can hide in the cellar hole if needs be. John and I can keep watch and watch about," came the voice of Father Garnet. "It is good to have had the chance to stretch out, eat well and get warm, but we are used to discomfort when it is necessary."

Jemma cursed quietly to herself and willed someone to offer an alternative plan.

"Father, why not come to Huddington with us? It is some time since we were searched and we have recently kept out of trouble, paying our fines and keeping quiet. You should be safe with us."

""Thank you, Robert, but I think we are safer here at Shurnock where all think it is empty and no one searches at all."

Jemma's hopes had risen but now they fell again. The priests sounded peaceful and kind, trying to prevent violence but would that be the case if they saw her as a threat to their lives? There was the sound of many people moving about and she realised the men going to Coughton were getting ready to depart. In a rush of adrenalin, she fled to the trees and hid behind an ancient willow, watching. There was little to see but she could hear men crossing the yard area, still arguing. The voices increased in volume and were hushed by more cautious members of the group, only to rise again. She heard the clink of bridles and the barn door being opened, Some horses must have been tied beyond the house because there were now more horsemen wheeling than there had been horses in the barn, breath steaming in the cold night air. Most of the horses disappeared over the far bridge but Jemma shrank further into the trees as two horses came towards her, crossed the moat and trotted the track, turning south on a track Jemma had not yet used. The dissenters, returning to Huddington. Was that Robert Wintour with someone who had remained silent?

The house was now quiet, silently lit by the flickering flames and Jemma rubbed a weary arm across her face, wishing she was able to share the glowing warmth of the fire. She still stood in the shadows of the trees, wondering if she dare return to the barn with Cassie and sleep there. Her mouth turned down as she thought that the cloak had probably vanished with its owner. She was about to stand to retrieve Cassie, when she heard the clink and jingle of metal and froze. Who was still here, invisible in the night? Had they realised she was here somewhere? Were they hiding, waiting for her to reveal herself? She stepped slowly back into the shadows and hoped that Cassie would stay quiet and not call out to her.

Out of the darkness came a darker shape. One man on a horse, his horse's hooves muffled in material so that he made no sound. He sat tall and straight in the saddle, a sword in a scabbard at his side. He took his horse across the bridge but then hesitated, just standing and watching. He then dismounted, fastened the horse to the bridge rail, and crept, as Jemma had done, to the shuttered window, half kneeling to listen. He remained stationary for some time, alert to the conversation within, and then crept backwards and returned to his horse, mounted and left.

Jemma watched him ride passed and vanish into the night. "Who was that?" she asked herself but could find no answer. It was so cold. She could not stay out all night, and nor could Cassie. Decision made, she fetched Cassie and led her quietly to the barn. It was deserted. The priests had no horses of their own. They had no reason to come to the barn. She must risk discovery or die of hypothermia. Discovery was the safer option but how she wished the priests had hidden in the priest hole and she could have locked them in with the barrel against the door, slept in the house and released them at dawn, possibly without them even knowing they had been imprisoned overnight.

It was almost impossible, without food, drink and fire to remove the chill from her body. She jumped up and down, pumped her arms and pulled the remaining hay as close to Cassie as she could get without being accidentally trampled and did her best to sleep. It was now 10 o' clock. She curled small and tucked her head in tight, hood of the hoodie up to stop the heat leaving her head but it was so cold, she had to keep getting up and running around the barn, burning energy to create heat but depleting her stamina at the same time. Were the priests going to stay for days or was this just an overnight stop? Who was that man on the horse and would he bring others to capture the priests in the morning? If so, she would need to be gone before they arrived.

She was awake again at 6 o' clock and gave up trying to sleep. Where had the priests slept? She was so hungry that she considered sneaking into the great hall and trying to snatch her cheese and bread but then thought of the nuts and flour and apples in the cellar. If they had slept in the house, she could get to the cellar, but if they had decided the cellar, though cold, was safer, what then? She had to eat. She crept first to the shutters but could see nothing in the dark room within. The fire was out. She didn't dare enter. She slipped to the cellar, and took a breath to steady herself before opening the door a crack as quietly as she could. She pushed her head in, looking round quickly and was relieved to find it empty. Hurrying in, she grabbed handfuls of nuts and stuffed them into her mouth, feeling like a squirrel as her cheeks bulged. Then she snatched some apples, filling her pockets before filling her cup with cider and drinking it down. Finding herself thirstier than she had expected, she took another cup. What could she put the flour in? She had had an idea to mix the flour with water and then make a fire to cook it on, the nearest she could get to bread, and more filling than the nuts and fruit. Her dish was in the house. She gulped the cider and half filled the cup with flour. She peered carefully out of the door and, seeing no one, sprinted back to the barn, now adrenalin filled, afraid of being spotted by either the priests or any one coming to capture them. She fetched Cassie. Which was the best way to leave? The front entrance was nearest but in sight of the windows and doors whereas the woods were further but along the blank walls of the house, out of sight of the windows and doors. She opted for the wood, leaping into Cassie's saddle and leaving as quickly as she could, not even looking over her shoulder to see if anyone was watching.

Once on the main track, she needed somewhere to hide while she lit her fire to warm herself and cooked her flour. No good going to Brian's farm. Cassie plodded on. There was another track here, that once led to a Nature Reserve. No, she thought, it *will lead to a Nature reserve*, one day, in the future. Where did it go now?

179

She turned Cassie and they went exploring, their eyes now adjusted to the before dawn gloom.

"At least there's no fog today," she told Cassie.

Cassie's head nodded as she stepped on. There were fields, here, full of sheep,and then a wide arc of trees spreading back into a thick wood spreading further than the eye could see. There were no houses in sight. She turned into the trees, and dismounted, gathering wood. Somewhere ahead of her, the stream that fed Shurnock's moat must run and become Bow Brook. She needed water to add to her flour and for Cassie to drink. They walked on and, listening carefully, heard the bubbling of running water. Finding the stream, she dipped her cup and allowed Cassie to drink before disappearing back into the trees and setting up her water heater. No solar power. She grimaced and resisted the temptation to hurl the batteries down. It wasn't their fault the last day had been all fog and no sun and that she hadn't been able to set the solar units up anywhere while she tried to find work. She still had matches due to her habit of always collecting her survival kit back together. She shaved her sticks to find dry wood beneath the frosty damp surface and struck a match, relieved to get the fire going with one strike. She whispered a thank you to her dad and Seb for suggesting she added the water heating cylinder to her kit. She would not need to have a very big fire to heat her water. It boiled quickly and she stirred flour and water together making a sort of fat-less pastry, and wound it onto a stick to cook it over the flames as she warmed herself. Cassie watched with interest. Jemma ate an apple while the pastry cooked and then peeled it off the stick and ate it, thinking it a luxury, but wishing she had thought to see if the hens had laid any eggs. She took a half gasp. Where were the hens? If they had been in the barn, they had stayed hidden and quiet all night and she hadn't fed them. She thought carefully. It wasn't safe to go back to check them. Either they had run away when the riders came or they were hidden and safe, or......the riders had taken them. Jemma shied away from the thought that they may have been eaten, and tried to comfort herself that there had been no smell of cooking meat. Later, she would go back to look for them. Another, happier thought came to mind. They may have gone back to Brian and the cockerel, only a run through the hedge for a hen if they had escaped the barn.

It was another grey day. Not fog, but thick cloud. The sun had risen but was nowhere to be seen. Would there be work anywhere today? Not in these fields of sheep. She couldn't work at Shurnock. She was not sure of the village's loyalties. Catholic or protestant? She wanted to know about the man on the horse and the people in the house. They had obviously been Catholic, also violent, angry and perhaps a little bit frightened, but it would be difficult to ask questions without raising suspicions. For the first time, she started to think about what they had been saying. Last night she had been too cold and tired to think of anything but how to get warm and where to sleep. Now, she remembered the angry voice, so hurt by things of the past, the execution of his cousin and the payment of so many huge fines by so many members of his family. So angry that he was prepared to kill the queen? Had he said that, or did he just wish to, in some way, remove her from the throne and put some other person in her place? Who was there left in line to the throne who supported Catholics? Was Mary, Queen of Scots still alive? Jemma thought she was already gone. What other names had she heard? She thought there had been more than one Robert in the conversation. One, the angry voice was Robert Catesby and the other, his cousin, Robert Wintour who had not wanted to rebel. Brian Cuffe had sounded a logical man and from Robert Catesby's scorn, not a natural fighter, whereas, the last man from Kidderminster had sounded like a practical soldier.

Still thirsty, she went to fetch more water and boiled it on the last of the flames, wishing she had coffee or even tea or mint to add but telling herself to be grateful for the boiling to kill germs and the heat to give her warmth. If the priests were going to stay at Shurnock, she thought worriedly, how was she going to eat? It was, what? Tuesday and a long way to the Saturday market, and without work for herself and Cassie and, even no hens, she was in danger of starving. She looked around at the bleak open fields. Almost everything was harvested and stashed away undercover. The only thing she could think of was a midnight raid on Shurnock's cellar to take more nuts, flour, apples, turnips and potatoes. If she brought Cassie close, she could fill the saddle packs, but her kettle and saucepan were still in the hall so she had no way to cook except using her cup and the water boiler, and no real shelter, except to risk the barn. She glanced around the wood she was hidden in. Could she build a shelter here and survive in it until the priests left?,,,and how would she know when they had gone? Every possible solution seemed to lead to more questions and more difficulties. If only she had fallen through time to summer harvest or autumn fruit, with enough warmth in the air to sleep under the stars. She looked up at Cassie, her face strained. "I don't know what to do Cassie. How are we going to survive?" She drummed a hand against her thigh, fist clenched tightly. "I must think of something, but how can I? I don't know enough. I don't know who I can ask for help. Even though Margery and Will are nice,

I can't ask them to share their food when there is almost nothing left until the new crops grow. If there's no work to do, no one can pay me. Do you think I could ask to be a maid in the big house? I expect they have enough already and anyway, they would want to know why I was needing a job there and not tending my family's land." She shook her head, angry, frustrated and frightened, almost panic stricken. She jumped up and strode round in circles, trying to remove the pressure build-up of emotion so that she could think logically, but so tired and hungry that any kind of thought was difficult.

There was William at Coughton, she supposed. He could perhaps let her sleep in the stables there. Who knew if there was excess food being grown with that big house empty. There might still be someone keeping account of the yields and selling the excess to pay the bills and fines, She did not want to get William into trouble, and then she remembered the plotters were going to Coughton last night. How long did they intend staying there? It sounded from the last man that it was only one night before going to meet Lord Essex somewhere, but she was not sure she had that right. She felt so angry at her inability to cope. "Come on Jemma. You're grown up. People are bringing up families at your age. You only have you and a horse to look after," but still she struggled to make a sensible decision. There were too many unknowns. "Right," she thought. "Let's take one thing at a time. Right now, you can go to Feckenham and check there is no work. If there is, you have money and can go to Alcester to buy food. If there is not, you can ask Margery and Will if they know anyone else who might need Cassie's help and will pay, and if they don't, you'll have to go back to Coughton and ask William. If all that doesn't work, maybe someone in Alcester, or Stratford might need a horse to pull a wagon".

She felt better for having a plan, even knowing that all her ideas might fail, but she would not think about that yet, nor how she would find out about the priests leaving. "Come on then Cassie," she said hitching up her skirt so that she could get her foot to the stirrup and pull herself up. She looked around, making sure the fire was dead and she had all her kit and they set off for Feckenham.

There was a group of villagers clustered together by the trough, serious faced as they discussed something important, but, as they saw Jemma, they pulled apart. What had she interrupted? More plotting? She pretended not to have noticed, wishing she was trusted and part of the community. Hugh and Ned were there, and Margery. No sign of Will or the Richards and Johns.
 "Good morning," Jemma tried. "Is there any work today?" Hugh shrugged. "Don't think so. There was supposed to be more seed to come, but the cart is not arrived. Will has gone looking toward Droitwich and John is gone up to the ridge to see if it's mebbe lost a wheel or summat. You might a seed Dicken gone up your way toward Alcester. " Jemma shook her head but didn't try to explain. Ned and Hugh looked at each other and then at Margery. "We wondered, did you see anyone else on the road?" Hugh said.
Jemma wasn't sure whether to admit she had come from the track south instead of along The Saltway. How important was it if she had seen anyone? They looked worried.

She shook her head, but said, "I didn't stay on the main track today. Cassie and I went exploring down to the wood and stopped to look at the sheep so we may have missed people on the road. Who did you think I might see?"

The villagers again exchanged glances and it was Margery that made the decision to include her. "You may have seen my John, or you may have seen a gentleman on a black horse, who would be Arthur Throckmorton. John went out last night and has not come home. Arthur, we think was out on the roads last night and perhaps this morning on the queen's business."

She stopped, suppressing emotion and gripped her hands together as if to divert it and hold it captive. "John holds Arthur and his family responsible for his father's death and his uncle fleeing to France where he died, too. I am afraid of what he might have done, knowing Arthur was out alone."

Jemma thought of the men at Shurnock and wondered if John had been among them. The man on the horse must have been Arthur Throckmorton. Margery was studying her face.

"You know something," she said, reading it in Jemma's face.

"I got lost in the fog yesterday," Jemma explained, "and I was late on the road. I saw a group of horsemen riding from Shurnock towards Alcester but I don't know if John was among them. Then I saw another horseman alone but he only looked at Shurnock and then was gone. I don't know if he came past the village or went South, but that was all last night. Not this morning."

Ned looked at Hugh and nodded as if confirming something they had discussed before. "Catesby, and his hot heads," he said disgustedly. "Tis one thing to be of the old faith, but to keep rioting is to bring more trouble on us in the village."

"Aye," Hugh agreed, "But 'tis not like young John to get involved."

185

Another villager that Jemma did not know said,"He would not want more of his kin harmed. If he saw Arthur, he may have gone to warn young Catesby, or perhaps Tresham or the Wintours."

Margery nodded. "That would make sense. Is there anything we should do, then?"

The group seemed to be communicating by mind rather than voice as they all exchanged looks, and then Ned said,

"'Tis Will who's the thinker and he's not here. I say, wait to see if young John comes home on his own or perhaps Will or Dicken or our John will meet him while they are looking for the seed merchant and bring him home with them. Nothing we can do but wait. If we goes all a-looking then when the seed comes there's no one to plant it, and more has to go chasing to bring everyone home."

Jemma felt deflated, hollow inside. She hadn't admitted to herself how much she had wanted to work with the villagers, part of a team, all looking out for each other and pulling their weight. She looked at Margery."Do you know if anyone else needs any help with a horse?" she asked hopefully, but Margery shook her head. "This time of year, there's little to do but wait, lass," she said.

Jemma nodded glumly, and turned Cassie to head back to the main road, that little lump of hopelessness building in her throat. She sensed Margery watching her, worried and sympathetic, but there was little she could do to help. Jemma reached the junction and considered trying west, just asking anyone she met for work, but then thought about the strips of land she had seen off the road to Inkberrow. She would ask there first. She turned east, trotting rapidly to the hill, slowing to a walk for the ascent and then trotting again on the downward side. As she approached Shurnock, she peered down the drive. No horses, no people, no smoke from the chimney. It looked deserted but the priests were almost certainly still there. She turned south on the track she knew curved around and ended taking her into Inkberrow, if she went that far. There had been no sign of John or Dicken.

 The strips were well north of the small town of Inkberrow. These, too were empty of people. It was as if the whole human race had been swallowed up by the earth, leaving Jemma and Cassie to walk the planet alone. She was afraid to enter Inkberrow and draw more attention to herself. Afraid someone would ask where exactly her homestead was or for descriptions of the imagined bandits. She turned and went back to The Saltway. She would go to Alcester and ask for work in the shops she had visited to buy food and Cassie's rug and even try the apothecary and if all that failed, she would consider going to Coughton and asking William for help, although she still quailed at the thought of meeting Robert Catesby and his clan. If they thought she was a spy, her life would be measured in seconds.

She studied the countryside as she rode, trying to take her mind off the ordeal ahead of her. With her shyness and the knowledge that it was likely everyone would say no, she was finding the imminent future terrifying.

There were more birds. Some big birds were wheeling overhead, fringes of wings outstretched, mewing to each other. Eagles? Buzzards, or kites? How did one know the difference? There was another that she thought might be a kestrel, flapping its wings fast, but staying in one place, its attention on the ground below.. Her mum had told her how they were the only bird that could hover in one place, searching for prey and then dive to snatch their meal. A

187

fox slunk across the track and disappeared into the trees, his coat glossy and deep red. There were more squirrels, all red with their bright eyes and bushy tails. She feasted on each sighting, feeling exhilarated and calling in her mind, "Mum, mum, if only you could share what I see. So many special animals you told me were gone forever, and they are here, before my eyes."

If only her mum was here to see them with her. She sighed quietly and shook her neck and shoulders, trying to shrug off the black thoughts and continue to enjoy the moment. There was a cry of alarm and indignation almost at her feet and a brightly coloured bird with a long tail and short wings jumped into the air and flapped into the undergrowth. Again, she wished for that book with the bright pictures and descriptions of so many birds. Pheasant or partridge. If only she had paid more attention. She had reached the houses on the edge of the town. Smoke wafted from chimneys and caught in her throat, making her eyes smart and the smell of unwashed bodies and sewage assaulted her nostrils.

She asked everywhere, plucking up courage for another "No," before entering each shop. Only if she had had a cart would she have been useful but she had no money to buy one and no wood or tools to make one. She remounted Cassie feeling more depressed than ever before in her life, numb and almost shocked that she had not achieved any work. She realised she had never had to face failure before. Always her family and teachers had set her tasks and challenges she could succeed at if she persevered. She now had only William to ask and with that was the danger of Catesby. She wondered if, as a woman, she would be beneath consideration as a spy. Apart from the queen, how important were the ladies in the eyes of the men? If they were just there to produce and look after babies or cook food and clean, she might pass unnoticed, although she wasn't dressed correctly for a housemaid. Cassie was trying to take her back to Shurnock and there was a bit of an argument when Jemma insisted they took the Coughton road, Cassie having learned the night before not to trust her rider when it came to direction. However, when Jemma said "We're going to see William," the ears swivelled and Cassie allowed herself to be steered to the right. What an intelligent horse, Jemma marvelled.

At the end of the long drive, Jemma hesitated. Was she being stupid? Should she just go back to Shurnock and pinch some more nuts and stuff. She could survive another night in the barn couldn't she? In the end, it was the need for advice that forced her on. William might know how often the priests changed their hiding place. He might have overheard the plans of Catesby and Tresham and know if or when they were headed for London.

The house was still silent as Jemma approached. If she had heard voices she would, almost certainly have turned back. Searching for signs of occupation, she saw smoke issuing from a chimney, but there were no flickering candles lighting rooms dark in the gloomy afternoon. Nibbling her lip, Jemma walked her horse on and into the stable yard. If there were horses here, she would turn around and leave, but, although there were wisps of straw where none had been before and horse droppings not yet removed, there was no sign of life. It seemed the men had come and gone. Jemma dismounted and led Cassie into a box, out of sight of casual eyes. There was even hay hanging in a net and a bucket half filled with water. "I'll go see William, and if we're staying, I'll come back and unsaddle you, OK?" she asked Cassie who was happily pulling out mouthfuls of hay.

Jemma shut her in and hurried into the garden. It was almost dark, but only 3 o' clock. She found William putting tools away. He heard her coming, and looked around. "Jemma! Hello. Are you back to ask about work? I have not yet had time to ask at the villages. Last night, a whole bunch of relations of Sir Thomas arrived demanding beds and food, wine and hot water. With the staff all gone, I have been acting as butler, wine waiter and boot boy while my wife and daughter cooked, served and made beds. I had to ride to Alcester for supplies this morning for their breakfast and they were in such a great hurry I was urged to gallop. How can one gallop with a cart of food? Anyway, they were gone again by mid morning so some of the food I bought for luncheon is still here – they took what they could eat cold with them – and Anne is cooking us a feast."

He looked at Jemma's pale, strained face.

"Will you eat with us? My wife would like to meet you, I think, and my daughter, too, although I have told them nothing about, well, about things that are difficult to explain."

Jemma's face became one enormous grin.

"If you weren't married, I would kiss you," she laughed. "There are priests hiding at Shurnock, and I came mostly for advice, but William, I am starving, and yes please, can I eat with you?"

William looked startled. "Did they see you? How did they not find you in the house?"

Jemma found she could laugh now about the terrors of the day before as she explained how she got lost in the fog and walked into a barn full of horses. As she told of the voices in the hall, William looked serious and then horrified.

190

"If they had caught you listening, they would have killed you," he said. "If you meet them again, just get away as fast as you can. Come to me if you have nowhere nearer to go for help," he said.

They were walking, now, towards the stable yard, where Jemma removed Cassie's saddle and gave her a brush from the brushes in the groom's storeroom, while William went to tell his wife that Jemma was joining them. As Jemma left Cassie, William called from a door into the house, and Jemma was led to a kitchen with a good fire burning, a black iron stove, the smell of bread and some kind of stew bubbling away in a cauldron. It smelled of luxury, a poor man's idea of heaven. Jemma felt she could cry with happiness as the bands of tension exploded and dissolved within her. Tonight, she was safe. Tomorrow, she would be strong enough to face another day. There were seven of them at table. Jemma and all the staff of the empty house, left to keep the grounds tidy and the rooms dusted and aired.

Jemma ate ravenously and the atmosphere was that of a party with unexpected excess food to eat. It was as if those left were trying to overlie the anger and aggression of the visitors of the night before with laughter and smiles. As the last of the food vanished, and cups were drained of cider, the talk became more serious.

It was William's wife, Anne, who began. She looked from Jemma to William and asked, "What will happen if the rebellion fails? Will this house be ransacked again?"

William gave her a lopsided smile. "Who is to know,?" he replied. "So far as I know, Sir Thomas is not involved being away at his own home. Blount and Catesby are the main drivers of this bunch, but I think that they are small fry compared to Lord Essex, so we may be left alone. I only worry that Arthur may stir up trouble. The rift between his father and Sir Robert and Sir Thomas became so great at the end that Arthur now hates all Catholics to the point of obsession. His zeal is frightening, almost beyond reason."

William suddenly realised young Edward was listening and watching with fear filled eyes. He broke off and looked at his daughter.

"Kit, our young 'un looks ready for his bed, kept awake by the goings on of last night. Should you take him home?"

He looked directly at his grandson and said firmly, "Whatever happens to the big family, we keep our heads down and do the job we needs to do. The soldiers know that. They do no harm to the likes of us. You can sleep safe, I promise."

Edward looked as if he was searching his grandfather's eyes for truth, and finding it, ran around the table to give him a hug and a kiss, kneeling on William's knees to reach his cheek.

"I love you, Grampa," he said impulsively.

William put both arms around Edward and hugged him back, infusing protection and support and love.

"Off to bed, young man," he said.

Edward and Catherine went to the door, hand in hand and left, chattering together about Jemma. They could hear the high voice asking perceptive questions about Jemma's clothes and voice and how tall she was. Catherine's replies were too quiet to catch. William and Jemma exchanged a look of relief that Edward had been too interested in his food to ask the questions at the table.

Jemma said, "Could I sleep in the barn here, tonight and I will be gone before breakfast tomorrow?"

William looked at his wife for approval before saying, "I had thought you might sleep in the house, but perhaps the barn is safer. Who knows if any of the plotters will get cold feet and return, wanting another bed here for the night. Where will you go tomorrow?"

Jemma was feeling braver with the food and warmth.

"I will try to find out if the priests have moved on. I was thinking, that from their tone, they are men of peace. If they are still there, I might ask that I can stay with them, that I mean them no harm but need shelter there while I work with the Feckenham villagers. What do you think?"

William looked down at his cup, turning it round and round between finger and thumb as he thought. "Father Garnet does always speak peacefully. The John you speak of is probably Father Gerard, who is, I think very intelligent and would listen and reason, and would only cause you harm if he believed you a threat. There is some risk there, but I think you could convince him you would do no harm."

The cup kept turning. William was still thinking. He raised his eyes to Jemma, "But what if Catesby returns or one of the others to move the priests on and you are found there?"

Anne said nothing but she raised her hands to her face, hiding the horror this thought brought to her. Jemma looked from one to another, feeling desperate. "The priests will be watching for danger. If they see anyone coming, I can run and hide in the woods again. If I can only sleep there one night, and take food and my kettle, I can build a shelter in the big forest and sleep there until they are gone, but William, I must return to Shurnock. It's my only chance of getting home."

William looked to his wife. "Do you have any thoughts, Anne?" he asked.

She shook her head. "I think there are things here I do not understand. Why Jemma has no roof of her own, and why living at Shurnock may help her get home, and I do not want to know. Like young Ned, I notice things to question in your clothes and voice, but I do not ask. Knowledge can be a dangerous thing, I think Coughton is a dangerous place for those who stand out or who cannot answer simple questions. I do not think Jemma should stay here, where soldiers come to hunt for priests and recusants so often, but," and here she turned to Jemma, "we will give you food whenever you have need. You have only to ask, and I can think of nothing more to help you. Just always be cautious and say always as little as you can to stay safe."

Jemma nodded. "Thank you," she said. There was nothing else to be said.

They were all tired. Darkness had descended even before the setting of the sun and William used a lantern to light Jemma to the barn and bring covers to add to her warmth. He lifted the lantern high, forcing the shadows to flee from the brightness. "You will be alright, here. If you are gone before we awake, take care and come whenever you have need."

He placed the lantern carefully on the floor.

"Thank you, William," Jemma said, wanting to hug him as Edward had, in gratitude and in the need for human touch, for reassurance and security, but she felt this would shock him and make him uncomfortable, so she settled for a light squeeze of his arm, before he left, pulling the door shut behind him. Jemma wasted no time, settling under the covers and blowing out the candle, descending into sleep within seconds.

The early night had made the world a better place. Jemma rose while the sky was still black, using the lantern to light the stable box as she saddled Cassie. She was going to try to reach Shurnock at dawn before the priests would be properly awake if they were there, and before other travellers would be on the road. She wondered if John had returned and whether the seed had arrived and where Arthur now was. How she wished for an internet connection or even a TV or radio news channel. The road seemed easy in the pre-dawn light. How had she got so lost in the fog? Arriving at Shurnock, with the pink rim of sun wash beginning on the horizon, she slid off Cassie's back in the road. "Wait here, girl," she instructed her mount. "I have to go quietly and do some creeping around looking through windows."

She ran almost silently towards the house, just the minutest thud of boot against earth. Should she just walk in, or check around first? She was going to have to confront the priests sometime if they were still here. Maybe she had better look around for signs of others joining them first, or was that just an excuse to put the moment off? No, it was sense, she decided and flitted around the house, peering through those annoyingly distorted glass panels, seeing nothing in the room. There were no obvious tracks of men or horses and all the shutters were closed as they had been before. No smoke from the chimney. She checked the barn. The hens were there on the bales of hay, gurgling at her as if reprimanding her tardiness in feeding them.
"You're OK!" she said with relief and hurried to throw some grain for them.
"Oh", she added, delighted. "You've even laid me an egg." but there was no time to collect it and take it to Cassie for safe keeping.

It looked like, either the priests were gone, or at least were here alone. It was time to confront them. She ran to the porch door, and opened it before she could find any more reasons to delay. The hall was empty. Things had been moved around. There was more wood by the fireplace and sacks of nuts, carrots and apples, tucked behind the door, out of immediate sight. Jemma went across the room and felt the ashes. Cold. She returned to the staircase and looked up the spiralling stairs. Should she just light the fire and cook her egg, listening for noise from above, or should she go up and if they were there get the meeting over with? They might panic if they felt cornered up there and come rushing out with a sword or a knife or something. If she just lit the fire, they could choose whether to slip down the stairs and escape or confront her. That seemed a better plan. She cleared the ash from the grate and laid the kindling, grateful to whoever had gathered it. She noticed her bread and cheese were gone. It was a fairish swap, she supposed.

With matches and dry wood, the fire lit easily and Jemma slipped out to fetch water, enjoying the luxury of having both saucepan and kettle. She also collected her egg, resisting the temptation to throw it triumphantly in the air. Her very own hens' first egg. Yes! But she wasn't going to risk a fumbled catch and a smashed egg. She made more noise than necessary, banging the latch on the door as she entered and scuffing her feet. If there was anyone up there, she wanted them to know she was here, but not hunting for them. She stuck the egg in the kettle and hung it to boil while she fetched herbs, almost whistling with the normality. She felt sure everything would be OK, but couldn't logically explain it. While she waited for the water to boil, she hurried out to the road and brought

Cassie in, tethering her under the apple tree. She wanted the priests to see her, but not anyone passing on the road. Still, no one had appeared. Had they gone? Or had they seen her coming and were now hiding in the priest hole? She decided the best thing was to keep her senses sharp but carry on in as normal manner as possible, and was soon eating her egg and drinking mint tea. The cloak was gone, which was a shame. So was the straw she had strewn by the fire. She was sitting at the table on one of the hard chairs to eat. Better for her posture, but much less comfortable.

It was as she finished that she heard the sound of voices filtering down the stairwell. They were up there. Should she call out? Did they know she was here? She finished the egg quickly. If she did have to run, she would do it with no food wasted. Then she repacked her survival kit and put it around her waist. Looking around, she opened the door to the herb garden and put the kettle outside, hidden amongst the rosemary so that she could either grab it and use it as a weapon, or come back to get it later if she chose just to run. There was nothing more to do. It was time to ensure they knew of her presence.

She went and stood at the bottom of the stairs and called in a voice that wanted to whisper. "If anyone is up there, I mean you no harm. I have to live here, too."
She waited, uncertain what to do. No one replied.
"If you need to stay, too, I am happy to share," she suggested hopefully. There was another pause of silence, and then the rustling of someone moving in straw and footsteps across the wooden floor above her. She couldn't help holding her breath. Another silly automatic response. Fight, freeze or flight. Why freeze now, when if she would need to run or fight, she needed a body filled

with oxygenated muscles? She tried to force air from her lungs and take another breath, her instincts fighting her rational mind.

The priest that appeared was bent but not old. He wore a ragged cloak that made her think tramp, but the face was alive with intelligence and held a calmness that she had not expected in someone constantly in danger, constantly on the run. To her surprise, he moved forward and sat on the top stair and smiled at her. "While we talk," he said, "I will stay here and you can stay there and neither of us will need to feel frightened,"
Jemma giggled. It reminded her of her reaction to the big black spiders that always startled her as they ran across the room. She had said much the same thing to them and it had normally worked. "OK," she said.
 "Is that a new word of today's youth?" he asked, smiling. "I have not heard the term before."
"I mean, that is acceptable," Jemma said, liking this man with his enquiring mind, and slight sense of self mockery.
"Good," he said. He studied her carefully and then asked "Do you know who I am?"
Jemma thought it was best to be honest. "I think you must be either Father Garnet or Father Gerard but I don't know which."
He nodded approvingly. "I am Father Garnet. And can I ask your name?"
"Jemma Martins," Jemma replied without hesitation.
The priest mused a short time, searching his memory.
"I do not think I know that name," he said. "but I will not ask too many questions and then you won't ask too many, either. That seems fair."
Jemma had a strange desire to giggle again. This man was good at putting her at her ease. She remained silent. Waiting for his next question.

"So," he said. "Our bargain is, that we share the house and food and neither of us will tell anyone else of our presence, yes?"

Jemma nodded carefully, "Yes, but I have a horse to feed and must go to the village for work if there is any to do."

"Hmm," said the priest. "That may be a problem." He scratched his bearded jaw, thinking. "We will be quite nervous of you accidentally letting slip our presence. I have a counter suggestion that you remain here for just two, maybe three days, when we will in any case be moving on and we will share our supplies with you. There is a servant bringing us food from elsewhere and I will ask him to replenish your horse's food supplies generously before we leave. How is that?"

Jemma studied his face, her eyes then sliding down to his clothes, noting that despite his stoop, he was still muscular. She thought that if she tried to run she might not get very far before she was recaptured and she might then find herself a prisoner restricted to one room, or even tethered with a rope. If she agreed, she would have shelter and food and if the priest was true to his word, even more food for Cassie. She tried to consider any more repercussions. What if she was found with the priests? Could she claim she was imprisoned and was not trying to help them? Two days. What if someone from the village or William came looking for her. Would that endanger the priests or even cause someone to be killed? There were so many people involved, people whose characters she did not really know, that it was impossible to predict the results of any course of actions. Just now, agreeing with Father Garnet seemed the best thing to do, and then she would have breathing space to think some more, or even reason with him more if she changed her mind.

"Yes, " she said. "I agree."

The priest put his hands together in a silent clap of pleasure and glanced around the top of the stairs, back towards the upstairs room, apparently seeking approval from his hidden companion. He nodded as if in response to the other man's agreement and turned back to Jemma.

"We will come down now and join you, Our prayer session is over and we are ready to eat. Will you be joining us?"

Jemma actually smiled. " I have already eaten an egg, but if you have bread, I would love some."

"Ah, alas, no bread, only hard biscuits which last longer, but there are enough of those to share as I am afraid we ate your bread." Father Garnet replied, getting to his feet and descending lithely.

His level of fitness was greater than Jemma had ever seen in a churchman. He saw her astonishment and chuckled.

"One has to be fit to run across fields away from the queen's searchers and one has to be agile to climb into priest holes. We exercise regularly because of this."

The other priest had come into sight, his clothes were a fine cut, but mud spattered, and Jemma felt her eyebrows rise. She had expected the black or brown cloak of a monk, rather than the clothes of aristocracy. He was of a more serious character, his face set and stern, but handsome in features. Jemma sensed he had seen a great deal of violence and death around him, only his faith keeping him strong against overwhelming despair, Too many betrayals of trust, even in friends, never mind a strange girl only just met. They brought another sack of food down with them and Father Gerard knelt at the fire to replenish the burning wood, then silently checked the kettle and took the saucepan for more water. Father Garnet sorted two platters and placed them next to

Jemma's dish, laying biscuits in each and then adding nuts and apples, sliced with a wicked looking knife which had Jemma swallowing nervously. An observant man, he noticed and shook his head with another smile. "Violence is not my way. You have nothing to fear."

Once the water was boiled, they all sat at the table and Jemma found herself ducking her head in prayer out of politeness to her two new companions as they offered a prayer in words Jemma did not understand.

"Was that Latin?" Jemma asked as they ate.
Father Gerard's hand paused in mid air and he glanced at his comrade. Father Garnet nodded. "Have you not heard it before?" he asked.
"No," said Jemma. "I was never taught it. Only English." She almost added and French and Spanish and a little German, but suddenly realised that most Tudor girls, except those of the very rich, would not have the chance to learn foreign languages and stopped herself. Father Garnet shook his head sadly.
"And yet, only fifty odd years ago it was the language of all church services and everyone spoke at least a little Latin."
He gave a small sigh.
"Does it really matter what language we pray in?" Jemma asked unable to restrain her interest.
Father Garnet, sat back in his chair and considered her. "That is a very sharp question," he said. "The answer is no, but all the words of God and the discussions and teachings of the theology we use are in Latin or Greek and so, if we lose these languages, we also lose the teachings of what God's word means. To keep the language alive, we must speak it and understand it. It is the language of the pope and if we all speak it we can

talk of God's word with people from all over the world. If we lose the common tongue, we can no longer make our meanings clear."

Jemma found herself fascinated by this intelligent speaker and his silent companion. She nodded thoughtfully.

"But, if you just prayed in church in English, wouldn't the queen accept you and then you wouldn't have to hide any more and you could just think in Catholic and then no one would have to be imprisoned or fined or executed, would they?"

Father Gerard was looking at her with a mixed expression, part admiration, part fear and she suddenly wondered if he thought her some kind of demon or witch, rather than just someone with a quick brain full of curiosity and enquiry. Father Garnet, on the other hand was looking delighted. He turned to his comrade. "John, we will be able to spend the whole day in debate to pass the time. What luck. And by the end of the day we may have a new convert."

The other priest snorted through his nose. "You carry on and I will keep watch. It would be unwise for both of us to be engrossed in debate with so many spies in the area. You can take a turn out in the cold later, Henry."

He rose from the table and exited with a clang of the latch and a bang of the door.

"Shall we continue our discussion upstairs?" the priest asked. "The wooden floor is warmer and there is less draught from the doors and windows."

Jemma hesitated. "Are you not frightened of being trapped up there?"

Father Garnet shrugged. "One cannot spend one's whole life being frightened. I would otherwise spend my whole life lurking uncomfortably in a dark, cold priest-hole. I tend to use the luxury of a warm room whenever the chance arises and trust in God and Gerard to keep me safe. Come, let us discuss your views on God with freedom while nothing but the walls can hear us."

He led Jemma up the stairs and they settled on the pallets of straw to talk.

The debate was free and fast with Jemma trying to fight for freedom to choose no god or any god and the priest arguing that there was only one true faith and it was essential not to be turned from God's true path. He had such a steady way of talking and never got heated and his grasp of the bible was amazing with the ability to use his knowledge of nature and wars to back up his points. Time flew by until they were startled by the rattle of the latch and Gerard returned, pale and gaunt with cold. "There have been some soldiers on the road," he said, "But none looked this way. I wonder if it is to do with Essex and Blount's escapade."

Jemma realised, suddenly that she had been thinking about Robert Catesby as the leader of the gunpowder plot, but that was 1605 and this was only 1601, and February, not November. Lord Essex, she thought was another rebel who failed and was executed. Was this the Essex rebellion? It hadn't seemed important, just a paragraph or two in her history book, whereas Guy Fawkes had pages. People were going to be imprisoned or executed for their beliefs but Jemma could do nothing to stop it.

"I'll take a watch. You get yourself warm," Father Garnet said and, adding a dark cloak to his garments, left the house.

Father Gerard spoke gruffly. "I must eat and then sleep, madam. Please take no note of my manner. I do not have Henry's resilience. Perhaps my faith is weaker but I find this fleeing from place to place, this jig to avoid capture exhausting and I must rest when I can,"

Jemma tried to imagine what it would be like, trying to convert people to a forbidden faith in secret, never sure if they would report you and see you hung, constantly dodging priest seekers, never able to stay in one place for more than a few days. Even living at Shurnock with the support of Margery and William had been traumatic and reduced her to tears. She could never live as these two men did. "I will leave you in peace," she said and descended the stairs.

Opening the door, she went to talk to Cassie, seeing Father Garnet watching her alertly in case she might try to leave, but she had nowhere to go and could see no point in reporting the priests to anyone.

The cold eventually drove her back indoors, the light in another cloudy day fading from grey to black. First, she led Cassie back to the barn and fed her and the hens, and then went to sit close to the fire, watching the flames almost trance-like, blocking out the feeling of imprisonment, knowing she was being carefully watched, blocking out the knowledge of imminent violence. Essex, Catesby, Blount, Tresham and one of the Wintour brothers against Raleigh, Cecil, Cobham and the queen's soldiers, each fighting for a set of principles not worth the battle. What was the matter with mankind that they couldn't live peacefully together?
She found her eyelids drooping and took off her hoodie and her hidden trousers to make a warm nest to snooze on, and slept. Her mind felt secure with another person on watch, even if he was a sort of jailer.

She woke in the dark to find herself covered in a cloak and the fire a dull glow as the last remnants of wood burned to ash. It seemed that every time she slept she woke in a different place, disorientated and confused. Her body felt relaxed and protected and she lay still, putting her thoughts together. Was anyone keeping watch during the night or did both priests sleep? Was there anyone out there in the night spying on them? She felt too tired to care, her adrenalin drained, energy spent. Her eyes closed again and she slept once more.

Chapter 10

She woke to lethargy. Never before in her whole life had she spent time doing nothing, but now the day stretched ahead with nothing to do. There was breakfast to eat, and lunch and an evening meal but she could not leave Shurnock. Once Cassie and the hens were fed, there was nothing. She sat up slowly, wondering why she had so little energy, expecting that the restful day of yesterday would have given her more stamina and bounce.

She had enjoyed the discussion with Father Garnet, his mind so quick, his arguments convincing, but she still remained an atheist, she thought. She wondered how much she had told him of science he had never witnessed, of flying in the sky and rockets to the moon so that she knew there was no heaven just above the clouds and asked how so many could live forever in heaven if the world population was to grow so large, and, in frustration, she had asked how any god could allow their world to become so crowded that the whole earth and all his creations would be destroyed. She knew, that if she had said these things to Father Gerard, he would have reacted with anger and fear and probably accused her of witchcraft, whereas Father Garnet had sat back, listening quietly, absorbing and sorting facts, not even challenging her knowledge of the future. So much for guarding her tongue, she thought wryly, but then, what could a priest do with the information when he himself was in danger of imprisonment or execution? Who would believe the things he told of her? It had been a relief to talk freely, but what of today? She rose slowly, and, shivering in the cold, damp room, she relit the fire. She wished she could recharge the solar batteries, but if Garnet saw them, he would want an explanation and Jemma thought that explaining solar power even to a priest was risking the whole future world with an invention too soon for the world to accept. Her match supply was getting low. She would soon have to learn properly how to use a flint. She could hear the priests praying in the room above as she went to fetch water in kettle and saucepan and set them to boil.

Opening the barn door, she greeted Cassie and the hens and fed them. The hens had given her more eggs, two nests on the hay bales. She thanked them, grateful that she could add to the priests' food in some small way. She stroked Cassie's head and promised her a good grooming later, leaving her for now in the barn, with the door ajar to let in light and sound, but too small a gap for the hens to slip through.

How odd it felt to be cooking for these two strange men, she thought as she created the flour and pastry mix and boiled three eggs for them to share. She heard their feet on the stairs and greeted them with a smile as they entered the room. It was good to have company, people to talk to. If only, she thought, we had glass windows in here and could open the shutters to let in more light, it would feel more like home. She laughed at herself, recognising that human trait of always wanting just that little bit more. If she had the glass windows, she would then want the comfy armchairs and the soft beds. "Be grateful for what you have," she admonished herself.

Despite the upstairs prayers, the meal began again with a Latin grace. Jemma supposed they were only doing as she had just done, being grateful for what they had. There was little difference between them except in method and language. They ate slowly, all aware of the long hours ahead, the lack of need for rush, and enjoyed the food more for taking their time. Father Gerard seemed to be revising his views of Jemma, giving her more respect, she thought. After the meal, he said, "We normally spend two hours now in quiet meditation. I hope you will not mind us ignoring you. The time is important to us." Jemma shook her head. "I promised Cassie, I would give her a good grooming so I will be in the barn for the next two hours, and perhaps I can take my turn as lookout while I do

it."
"That is good," Gerard said, and actually smiled.

It was good to spend time with Cassie. The long sweeping strokes of the brush were a kind of meditation, too, watching the coat lose its matt look and begin to shine. Seeing Cassie relax and lean into the brush, almost resting a hock on Jemma's shoulder as her back was brushed until Jemma's shoulders developed a burning ache with muscles well worked, relaxed Jemma's mind too. She knelt and picked the mud and hay out of Cassie's coat around her legs, and then turned to her mane and tail. At last, she stood back and admired her beautiful glossy horse.
"Good enough for a show, girl," she said, reaching up to rub Cassie's ears."I do love you."
She looked at her watch, 11.30 already. Perhaps she could start preparing some soup, and it was just about warm enough for Cassie to be outside for a while. She led Cassie out, saying, "Now don't you go getting muddy when I've made you look all smart. No rolling in the mud."
She knew, though that Cassie would make her own decisions.

In the house, she found the priests already peeling and chopping potatoes and joined them with her own folding knife. Both priests gave it sidelong glances, silently noticing the springs and neat rivets and how the blade folded away but asking nothing. It was companionable and peaceful and Jemma again marvelled at how they could remain so calm within the tumultuous times they lived. As the soup simmered, they sat quietly with their own thoughts, only Father Garnet breaking it to say a servant should appear this afternoon with more supplies so Jemma need not be afraid of someone coming. Again, they ate slowly after grace and, after lunch, Father Garnet and Jemma discussed the stars, the moon and the sun, neither giving ground on their beliefs, but Father Garnet expressing amazement of Jemma's knowledge.

"I know of no other woman with as great a knowledge as you. Only the Vaux family have women of great strength, curiosity and book learning, but then, their father was also a man of great knowledge who believed his daughters and their children would have great power in this country and tried to give them the wisdom to use it wisely. It would be a wonderful thing, Jemma, if sometime you could meet them. They would enjoy your thoughts."

Despite the discussion, Jemma felt caged. The priests had demonstrated their trust in her by allowing her to go to the barn with Cassie while they meditated. It was as if the cage door was open, but some invisible force prevented her from flying free and she found it difficult to contain the restlessness within her, almost as if sensing some great danger ahead from which she should flee, but not knowing when or where to go. The temptation had been there as she put Cassie to bed and fed the hens again but the night was too dark and cold. She found it difficult to eat the evening meal when she had not yet burned the energy from lunch and wanted to whizz around the house to remove some of the building adrenalin. The priests produced a chess board and challenged her to a game in the candle light, the winner to play the other priest. She was delighted, and found herself evenly matched with Father Garnet, but easily outplayed by Gerard. The pieces were beautifully carved and after the games, she took each piece up and gazed at the smooth carving, worn by many players fingers and their characterful faces. The servant had been and gone, with instructions to bring more hay on his next visit and they were preparing for bed when there was a banging on the door. They looked at each other, surprised and questioning and before they could rise, the door opened and Margery walked in.

They leaped to their feet, certain that a visiting after dark must be for bad news. Margery looked at Jemma with surprise, if not shock, but turned immediately to Father Garnet."Father, there is trouble coming. My grandson, John, saw Arthur watching this house three nights ago, when I think you came here, and afterwards, John followed him. First Arthur followed one of the Wintours back to Huddington, then he went to see Justice Leighton and Martin Culpepper and John heard them discussing young Catesby and the priests staying here at Shurnock Court. It sounded like they intended to leave you as a trap to try to catch Catesby and Tresham concealing you elsewhere. John was going to come to warn me, but then Arthur said he was going to follow Catesby as he thought there was some conspiracy about to begin and he must find out more, so John thought it best to watch Arthur. He stopped only long enough to grab supplies and money and galloped after Arthur." She shook her had over such impulsiveness, but carried on with her tale. "It seems that Catesby and several other young men have joined with Sir Blount and they were headed to London for some kind of demonstration against Lord Cecil to be led by Lord Essex. John spoke so fast of it all and was so tired as he was speaking that I could not get the hang of the whole story but it seems they all went down to London, one following the other and Catesby was being his normal hot headed self calling for battle and murder, along with Blount and there was some such rubbish about a play written by that scoundrel, Shakespeare that would make the queen sack Cecil, but somehow it all went wrong and Lord Egerton and Knollys went to arrest Essex and found all the hotheads baying for revolution so that Egerton was going to arrest Essex. Then it all seemed quiet with no one going in or out and Arthur loitering in one part of the street and my John watching him from round corners and the word came out that Egerton was being held against his will and Arthur vanished off, John thinks, to warn Cecil and the queen. He did not dare loiter any longer for fear he would arouse suspicion, so he left to eat and think and decided he had best return here to warn us of what was happening and the danger to you." She broke off and a smile flashed across her face briefly and then was gone. "My grandson always means well but things don't always work out for him. He got lost in the dark, around midnight and ended up on the wrong road, headed, he thinks for Suffolk and had to stop and sleep in a barn until daylight when he could ask his way and return here. He is exhausted and was very hungry so I made him tell me the tale while he ate and as he talked, his head nodded and he was asleep on my hearth so I thought it best to bring you the news and ask if there is anything we should do."

Jemma felt like she was in a film of some sort, unable to believe what she was hearing. So much intrigue, and how did the bit about the play fit in? The trouble was, the film was real life and if Robert Catesby, Francis Wintour, Tresham and the others were coming back here, what would happen next? Would they succeed in their revolution? It seemed to Jemma, not very well planned and if Arthur had managed to warn the queen of a plot before it even began, would they even have managed to leave the house of Essex? Jemma was having difficulty working out times and distances. If it was a hundred miles to London, how long did that take by horse? It had taken John almost a day, but he had got lost on the way. If the rebellion worked, no one would return for days, would they? They would be celebrating their success in London. If there was a battle in the London streets, and Essex lost, that would have happened this morning and the losers would be already running away if they had managed to escape. Would they come straight here? Probably not. It would be too far to gallop in one go and there must be other supporter's homes they could hide in overnight instead of exhausting their horses, perhaps breaking a leg, dashing around in the dark. What would Arthur have done after he alerted the queen? Stayed to fight or come back here to try to round up the priests?

She had been thinking so deeply that she had missed some of the conversation but it seemed the priests were following her thoughts. Father Garnet was looking thoughtfully at the shutters, assessing the hours of darkness and the cold of the night. Margery waited quietly for their decision. Father Gerard seemed to be focussed inwards, studying the thoughts in his head. Jemma wanted to scream at them. "Quick! Decide what to do. We need to do something."

At last, Garnet spoke. "We cannot leave without a horse that knows the roads and tracks in the dark, with not even a moon to light the way. It is too far to walk the marshes to Huddington, and Coughton will be searched as Arthur knows Catesby stayed there. We may need to go to Baddesley, or Harvington and we cannot walk that far without shelter."

He looked at Jemma. "We cannot take your horse. She does not know the roads, and in any case, you have need of her."

He turned to Margery. "I think we must ask another favour of young John, who has already done so much, and ask him to ride, tomorrow as early as he can to get us a horse from Huddington, and we will either go back there or ride on to Harvington. If he can go early, we may slip away in the first light, unseen."

Margery nodded. "I thought, myself, that you might ask this. John could lend you his horse, but it is as exhausted as he is. He should not have ridden it so hard and will barely carry him to Huddington tomorrow, and of course, he would then have to get it back from there somehow. I had best get home before he wakes lest he try something else not knowing we have made a plan."

Father Garnet put out a hand and took Margery's. "Thank you for coming to us this night. I wish that we could escort you home, but as you know, if we were seen, it would only make things worse for you. How I wish the queen had not changed her ways and become so hardened to us Catholics who only wish to continue in the right faith. I am truly grateful to you and your family."

Margery sniffed, as if to make little of her actions. "I had best go."

She moved quickly across the room, raising her shawl against the cold and with no fuss, disappeared into the night. Garnet looked at Gerard and Jemma and slapped his knees.

"Best sleep while we can," he announced and made for the stairs.

Gerard followed, turning at the door to wish Jemma a goodnight, his mouth twisting into a cynical smile. Jemma's goodnight reply was uncertain. Would any of them be able to sleep? She did not know how the priests could sleep upstairs where they might be trapped. At least, in the hall, she could run from a choice of three exits.

Her sleep was restless, waking at the drop of ash in the grate, or the creaking of the great beams as they cooled, changing the stresses of floors and panels that cracked sharply as they moved. She felt the darkness pressing in on her and had to get up and pace the room, even opening the door to find the night quiet and the stars hidden behind a blanket of grey cloud. Even the stars that normally reassured her and gave her peace were hiding. She returned to her covers and tucked herself in, shut her eyes and tried to stop the circling thoughts of fear and uncertainty. There were uneasy dreams as dawn approached and she was glad to be woken by the priests descending and lighting the fire, their voices gruff as they prepared for their evacuation. No one had discussed what Jemma would do. Was it safe for her to stay if Arthur was going to bring soldiers to search the house? No, it was not. Would Margery shelter her, knowing she had been with the priests or should she go back to that plan to build a shelter in the forest? She had best get her own supplies together and make Cassie ready. She rolled her wrist round and saw it was just after 6, still dark outside, but by the time they had eaten there would be light enough to see. She sat up and put the covers she had used with the priests' sack wrapped rolls. How she wished she had another cloak for herself. Her layers of clothing and her sheepskin jacket provided just enough warmth, but there was a subconscious sense of protection in a cloak that you could sleep in. They ate hard biscuits and porridge and drank herb tea, and Jemma once again filled her pockets with nuts and carrots and almost the last of the potatoes. She dare not dig more or there would be none for generating the new crop for next year. They had finished eating but no one had appeared, neither friend nor foe.

Jemma filled Cassie's saddle bags with food and tied on the saucepan and kettle, her survival kit still held a few meals. It was 9th February. A month before the leaf buds would break and real foraging could begin. She found herself riding a roller-coaster of emotions. First up, sure she could survive with just a little help from William, and then down as she counted the days to survive and the tiny supplies she carried. The trenches she dropped to were black with despair.

They were ready to go, only waiting for John to appear with the horse. Jemma could have gone, but she waited too, hoping for some news of Arthur's whereabouts and how Essex had got on in London. If only they were all still in London, and Arthur was in hiding, the queen having sided with Essex, there would be no need to run, but Jemma knew her history book had not told the story that way, even if she could not remember the detail. It was not as if she had done anything to change that part of history, though, whether her discussions with Garnet would tweak history, she did not know.

Someone was running down the track from the village. As he got nearer, they saw it was Dicken. They moved uncertainly to meet him as he puffed to a halt. He bent his head to his knees, putting his hands down to stop them trembling.
"Come to warn, you," he gasped. "Sir Arthur is back. He'm already been to Leighton, but he send him away saying it too early, so now he'm gone to Culpepper at Astwood. Missus Throckmorton say to warn you."
He stood straighter as his breath returned.
"John has gone for horse at 6. Should be here any time. She say to stay hid, but be ready to go."

The priests were solemn as they exchanged looks. Garnet looked at Jemma. " I think you had best go. You do not need to be associated with us."

Jemma hesitated. "You might need Cassie to take you away if Arthur comes. She can gallop if its only a short way. She might take you as far as Himbleton, and Arthur doesn't know I've been with you. I can just go and hide in the church or somewhere while they are searching here. I can walk there." The priests exchanged another look. "Are you sure?" Garnet asked.

Jemma nodded firmly. Garnet turned back to Dicken. "Thank you for the warning. You had best walk back across the fields to the village. Don't get mixed up with Catesby or Arthur. Go now."

Dicken wasn't one to argue, and obediently turned, loping down the track and disappearing into the woods to follow a fox run going in the right direction.

"Get Cassie ready to go," Father Garnet ordered, and John, you go watch the track east, while I will watch west. Let us hope we see John before anyone else."

They split in their three directions, Jemma bringing Cassie out of the stable and, as she stood with Cassie saddled and bridled, she felt the fierce ache of remembering. She had stood just like this, waiting for her mum to run from the house more than 400 years from now, except that then there had been two horses ready to go and now there was only one, and if there was to be fighting, it would be with swords, not electric laser weapons and the two men involved would again be men of peace, but this time armed only with the knives they used to peel and chop potatoes. She felt that sense of urgency swooping over her, engulfing her and heard a shout from Garnet.

"John's coming."

Relief washed in and she called on to Gerard, "John's here," She heard Gerard running back towards her and led Cassie so that they could see John approaching. He was galloping Ned's horse and leading another with packs of food attached.

215

As he reached Garnet, he rolled from the saddle. "Quickly," he gasped. "I could hear more horses coming from Astwood. Mount up and go. Wintour will meet you at Inkberrow. He has his men out watching for a safe route and will lead you through."

Garnet was leading the horse to the mounting block, and altering the strap length of the stirrups. Gerrard was almost back down the drive when there was the sound of galloping on the track and a horse swerved into the end of the track behind him. This horse was sweat soaked and stumbling, foaming at the mouth and its rider looked tattered, pushing his horse desperately for more speed. More horses appeared behind, one ridden by two men, their clothes torn and all covered in mud. Cassie backed off to the end of her rein in panic and Jemma had to fight to hold her.

"Get up, man," Garnet was urging as Gerard tried to climb up behind Garnet, the horse objecting and John Throckmorton having to go to hold it steady, while his own horse danced in fear. The lead horseman was shouting to them and Jemma saw it was not Arthur but the returning rebels from London. The priests were mounted and Jemma now hopped alongside her frightened horse, getting a foot into the high stirrup and using all her strength to lift herself up into that saddle so far above her head. John had mounted too and had turned his horse for the village, it's eyes rolling in fear of the shouting men behind him, but as he crossed the bridge, more horsemen appeared at the end of the track. This group were more disciplined, their horses fresher and John turned quickly south, following Wintour's path. Garnet had had difficulty controlling his mount, but it now saw where John had gone and made up its mind to follow the horse it knew. Cassie was terrified. Too much noise and confusion, she backed up as if trying to return to the barn and Jemma could do nothing as the two groups of horses approached, neither yet in view of the other. If she could only get Cassie to follow John, there was a chance, but the gap was reducing rapidly and she had little hope Cassie could outrun Arthur's posse, even if she might escape Catesby.

Cassie refused to move, and in desperation, Jemma slid back to the ground, grabbing the rein and pulling Cassie forward. Cassie followed her unwillingly, instinct telling her to retreat to the barn where she had always been safe, training insisting she follow her small rider's commands. They reached the moat bridge and Jemma pulled her on to face south away from the oncoming horses, partially hidden by the trees. Cassie saw the path of escape in front of her and started to walk more easily and Jemma flung herself upwards around her horse's neck, a thing she would have said was impossible, if it had not just happened, and uncharacteristically kicked Cassie into more speed. Cassie leapt forward as horses came into view behind her and Jemma swung around in the saddle ready to ward off the attack of the nearest rider, and, as Cassie leapt, Jemma felt a blur and ripple of change and the horseman was gone. There was a baa of sheep near by and the rev of an engine, followed by brakes being hauled on and an angry lady's voice shouting, "I nearly ran you down. What were you playing at?"
Jemma was reeling from her disorientated senses. Where did all the horses go? The air was still cold, the ground frosty. Shurnock stood behind her, its chimneys silhouetted against the early morning light. Jemma's breath whooshed out. The chimneys. When she had looked behind her just seconds before there had been just one chimney above the fireplace of the great hall. Now there were five sprouting from the centre of the house. The woman had leapt from a small van, almost at Cassie's feet and was advancing angrily. "Were you hiding in the barn? What made you suddenly bounce out like that? I could have broken your horse's legs!"

Cassie was backing now, from the angry lady, who seemed to realise she was upsetting the horse and tried to stuff her anger back into its box. She reached up to take the bridle and patted Cassie's nose focussing on the horse, rather than the rider she held to blame. "Sorry darling," she said. "I didn't mean to startle you, but you gave me such a fright. Hush now. It's OK."

She looked up at Jemma, the anger in her eyes fading, but still judging. Her eyes raked over Jemma's clothes and she looked puzzled by the sacking skirt, but then focussed on Jemma's bare head. "And where's your helmet?" she snapped. "Even shire horses can buck people off and kick them in the head you know."

Jemma did know, but she was at a loss to explain. She looked around her, taking in the fields of sheep, the neat wooden fences and stiles with footpath signs and found herself speechless. Was she home? The snow had gone, but there were no floods, The fields were full of grass and sheep, so many sheep. She could hear birds singing as they never sang in her real time. The lady was still waiting for an explanation. Jemma shook her head, found her voice,"Sorry," she said huskily, "I didn't mean to frighten you or make you angry. I- I -I suppose I was just thinking about other things and I wasn't expecting anyone else to be here and, and things have been a bit difficult recently so I wasn't concentrating and I like to ride Cassie when I need to sort things out in my head and I must have forgotten my helmet. I'm very sorry."

The lady's face had softened. "I can't say I haven't done the same in the past," she said, "But I suggest you now dismount and walk your horse back carefully. I'm sorry I shouted but I really thought I was going to hit you and that scared me." She looked at Jemma's face. "Are you alright?" she asked.

Jemma didn't know if she was alright or not. How did she ask what date it was and who lived in the house and if she knew her parents and oh, so many other questions, but at least there was no one chasing her. She was safe from those aggressive horsemen and the dangers of treason, and harbouring priests, of torture and execution.

 "I think so," she said. "I'm feeling a bit disconnected," she added honestly.

The lady gave her another all over look, and suddenly dipped into her pocket, coming out with a piece of card. "There's a number on here which might help you, " she said. "All us farmers have been given it in case we have mental depression problems. You'd think, being out in the sun and the fresh air we'd be OK, but we do get terrible fits of depression, so this is a help group for when we need it. I can get another card, so you have this one."

She stretched up and Jemma took the card automatically with another thank you. The lady turned back to her van.

"Better see to these sheep," she said.

Jemma dismounted as if she was sleep walking and then stood, unsure where to go. Should she just walk back to the house, and put Cassie in the barn? What if it all belonged to someone else? She took a hesitant step forward and Cassie followed quietly. The lady was humping bales out of the van and dragging them into the field where her sheep, with small lambs baaed and ran hopefully towards her. Jemma recrossed the moat and found the paths gravelled and edged with neat flowerbeds. There was no barn. Only a covered over swimming pool in the barn yard and the familiar cherry tree and grape vine, The moat was part filled in and there were sweeping lawns where she was used to reservoirs and dykes. She took Cassie on round the house. Everything was quiet. A vast lawn swept from the kitchen wing with its marker date, 1606, to the moat and the apple and pear trees were there, hollowed out with age. Jemma swallowed hard. So nearly home, but this must be before her family arrived, before she was born. If she knocked at the door, it would be someone else who answered it, not her mum or her dad or Uncle Seb. She turned and clung to Cassie and the tears welled up and fell uncontrollably. How could she go on and on changing time and never knowing what time she would end up in? Should she keep trying or just move right away from Shurnock, Try to make a life in whatever time she was now in. With the world blurred with tears, she turned and pulled Cassie across the lawn to the moat so that she could drink if she wanted. Still holding a long rein, she dropped to the ground, pulling her knees up to her chin and looked out across the sparkling water, lit by the early morning sun. There were birds everywhere. Ducks quacking and swans, so graceful and elegant, their heads held aloof above the squabbling flocks of other birds that Jemma thought were geese. There were tiny black birds swimming, with a white patch. "Coot," one said and Jemma remembered her mum saying lots of birds were named for the sound they made. The sight blurred again as more tears fell. Jemma felt that she would like to just sit here and give up. Just wait until she dissolved into atoms that might hover forever in this space until her family came and she could be with them. She could hear the van growling slowly up the drive towards the gate to the road and hoped it wouldn't stop, that the lady would leave her alone to struggle with her thoughts. But instead she heard the engine fade and the door open. There was the crunch of feet crossing gravel and then silence as they walked across the grass to stop beside Jemma.

"Are you really in trouble?" the lady asked and gently put a hand on her shoulder. "Do you want to come with me and perhaps talk a bit?" and suddenly Jemma knew she did. She needed to tell someone honestly all that had happened and she didn't care what they thought. If they thought she was loopy, nuts, crazy, at least she would have help and not be alone any more. She looked up at this kind person who was prepared to help and said, "I don't think you will believe what I tell you, but yes, I do need help and I do need to talk. Will you listen?"

The lady gazed at her sympathetically and then looked around vaguely, her eyes unfocussed as she thought, and then looked back at Jemma. "It'll be cold sitting here. Would you like to sit in the van, or if its a long story, should we go back to my farm? I just keep some sheep here, but I live further along the road."

She looked at Cassie, and then towards the road. "The road

gets busy from now until 9.30. I don't know how your horse is with traffic, but with you not having a helmet, I don't think you should take her along the road, riding or walking, The stables are empty here, just now, and so is the house so how about we put her in one of the loose boxes and I take you home in the van and then we come back later with a helmet for you, and I'll ride my horse for company?"

Jemma felt panic rising at the thought of being separated from Cassie and her lip trembled as she fought more tears, knowing this lady was doing her best to help. The lady watched her struggle and said quickly, "OK, I have another idea. Let me go back to the house and fetch some hot drinks and something to eat and you wait with your horse in the stable block and I'll be right back with a blanket or two and we can chat there while we eat?"
Jemma gave her a wobbly smile and wiped away tears. "Yes," she said. "I'd like that. Is that really OK for you to do? You don't mind? I mean, you must be busy with the farm".
"I'll be right back," the lady said, without answering Jemma's questions. "Go get warm in the stable."
She waved he arm back to the block of buildings Jemma had passed almost without noticing and hurried back to her van, rattling the door shut and starting the engine. Jemma watched her go, still feeling numb, blank inside, but no longer aching with despair. Automatically, she did as she'd been told, glad to have someone else making the decisions.
 "Come, Cassie," she said, pulling the reins and Cassie settled in behind her as they walked back passed the house, finding a row of neat stable boxes, one with bales of straw, the rest empty. Jemma wasn't sure if the straw was for some other animal so led Cassie into an empty box, but pinched some of the straw for Cassie's comfort, and stood, stroking her and hugging her head, feeling relief that Cassie and she were still together, that she hadn't slipped through time alone.

After a while, she slipped out of the box and went to look at the house. As the lady had said, it was empty of people, but looking through the windows, she could see there were carpets on the floor with a table and chairs in the great hall. The kitchen looked glossy and all electric, with high stools to sit on at a breakfast bar. She tried the door latch, still hoping that she could enter the house and find her parents there, waiting for her, but everything was locked up. She could hear the constant buzz and roar of cars and lorries battering the tarmac as they sped along the road and was glad Cassie was not having to deal with that. She found her mind had shut down, only allowing her to live in the moment, preventing thought about the past or the future. She mooched back to the stable and heard the van approaching from behind. She supposed she ought to be thinking what to say, but the blank in her mind was like an avalanche, a whiteness flowing over everything, blotting out memories and thoughts and she watched the lady climb from the car, feeling as if, any moment she might just evaporate and drift away into space.

The lady smiled, and called, "Here, take these rugs. There's a blanket there, too and I'll bring the hamper. My name's Sara. Do you want to tell me who you are and what your horse is called as we'll be sharing a stable."
Jemma held her arms out and took the rugs. "Jemma," she said, "and my horse is Cassie."
Sara lifted a large picnic basket and said cheerfully, "Don't be disappointed. This hamper is only half full but it was handy for carrying things in."

She dumped it in Cassie's box and took the rugs out of Jemma's arms, spreading them competently and waving Jemma to sit, holding a blanket ready to wrap it around Jemma's shoulders. Jemma still moved automatically, aware of the comfort of someone else's arms as she was wrapped in the blanket and wanting to hold on and never let go. Wanting this moment of being protected to last forever, but Sara had stepped back and was kneeling to open the hamper, taking out two thermos flasks and two mugs and a packet of biscuits and then a cake. It all seemed unreal and Jemma wondered if she was still really in 1601 with the priests and this was a dream. If only it had been a longer dream and she could wake up in 2046 with her mum calling her to breakfast, but she remembered the awareness of cold, the heat of fever, the pain of hunger and knew they were not the stuff of dreams.

"I brought coffee and tea. Should have asked which you liked," Sara said, waving the two flasks."And I can't stand the taste of coffee in plastic cups, so I bought mugs, too. Which would you like? I've got milk and sugar separate."

"I like them both. With milk, please," said Jemma.

"Coffee,then," decided Sara and added sugar without asking. Jemma wrapped her hands round the mug, enjoying the feel of warmth and the smoothness of an ordinary pottery mug. She inhaled the smell and took a small, careful sip. It tasted wonderful. No taste of smoke, no taste of herbs. Just pure coffee. She sipped again as Sara unwrapped the biscuits and offered her the pack. Jemma stared at the plastic wrapping and reached out uncertainly to take a chocolate coated digestive. The wrapping stirred a memory of when she was tiny and standing in a shop somewhere, rows of biscuits in circular tubes. Normally, biscuits came in metal tins. She tried to remember where she had been to see the tubes but it was too long ago.

"You can have more than one," Sara said. "Here, I'll put the packet next to you and you can help yourself."

She took a couple of biscuits for herself, poured another coffee and wrapped herself in a matching blanket. Looking at Jemma's face with unblinking eyes, she said, "You can tell me anything and I won't judge."

Her face twisted with deep emotion and then returned to a half smile. "My brother committed suicide three and a half years ago. He found it difficult to ask for help. I'm glad you have asked, and I will give you all the help I can."

Jemma nodded but she didn't know where to start, how to hollow a little bit of explanation out of the whole avalanche without the whole thing tumbling on top of her. She sat there, gazing silently at her hands on the mug, watching the biscuit melt in the cup's warmth.

Sara drank her coffee quietly. "Eat your biscuit. Before it melts," she advised and Jemma obeyed.

Everything felt as if it was happening a long way away, maybe even to someone else and she felt frightened as the distance seemed to grow. It was as if she was in a tunnel on a fast train going into a hill, the light fading behind her.

Sara saved her, wrapping her palms around Jemma's hands, pushing them firmly against the mug so that the heat bit in. "Jemma, I'm going to ask you some questions, just to get you started. You can tell me if you don't want to answer any of them, OK?"

Jemma nodded.

"Have you run away from home?" Sara asked.

Jemma hesitated. "No," she said. "I want to GET home, but I can't find how."

Sara blinked, thinking. "So, are you lost? Do you know where your home is?" She had a sudden thought. "Have you, maybe, just moved house and don't know your way around?"

Jemma shook her head frustratedly. "I used to live here, at Shurnock Court, but then everything changed and, and..... and I don't know how to explain why, but I don't think I'll ever be able to find my mum and my dad again."

She raised eyes that seemed to have too much depth, too much horror, "I don't know if I have somehow changed things so that they can't be here."

Her eyes brimmed with tears again and she, angrily tried to wipe them away as they overflowed.

Sara sat back, baffled. "Do you mean you had an argument? Said something that will have hurt them too much? Done something wrong?"

"No," Jemma hicupped. "I told you, you wouldn't believe me, but, ...but I fell back in time, and I think I've managed to come forward again, but not to the right place. I wanted to reach 2046, but I haven't have I?"

There. It was said. Jemma felt relief that the truth was out. Now it was up to Sara, what she did with it.

Sara sat still. "What a strange thing to have said," she thought. "How on earth do I move forward from here?"

Sara had joined The Samaritans after her brother's death to try to help others struggling as he did. She had training, but nothing to help her with this. She could see in the tautness of Jemma's face and the exhausted, thin body, clothed in mud caked clothes that things were very wrong but if she called in the authorities, she would lose Jemma's trust. She was pretty certain that the last thing Jemma needed right now was an official enquiry with probing questions, small white rooms and too many eyes watching her. It was possible Jemma's mind had made up the going back in time story to mask something even more terrifying, but Sara wanted Jemma feeling stronger before they peeled back the layers, or removed the shield Jemma's mind might have raised.

She made a decision to work on the present troubles. She would get Jemma fed, washed, warm and let her sleep if she needed and then Sara would talk to her supervisor at The Samaritans about what to do next. The biggest immediate problem was how to get Jemma and Cassie home.

She pictured the local footpath map in her head. There was a way off the busy roads, but it was a long way round. They could cross The Saltway, go up the hill track and right at the barn, and then swing right again to come back to the farm. She looked at Jemma's tall thin frame and wondered if there was enough energy remaining to lead Cassie that far, or should she allow Jemma to ride? She had brought the spare

225

helmet and Sara reckoned she could walk in front, or alongside horse and rider and then come back for the van. Thank goodness the lambs were already born and developing well and the weather was not too cold. This was the only lull between the busy seasons – more lambs in March and then the medical stuff began, along with the shearing and moving from winter to summer pastures and the sheep markets and so on until the next winter came. Thank goodness, too that the pandemic was in a lull and there were no worries about social distancing and the wearing of masks. She refocussed on the young, blank, face.

"OK, Jemma, I think maybe it would be good if you finish your coffee and, here, have a piece of cake to keep your energy up. I think we can get back to my farm across the fields so Cassie won't be spooked by the road, and then you can have a hot bath, or a shower if you like and we'll take it from there. What do you think?"

Jemma again, turned those hollow eyes on her, but gradually she focussed and a spark of life leapt. "Really?" she asked. "Can we?"

Sara almost laughed. Glad to have found a way to connect, to pierce the armoured shell. "Yes, really," she said.
Jemma drank the coffee and ate the cake she had been handed. As she chewed, the taste became more real. There was chocolate, and sugar and sponge. The train that had gone into the tunnel of darkness and shadow was reversing and bringing her back into the real world of sight, touch, scent, taste and sound. She took another bite and chewed faster, revelling in the tastes of this time, this world, so close to her own. Now she knew she was hungry. She could feel the food thawing her out, melting the ice that had encased her heart and mind. Warming her frozen soul. She licked her fingers enthusiastically and now Sara did laugh, watching this child coming back to life. "You can have another piece when I get

the van back, but you'll have to wait just a wee while. Come on. Let's get you to the farm."

She stood and put out a hand to haul Jemma to her feet, quietly horrified at how little she weighed.
"I have a helmet for you, so you can ride once we cross the main road." Sara said, as Jemma led Cassie out of the stable and Sara reached into the van, retrieving the hat from the passenger seat. She pushed it onto Jemma's head, watching as Jemma automatically adjusted the straps. They walked up the drive together, and Sara listened carefully for a lull in the traffic where they might cross safely, then quickly waved Jemma and Cassie across the road, running ahead to open the large double gate and let them through.
"You carry on," she said "and I'll catch you up when I've shut the gate."

Jemma led Cassie up the hill, and Sara swung the heavy gate shut before jogging after them.
"You can ride now, if you like." she suggested.

Jemma started to pull the sacking skirt up around her waist to make mounting easier and then paused, thinking. "I don't need this now, do I?" and tugged the ties undone, rolling the skirt into a bundle and tying it behind the saddle, reaching high, on tiptoes to fasten it tightly. Sara cupped her hands to make a step and lifted Jemma easily into the saddle. Looking up, she watched Jemma take the reins and felt happy to see Jemma's confidence rise as she and her horse became one entity, a perfect team, each looking after the other.
"This way," she said, and walked on up the hill. They were quiet, Jemma concentrating on staying just behind Sara so that Cassie could follow her lead, Sara thinking of her brother and wishing someone could have helped him as she now helped Jemma but also hoping she could get this right. How did one help a person who thought they had been lost in time and was convinced they had lived in a house that had been

empty and undergoing renovations for the last five years before being put back on the market? Surely she couldn't have been living rough all those years, and more? Sara was "new" to the village in villager terms, having moved here three years ago and had not got to know the previous owner, but surely someone would have made enquiries if a child of that owner had gone missing when, or just before they moved? If she could get Jemma's surname, she might be able to make some discreet enquiries. If Jemma was part of a drug trade ring and had somehow escaped, finding the truth might be urgent, but somehow, Sara didn't think it was that. Would she be in trouble if she didn't contact the police straight away? Was there anyone she could trust to hold back on officialdom but would confirm her good intentions when the truth came out? She started working through the villagers, one by one creating a mental list of "maybes" and "definitely nots."

Chapter 11

As Jemma relaxed into Cassie's stride, she looked about her at the rolling fields with the small copses of trees and felt a stronger sense of homecoming. This was a world she could understand. There were pylons and cables carrying electricity. Her own family had created all their own power, but she remembered these giant structures, standing derelict, the cables dangling and no longer transmitting power. The almost treeless fields were familiar. She had crossed them on foot as a child and stood on the hill tops gazing across the plain to the ring of hills which made a protective horseshoe in the purple distance. Often, she wondered what made those particular hills purple, and now she could see them again. How far off her own time was she? Were her mum and dad out there somewhere, as young children? Her mind throbbed and whirled as she imagined meeting them and saying she was the child they would have one day. Was that possible? Could it be done? Her brain threw up a protective wall, refusing to think about it and made her refocus on her surroundings. They had swung passed a barn and were now descending again, Sara opening another gate, and shutting it again behind them. There were buildings ahead of them now. Sara nodded her head at them, "That's my farm. You might meet my son, Martin, but only if he is not where he should be, revising for his exams this Summer in his bedroom. He does take time out, wandering around the barns to stretch his legs and, as he says, letting the info assimilate. I guess if he's not around now, you'll meet him at lunch. Don't worry. He's harmless. Barely notices anything that is not to do with rugby, nature or farming. He plans to be a vet and work in a wild bird sanctuary."

She grinned, but there was pride in the smile. "Got it all worked out," she said.

"My dad was a vet," Jemma said spontaneously "But he ended up a farmer."

Sara noticed the past tense, and made a note to check for qualified vets missing a daughter, perhaps now dead.

She considered a possible car accident that might have killed her parents and left Jemma traumatised to the point of returning to an old family home. "Did he have a practise before he took up farming?" Sara asked conversationally. "I think he just worked for someone else while he was training," Jemma said, "And then he met Mum and they started the farm, with my Uncle Seb."

Jemma felt like she was two people at once. One was having an ordinary chat with a lovely lady who owned a farm and the other was screaming in fright, but it was like the frightened Jemma was muffled in a blanket. Hard to hear. If she could just ignore her and keep living in the "now", she might be alright.

The farm yard was empty, just a mud covered tractor apparently abandoned and the normal debris of farm life, straw, mud, and a pair of wellington boots by the door.

"My horse is just round the corner, there, in the stable block and there are two empty boxes, so Cassie can have one of those for now," Sara said, leading them on. Once halted at the boxes, Jemma slid from the saddle and then took it off, before leading Cassie into the box. "Is it alright if I brush her down before we go in?" Jemma asked. Sara nodded approval. "It's good you look after her properly," she said, "I think, while you do that, I'll go back for the van. Take your time and I should be back before you finish."

She hurried back round the farm house and down the track to the road. It would be much quicker, that way, even if she had to dodge onto the verge to avoid the megalithic lorries. She wanted to think about how to help Jemma, but with so many vehicles whizzing about, she had to concentrate on not getting run over, and then not having an accident in the van. It seemed, the more people talked about the need to reduce car travel to avoid climate change, the more people leaped into their cars and cluttered up the roads. It was odd the way people never wanted to live anywhere near where they worked, sent their children to school, or shopped. Some idiot hooted their horn at her as she walked in the road where the verge vanished into a ditch. He had plenty of room to go round. She resisted the urge to yell abuse or stick her fingers up at him. Why sink to his level? He probably had problems of his own.

She reached the edge of Shurnock's land, crossed the road in a gap in the traffic and climbed through a gap in the dilapidated hedge, her work boots and heavy trousers protecting her from the brambles and stinging nettles. Looking at the house, as she strode across the sweeping lawns, she wondered about its past. Who had lived here over its centuries of existence? Say it was built in 1500, it would now be 524 years old. With generations 30 years apart, that would be 17 generations. She worked it out again, surprised that it wasn't more. Of course, people now didn't often live in just one house, maybe moving every twelve years or so. That would be lots more owners. She reached the van and stopped thinking about the past, except to wonder if Jemma really had lived here during her short life. She couldn't be more than nineteen, Sara reckoned, so not that many years to look back through. She gathered the blankets, rugs and hamper and chucked them haphazardly into the van and set off, waiting patiently for a lull in the traffic, knowing there would be one when the traffic lights in Droitwich synced with the lights in Alcester, so long as there weren't too many people pulling out of the side turnings along the way. Her mind had time to consider Jemma as she waited. It really was best to get a bit more information before contacting the police or social securities. If she had just got lost, or left a foster home at age eighteen and ended up homeless, there was no need to involve the police. If there had been a family argument, she might be able to let the parents know she was safe and discuss with them what should happen next. Being realistic, she knew reconciliation might not be an option, but she hoped, so hoped that a bridge could be rebuilt for a future reconnection. There were too many broken families out there.

Pulling into the farm track, she chugged up to the yard and parked next to the tractor. She'd only been fifteen minutes. Better check if Jemma was still with Cassie.
As she approached the stable, she could hear Jemma talking to her horse and stopped, feeling slightly guilty about listening in but thinking Jemma might tell Cassie things she would find hard to share with Sara. Unfortunately, they were discussing whether Cassie liked the stable and felt safe here, rather than the past or even a possible future. Sara called out,
"I'm back," and walked into Jemma's view.
Jemma smiled, and said, "I'm just finished."
Sara led the way into the house, leaving her boots next to the wellingtons, and Jemma copied her, noticing how muddy her socks were, and peeling them off feet that had become ingrained in the wool/cotton mix. She felt embarrassed at the smell and became aware of the stench of sweat from her clothes as well as the odour from her feet. She felt herself hunching small in an attempt to reduce the overall smell. It was as if Sara read her mind. She smiled and said, "I expect you want that shower, now. I can wash your clothes, too if you like. You needn't worry about smells. Eighteen year old boys smell pretty powerfully, and, as you know, with your dad being a farmer, it's impossible not to smell of manure coming home some days."
She indicated Jemma step into the house with a tweak of her head. "The shower room is this way. Chuck your clothes out and I'll bring you some of mine." She put her head on one side, assessing. "They'll be a bit short in the leg and a little baggy around the hips, but I think we'll get away with it."

She opened the door, checked Jemma could work the shower and went to find some spare clothes that were comfortable but respectable. No rips from barbed wire or working with the sheep, but not smart. She didn't have many of that sort, but eventually came up with some baggy bottomed jogging trousers, a checked woollen shirt and a sweater, lots of socks, darned at the heel and knickers. That would have to do. She knocked on the shower room door and shoved the clothes in, taking the clothes Jemma had been wearing and walking to the washing machine, checking for labels, automatically removing things from pockets. Some of the materials, she had never heard of. Others were of a fine wool and looked hand knitted or even hand woven. Her own sheep were a mix of special wool breeds and she was impressed by the softness and strength, even the waterproof texture of this weave. No labels on those, but she'd try a 40 degrees C wash.

There was a clattering on the stairs and Martin appeared, blocking the light with his sturdy, still growing frame, legs too long for his body. She knew boys went through this stage, but still found the stubbly chin and shaggy hair annoying. He was even still wearing his pyjama top.
"Hi Mum." His head turned towards the shower room. "Who's using the shower?"
"We have a visitor," Sara said.
She picked up a discarded shirt from an armchair and threw it to him. "Put that on. I'm about to cook up some bacon and egg sandwiches. Want some?"
"Yes, please," Martin said. "So who's the visitor?"
He followed Sara into the kitchen, putting the shirt on over his pyjamas.
"She's called Jemma. I found her wandering around Shurnock when I went to check on the lambs. Frightened the living daylights out of me, appearing from nowhere. Right in front of me, riding a shire horse, with no helmet."
She relived the shock of the moment as she described it to her son. "Still can't think how she appeared so suddenly."
"Perhaps, you were thinking about something else, and not focussing," Martin suggested.
Sara paused and shrugged. "Possibly," she admitted, "I don't

233

normally meet anyone there, except, occasionally the gardener so maybe I was already looking at the sheep. Anyway, I brought her home because something is very wrong. She looks like she's suffering from PTSD, to me. When I'd finished with the sheep she was sitting, in tears, hanging onto her horse and gazing out over the moat, so I asked her if she needed help, and she said yes." Sara stopped, hesitated.

Should she tell Martin about the going back in time bit? Was that fair to Jemma? On the other hand, if he knew now, he wouldn't look like he thought she was batty if she mentioned it later and that might help them both build a better relationship. As she grilled bacon and boiled eggs, she told Martin what Jemma had said.

Martin listened carefully. "Sounds like she's been having a rough time," he said. "What can we do?"

The shower had switched off. Sara started making toast and switched on the kettle."Get us some coffee, love," she instructed.

As Martin rattled around with mugs, spoon and coffee jar, she said, "I think we just act like everything is normal for now. I was actually thinking that this might be one of those fate things. I've been worrying you are spending too much time helping me with the farm when you should be studying and wondering where I could get some part time help so you can get your head in your books, and along comes Jemma who says her dad was a vet and a farmer. If she'll stay, she can earn her keep while we sort out what's gone on, and then we can just let the story come out when she's ready."

Sara concentrated hard on dishing out the toast and fishing the boiled eggs from the pan, not looking at Martin who had turned to face her, with the kettle steaming in his hand.

"Mum, you're not thinking of slave labour?" he burst out, slightly horrified.

"No!" she said indignantly. "She'll get a fair wage. I just think she might have been sleeping rough and we can give her a bed and food and, well, I think she might be too proud to

234

accept charity, and, to be honest, we can't afford to give too much charity either, with your university fees looming, so, this works, doesn't it?"

Martin began pouring milk and coffee into cups, thinking things out. "I guess so," he said, "But don't get into trouble with the police or social security service, will you, Mum? I mean, how does it work with national insurance and tax and stuff?"

"I'll have to find out," his mum said glibly.

They heard the shower room door open and close and Sara called out, "We're in here, Jemma. Come and meet Martin." Jemma appeared, shyly at the doorway as Sara slapped the sandwiches together.

"Just in time for the sandwiches, Jemma," she greeted her guest. "Sit down in one of the armchairs. We only use the table for celebrations. Jemma, this is Martin. Martin, this is Jemma."

"How you doing?" Martin greeted her.

Jemma gave a small smile. "Much better, thank you."

She stepped over to an armchair and sank into it, feeling safer concealed in the sagging cushions and being, first startled and then delighted at the softness supporting and enfolding her body. She felt, almost suspicious of the luxuries surrounding her. It felt as if everything she had longed for for what seemed a very long time were falling on her all at once and her senses didn't know how to cope with it. It felt dreamlike, unreal and she was so afraid she was going to wake up and find all this had not happened and she really didn't know how she would cope with finding herself still a semi prisoner of the priests in 1601 with no shower, little food, mud encrusted clothes, cold and with nothing soft to comfort her.

Sara was handing her a plate and mug emanating smells that set her mouth watering. She set the mug down and took a cautious bite of the sandwich, revelling in the tastes and textures, so true to the 21st century. So nearly home.

Sara and Martin were also sat in armchairs, munching toast and slurping their coffee. No one knew quite how the conversation should go and all were glad to have the excuse of food and drink so that they need not talk.

It was Martin who finished first, and licking his fingers, said, "Are you from round here? We only moved here three years ago, and with the farm being so much work, we don't get to socialise much, but I don't remember you from school."

Sara had made a startled movement as if to prevent interrogation, but realised Martin was asking a question he would have asked anyone he met for the first time. It might be a good way of finding out without pushing too hard.

Jemma replied without hesitation to the non-committal question. "I lived at Shurnock, but I only went to school until I was six, and then I learned from home. I thought everyone was learning at home."

Her forehead creased as she realised that she must be in the time her mum spoke of when most children went to school to learn. Martin gazed at his mum, unsure when she could have lived at Shurnock. Perhaps he was estimating her age wrong. Was there a time when everyone was home taught? Maybe the village school had been closed for a while and there had been no transport to the next school. He knew there had been times of cuts when that sort of thing had happened. If she had proved autistic or very bright, maybe that was why she was home taught. Maybe it was autism that had led to the present situation.

"I'm just coming to my 18th birthday," he said. "How old are you?"

"I just had my twentieth," Jemma replied, "at the end of January."

"My birthday is 17th March." Martin said. He glanced around the room, searching for inspiration. How to go on? "Mum says your dad was a vet. That's what I want to be."

Jemma nodded and was surprised to find that insulating layer between emotion and voice allowed her to answer without tears. "He liked being a vet, but he said it was more important to become self sufficient and use the farm to keep us all safe, grow our own food and animals. He did help other people when their animals were ill. It's just, the farm was more important."

It was as if a tiny part of her brain was knocking on a door shouting, "Why aren't you upset? Your dad is not here. Why are you just sitting here eating toasted sandwiches?" but it was muffled in layers of cotton wool, smothered and unable to break through to the top surface. It felt.....odd.

Martin was talking again. "My dad said farming was too tough and we shouldn't take it on, so he lives down south in a town and he's an accountant and me and mum live here. He's kind of right. Running the farm is tough, but I like it better than being shut in by buildings. It's a bit lonely sometimes, but I like having the sheep and horses to chat to. I sometimes reckon they talk more sense than humans anyway."

Jemma took another sip of coffee and thought about her family. Remembered her mum saying pretty much the same thing. "I think, maybe, global warming will force people to talk sense," she said. "Mum said when you're on the edge of survival, common sense either comes to the fore, or you cease to exist."

Sara and Martin exchanged a glance. They both cared desperately for the state of the world, but had not heard anyone put the problem so bluntly.

"I think your Mum and us might share the same view of politics," Martin said. "Does she belong to The Green Party?"

"She did." Jemma replied. "By the time everything was falling apart, she'd given up on governments and said we needed to concentrate on just helping our own village survive and the rest of the world would have to look after itself. It made her cry, she was so frustrated."

"You mean with Covid?" Martin asked.

Jemma shrugged. "I suppose that was part of it, but the fuel problems, too, and then getting food later."

The conversation seemed odd to Martin. Like they weren't

quite talking about the same world. It was like Jemma was in a parallel universe where climate change had happened faster than in the world they were living in now, and in Jemma's world, civilisation was already collapsing, whereas in Martin's it was a possibility looming on the horizon. He glanced at the clock on the mantelpiece and said,
 "It's been nice meeting you, but I'd better get back to work."
He stood on his gangly legs and headed back to his room. Jemma switched her gaze back to her mug, and then looked back at Sara."You've been very kind," she said and felt her mouth trying to close on what she felt she must say next."I feel a lot better, but I have to find some work and somewhere to live so I had better be on my way. Thank you very much for, ...for EVERYTHING. I wonder, could, I leave Cassie here for now? When I get a job, I'll pay you, I promise."
Sara came over and knelt on the floor, holding Jemma's hands in her hers and looking up into her face."I think, Jemma, we have been meant to meet. What would you think about working here, on this farm, and you can sleep and eat here, too if you like. We might even find a tad of work for Cassie when the tractor is playing up, which it does more and more often these days."
Jemma gazed down at the brown, caring eyes looking up at hers and felt warmth and relief wash through her. "Oh. Yes." she breathed. "Please, can I?"

Days passed. Jemma learned the routine of the farm and amazed Sara with her ability to fix and improve the machinery. At first, she was too shy to offer advice, but seeing Sara frustrated over costs to fix things, struggling to manage equipment that was built for a man and swearing over her weakness Jemma began to introduce pulley systems and winches to make lifting easier and used Cassie's strength to pull ropes that could lift straw bales and feed sacks. She felt happy, fitting in, and earning her keep. Martin would join them for herding the sheep into pens for medication and doctoring, cleaning maggots from hooves and checking the health of lambs as the new crop were born in March.

Gradually, the past weeks became a dream. Her mind refused to think how she had moved from 2046 to now. Her time in 1601 was a nightmare washed into oblivion. Looking at Sara's appointments diary she had found she was living in 2024.
There were shocks. So many cars! The reliance on gas for energy. How far people travelled for holidays and the amount of building on land people were going to need to grow food. It was alarming how much time people spent playing computer games and how reliant everyone was on computers and electricity to do the simplest of tasks. One day some fighter jets flew over and she nearly collapsed in fear. The aeroplane trails across the sky were things she had never seen before, beautiful, but so frightening with the amount of fuel Martin said they burned.
When she went to the village, and bought stores in the village shop, she would occasionally hear a name and look round to see someone she knew, but much younger than she had expected, and now she had another worry. In a year and a half's time, her mum and dad and Seb were due to buy Shurnock and move in. In two year's time she would be born. How could she exist at age 22 and zero at the same time? How could she live just along the road from her mum and dad without them knowing? In her head, she knew this could not happen, because, already, she knew who would own this farm as she grew up at Shurnock. By the time she was eight, it was no longer Sara and Martin. So far as she remembered, she had never met them before, but before she was eight, her life had been Shurnock and the small amount of time at school from age five to age seven. Grown up life was too far above her head to be relevant, and then, as she grew, only parents of school friends and the people she made regular contact with, like the people who ran the shop filtered into her conscious mind. By the time Jemma had reached eight, Martin would have been qualified. Perhaps he had fulfilled his dream to work at a bird sanctuary and Sara had moved to join

him, but what had happened to her, the grown up Jemma? The person she now was? Although Sara had so far ignored the need for papers and identification by simply providing Jemma with food, clothes and shelter and stabling for Cassie, if they moved away, Jemma would need to find other work and those pieces of paper that proved her existence would become necessary. Whatever story could she tell to explain her lack of birth papers or any other paperwork that was automatically created along the path of life? The little voice in the locked, muffled room occasionally shouted louder, demanding to be heard, insisting she face her past and future, but she couldn't do it. There was too much trauma, too much uncertainty and she just added padding, turned away from things too terrifying to contemplate and lived each day as it came.

Sara had searched the net for any "Jemmas or Gemmas" missing in Worcestershire or Warwickshire, and then the whole country, any age from 14 to 40. She had looked for vets dying in road accidents or murdered, even gone missing or drowned at sea but had found nothing that linked. The only "missing" story was that of a gardener in 2019, but that lady had been found and was anyway much older than Jemma. It was odd that it had happened at Shurnock Court, only five years ago. Sara vaguely remembered the police enquiring about it, trying to fit the jigsaw together after she had been found, questioning both her and Martin, who had only been fourteen then, and thought the whole thing exciting with searches with dogs across their land, but no one had mentioned a missing girl at the time. Try as she might, Sara could not fit the two events together. She even remembered another police constable visiting a whole year later saying the lady had been found, but they were still trying to work out what had happened. Nothing more had come of it.

Sara's mind returned to thoughts of a possible drugs ring or slave labour. Had that lady discovered something and been kidnapped for a whole year before returning too traumatised to talk of it? Was Jemma, in fact part of some slave gang that she had escaped? (If so, Sara could be in big trouble, she thought). But, then how had she ended up with Cassie? Bits and pieces came out in conversation. Her love and admiration for her mum and dad and Uncle Seb (She had searched hard for Sebastian, such an unusual name, but found nothing). In the end, she hadn't even asked The Samaritans for advice. She sensed that Jemma was burying her traumas because she couldn't yet face them and Sara was terrified that officialdom would insist on uncovering them, forcing them to the surface before Jemma was ready. Sara decided she would give Jemma six months if she needed it and then suggest professional help. She would be in trouble for keeping it quiet but Jemma seemed so muddled by time that the delay might not even be discovered. (Wishful thinking, she chided herself).

The one thing that brought Jemma out of her shell was climate change. Martin had passed his driving test and drove the pair of them to meetings of all sorts of climate change groups. Greenpeace, The Woodland Trust, the RSPB, and The Green Party, until Jemma pointed out they should cycle as the car was adding to the climate problems and they became a whole lot fitter.

"It's uncanny," Martin told Sara, as they warmed milk in the kitchen for the sickly lambs. "She speaks as if she knows what's going to happen. She's so convincing that even though I know the science and think she might be right, a little bit of me hopes that we will sort everything out, that we might be wrong, that the scientists have got it wrong, that the scientists will think of a way to stop it all happening, but Jemma talks like she knows how the glaciers will melt and the sea levels rise and she talks about the rivers flooding and winds that will take the electricity supply down and fires raging through the forests and burning all the crops and I know it has started to happen. I mean, like Bewdley and Worcester always flood, and places like Tewkesbury and London and York that didn't used to, but she says even the Bow Brook will flood the land because the Avon will back up and she's even shown us calculations and the figures look right, Mum. It's scary," Sara nodded. "She was talking to me about putting in reservoirs to reduce flooding and save water for the summer droughts so we have water for the sheep and buying solar panels for our own electricity, even a wind turbine and a hydro electric plant to put on the stream. I don't think we can afford all that, but I've applied for solar panels for the barn on the hill and the house. The government schemes are useless but she was so sure we would need them, and the prices of fuel are rising so fast that I'm getting them." She shrugged. "Who knows, they might pay for themselves in about fifteen years, and at least I will know I've done my bit to reduce climate change."

"I so wish," Martin said, fiercely, "That we had had a different government for the last thirteen years. Before that, it looked like we might have been going in the right direction, even though it was a bit slow, but in the last thirteen years, we've gone backwards, haven't we?"

Sara nodded and smiled wryly. "I always think of this government looking only to tomorrow and the next pound in their pocket, whereas the greens look so far ahead that no one voting can see the benefits of what they say. The other parties lie somewhere in between but, yes, for the future, we have the worst government possible. Money before sense. I used to write to them, urging them to take the money out of the equation and then look at what needed to be done through common sense and then make the plan, using money to make it happen. They couldn't even do that with the pandemic with people dying in thousands around them, so climate change has no chance."

Martin wrapped his arms around his mum and gave her a hug, knowing that she was thinking of her parents, both now dead. It had hit her hard, losing them just a fortnight apart when they had been so sprightly and healthy before Covid

242

struck. She had gone round in a daze for going on six months, and then, just when she was pulling it together, her brother had gone and killed himself, struggling on his father's farm alone, unable to cope with the anger of loss and the lack of support, even blaming himself for allowing his parents to get infected, and of course, having had Covid himself, he was finding the work almost impossible, impatient with the exhaustion that Long Covid left him with. Martin had been so angry with him. Not for dying, but for not asking Sara and him to help. Too proud to ask his little sister when they could have saved him.

Martin had expected his mum to fragment. He had stood ready to hold her together, but she had argued with his dad about the farm and then simply walked out with Martin, sorted the farm and joined The Samaritans for good measure. The anger still sparked against the wasted lives, but she was strong, whole again and, Martin reckoned, having Jemma here was helping. He had been worried about going off to University and leaving her on the farm alone. If Jemma would stay, everything would work out right (assuming the climate could be controlled he amended his thought).

Sara gave him a peck on the cheek. She smiled. "Elections this May. There's still hope."

Martin grinned. "Adrian has asked Jemma to speak at the Birmingham climate march on behalf of The Green Party and Jack and Laura are pushing her to speak for Climate Action. So far, she is saying she is too shy, but, my gosh, Mum, if she gets up there, I'm sure she will convince thousands to change their ways, whoever they vote for. She's so factual about everything."

Jemma walked into the room and they looked slightly embarrassed.

"I heard you," Jemma said, " and I appreciate the compliments, but, even though I so want to make things happen differently, to make people understand how urgent change is and what they have to do, I can't speak in front of all those crowds. They would take my voice away."

Sara was taking the warmed bottles out of the oven and putting them into three heat proof bags to take to the lambs in the barn. They walked across together, a bag apiece. As they fed the lambs, Sara said, " I used to be very shy. One day, I was told I had to do a talk to the whole assembly at school. I was terrified, but one of my teachers said, "It's easy. Just pick five friendly looking faces in different parts of the hall and speak three sentences to each one in turn. Everyone in between will think you are looking at them and including them every time you sweep your eyes from one face to the next". So, that's what I did and it felt like I was having a one to one conversation with each of those people and it went fine......I don't know what I said because I was too nervous to think about the words, but I managed the whole speech,"

Jemma looked down at the lamb she was feeding, sucking enthusiastically at the teat of the bottle. It sounded possible. Could you focus out a thousand people? If you had friends you knew dotted amongst the crowd to talk to? No one knew what climate change would do, except her. She had the knowledge of how so many could be saved by becoming self sufficient and setting up their own energy systems. She didn't know if it was possible to change the future to save a few more lives, even maybe millions of lives if only she could make everyone understand that to have a future they must make sacrifices now. She understood that the pandemic had already made everyone antagonistic about rules and limitations on what they could do, but, if she didn't try, all those people she could have saved would die in the floods and fires. Everyone who drowned or starved or burned, those deaths would be her fault. She swallowed hard and felt her face grow hot. She would have to try. If the words didn't come on the day, she would feel stupid, but that was something she had to risk.

"OK," she said hoarsely. "I'll do it. Not for any party, though, or group. Just to warn people, to ask them to lose a bit now, to save a lot later."

Martin almost dropped the bottle he was holding, in shock. "Jemma," he said. "You are amazing and I will give you a kiss when this lamb stops trying to take the bottle out of my hands and eat it."

It made them laugh. It was the first time Jemma had laughed since losing her parents and it surprised her. It felt good, but also shocking. Like she had betrayed their love. She almost wanted to apologise to them for being callous, but then, she thought, they wouldn't have wanted me to be unhappy for ever. If they could have, they would have urged me to get on with my life and make happiness wherever and whenever I could. They had chatted one night about the buying of Shurnock and how it had changed them, saved them from unhappiness. Carl's parents had died of Covid in September 2020 and Beth and Seb lost theirs in January 2021 as the pandemic escaped from London and washed across the country. They had all been angry, the rage consuming them, believing all the deaths had been unnecessary. Along with the inadequacy of the government to act against climate change, they were full of fire, furious at their impotence against a government that still talked only of money and not of lives. They had gone to a climate rally, met and agreed to buy a property between them, and that property had been Shurnock. It had filled their minds to the exclusion of the burning rage, and as they clinked glasses on the first night of their new adventure, Carl had said, "To the future. We can't grieve forever."

As her parents related the story to her, she had liked those words and stored then away to use whenever she was sad, and now they surfaced and added to her determination to do what she could. If she somehow changed the future, the marauders might never come. If she didn't change the future, well, she supposed she was part of the things that had happened and she had helped those she had seen surviving to get to that point. The rally was in four weeks. Martin got straight onto Greenpeace and Climate Action and Adrian at

The Green Party. "She's agreed," he e-mailed. "Can you get her a slot to speak? How long can she talk for?"

Jemma found there was too much to say. How could you compact the whole future of the world into twenty minutes? It was impossible. Martin did his best to help. "Look who else is speaking," he advised. "There's Greta and two famous naturalists. Adrian is going for the political angle. How about you concentrate on describing what will happen if we don't sort this out and then advise on the self help stuff. You're so good on crops and food and how to make energy without burning fuel and renewing resources. Why don't you do that?" Jemma nodded, thoughtfully and hugged him gratefully. "Yes. You're so clever, Martin. Thank you."

Chapter 12

The night before, Jemma's head fizzed with the things she needed to say. She had washed almost ritually, had Sara cut her hair and laid out her clothes. She was going to wear the clothes she brought with her from 2046 to feel closer to her parents, but not the sheepskin. The sun was going to shine and she reckoned speaking to all those people was going to make her hot. She had the speech written out and had read it out loud a hundred times, changing words here and there and then yesterday, had thought it was rubbish and wanted to start again. Martin had taken it from her hands.

"It's fine," he promised her. "Just start with what you've got and if you suddenly feel the need to branch off and add bits when you're up there, do it, but rewriting it now will only scramble your brain. It knows what you need to say."

She ran through the whole thing three times before she slept, still tweaking it, changing priorities a little, but Martin was right. It was all there, she could let it go. Her mind cleared, relaxed and she slept deeply, without dreams.

The sun through the window woke her. It was agreed, they would start the day normally. Eat, feed the lambs, check the sheep and then cycle up to the station at Redditch. Burning some of her physical energy would keep the adrenalin under control. She already trembled at what lay ahead. The routine helped, perhaps lulling her mind into a false sense of security. They ate a good breakfast, unsure when, during the day they would be able to eat again.

Sara was staying to look after the farm.

"You look just right," she reassured Jemma. "Smart but one of the people. I think they'll love you."

She impulsively hugged the girl in front of her, her face taut with nerves. "If you're like me, you will be feeling almost sick before you step up there, and then, as you glance round those faces you have planted in the crowd, the nerves will go and you will speak with that passion that fires you up and makes you care so much. You'll be fine."

Jemma hugged her back, grateful for the family that had welcomed her in and given her strength. Martin drained his mug and gathered their rucksacks. "Time to go," he said. "We don't want to miss the train and have to cycle all the way to Birmingham. Come on."

They hurried out of the house and set off up the hill to Astwood Bank, and then all the way up the ridge to Headless Cross and down to the station, where it was if the train awaited them. There were a few placard bearers on the platform, their dress ranging from tattered jeans and T-shirts to smart trousers and jacket. It was good to see the range of people who now cared enough about the planet to demonstrate. Martin sorted their tickets from the machine and before long, the train was off.

There was a debate taking place at the other end of the carriage about whether computers were a good or bad invention and Jemma listened with interest. They used too much electricity, People used them for frivolous time wasting activities like sending photographs of cakes they had made, or playing endless games and sent out misinformation or stole each other's money, but the pro computers argued that they were used for accuracy in calculations that saved lives through safer construction and engineering. "Only if the right figures are inputted," someone argued. They allowed people to learn about global warming and climate change and set up demos like today's, didn't they? "Well, yeah but we could a done that by telephone and newspaper and TV and radio and that," a girl argued.

"Newspapers use electricity to print and wood and chemicals so they're no better."

"Yes, but look at all the old computers dumped and leaking dangerous stuff into the ground or giving slum kids cancer when they dismantle them,"

"Well, maybe we should make computers we don't need to keep changing, then,,,,"

Jemma liked their active brains and genuine thoughts. She felt nervous about talking in front of such quick debaters. Supposing they didn't like her? Martin was watching her face and saw the cloud of uncertainty shadow her features.

"You'll be great," he told her. "Here, have a jelly baby."

"Where on earth did you get those?" Jemma said, with a smile.

"The shop," Martin said. "Just started making them again. Due to popular demand, I suppose."

"I only like the red and green ones," Jemma said.

"Uh- oh," said Martin. "I don't like yellow. Guess they'll be a lot left in the packet for Mum tonight."

It was a silly conversation but it helped free Jemma's mind from the mission ahead.

The train filled gradually as they meandered towards Birmingham. More banners and placards appeared, but also a crowd wearing striped scarves headed for football matches. Each group surveyed the other with curiosity, not understanding their motivation. The train was packed as it left University with the odd singsong chant. Martin reckoned it would be a lot noisier coming home. He also wondered about Covid. How many people were still carrying the virus in any one of its many mutations? He had so far dodged it and hoped no one was spreading it around. His uncle and grandparents had caught it via a sheep sale of all things and brought it back to Feckenham, where it spread via the local shop, but luckily the mask wearing and lack of parties had made its infection sporadic and it had died out quickly. By the time Martin and Sara had arrived, it was gone and the Feckenham community had become even more insular as a result of the scare that left three dead and five with long covid. He did not want to be responsible for another flare up and more deaths. He realised, he didn't even know if Jemma was vaccinated. It was too late to do anything about it now, except try to keep her out of the crowds as much as possible. He'd be doing that anyway, for the villagers' sakes.

The train stopped and they waited patiently for the wedge of humanity to disembark before descending themselves and following the scarves and placards up the escalator. Jemma thought vaguely that, in ten years time, the escalators would no longer be functioning. So many tiny changes yet to come. If only those changes had come sooner, the whole world would have survived. She shook the thought away. That was a past she really could not change.

As they arrived at the great square, Jemma gulped at the sea of faces crowded into the space, listening avidly to the present speaker. The words came to an end and their was an eruption of cheers and clapping. Martin led her around the edge of the crowd, as he had been instructed, to a cordoned off tent where they showed their cardboard passes and were permitted to enter. Ahead of them were seats and tables accommodating sandwiches and drinks where a few speakers sat chatting. It was easy to see who had already had their turn and who still waited from the body posture. Tense spines and stretched skin over cheekbones meant about to speak. Flushed cheeks, big smiles and too much adrenalin to contain said, "Job done." Jemma heard a name being introduced and her body jumped to attention. "Margot Bish is a local gardener and green activist...." the announcer proclaimed and Jemma felt her head swim. The lady who went through time was here, and talking, but Jemma would not be able to talk to her because she was to speak straight after her. The only chance was if she hung around to listen But would she?

She sounded fiercely angry as she berated the politicians for their lack of action. She spoke of how she was observing climate change in action. The number of bees were decreasing drastically. Plants, used to the old English climate were dying, unable to cope with soil being saturated with winter wet and full of air pockets in summer drought. She described leaves burning with their inability to protect themselves against the fierce heat of the sun so that the plants could not feed themselves and died. She explained how the changing seasons were destroying the balance between pest and predator so that damage to plants, including crops was increasing and warned of the new pests that invaded and survived as a result of the higher temperatures. She spoke of how the marshes that captured and held carbon were drying out and burning, releasing carbon to the atmosphere and exacerbating the problem and she begged people to accept that the problem was real, here, now and every little change that anyone made or failed to make could save or destroy the planet. The speech was short, blunt and full of impact and received more cheers and a murmur of anger against the politicians that were failing them.

She stood back from the microphone and gazed in awe at the hundreds of people brought together in fear and frustration and saluted them, before leaving the stage. Jemma felt dry mouthed and her legs trembled. Her turn had come. Margot gave her a grin as they passed. "They're on your side. Just say what you have to say. You'll be fine," she said, her cheeks flushed with excess adrenalin.
"Thanks," Jemma said and stepped into the sunlight. The crowd cheered and then fell eerily silent, waiting for her words. She put her speech down and adjusted the microphone and looked out at the multicoloured crowd. For a moment, the enormity of so many faces took her voice away and blanked her mind, and then, she saw the banner being hastily unfurled at the back of the crowd. "Yay, Jemma, Go For It" it said, and there were Martin and Adrian under it, giving her a thumbs up. She cast her eye over the masses and saw the banners of people she knew even though they were too far distant to recognise, and then, she saw her mum with Uncle Seb, and just a row behind her, her dad. Not as she remembered them in 2046, but as she had seen them in

photographs and video clips from before she was born. They were waiting for her to speak.

"I've been asked to tell you what the world will be like if we don't act now to reduce climate change, and I say reduce, because, already we are in the spiral where climate change cannot be stopped, only slowed so that we might have time to learn to live with the problems we have already created.

The earth is warming.

The government we have says they aim for zero carbon by 2050. Well. Yes. That will be easily achieved because we will nearly all be dead. Most of the planet by 2050 will be either a charred desert or ocean. You can see that it is already beginning to happen with fires in Spain and the south of France and tsunamis taking out islands that once would have survived.

The pockets of land that will be left will be so heavily populated that no land will be available to grow food and those who have survived that far will also die.

That is what will have happened if we do not change NOW.

So let's ignore 2050.

Let's think about doing everything we can by 2030.

We have just six years.

If we ditch the cars, halve the electricity we use, stop making products out of cheap plastic that have to be replaced every year and use every resource we have to create green electricity – solar panels on every roof, tidal power, river power to turn water mills as well as turbines, use of the wind in every way for windmills and wind turbines, then we have a chance.

If we change our emphasis from a growth economy, which is, of course unsustainable, to an economy based on regrowth we have a chance.

 Money used to be a piece of metal mined from the ground. Now it is a number in a computer, burning more fuel with every transaction we make. It is meaningless in terms of survival. We have to stop thinking about numbers in a computer, and think instead about growing enough food for the population we have on the shrinking amount of land that will be available as climate change bites.

We need to replace recreation that relies on electricity, that adds to the heat of the earth's surface, and find ways to entertain ourselves that do not require an input of power, other than that produced by our own muscles.

We need to relearn from our great grandparents how to manage household tasks without the flick of a switch.

If we only manage half of this by 2030. If perhaps, we cannot break ourselves of our electrical habits, or our holidays abroad or our need to leap into our cars to travel, or if we allow our government to prevent us from providing our own electricity as they have done by reducing grants and creating rules that only allow the rich to invest in green electricity, let me tell you what the world will be like in 2045.

Those who have listened and learned from the experts who talk to you today and who don't wait for a government that cannot work quickly enough, bound as it is by red tape and apathy, those will survive, but they will be living on the food that they grow, and making their own clothes as we once did 400 years ago. Even spinning the wool and cotton and weaving the cloth.

Travel will be by horse and cart or on foot. Even public transport will have failed because we did not act soon enough or fast enough. Our mains electricity system will have failed. Underground cables flooded, Pylons damaged to the point of being irreparable due to high winds. Many sub stations will have failed due to being under water.

Every winter, the rivers will flood by about 15 metres of depth. Streams and brooks will back up and flood. Birmingham and Redditch will be islands. Evesham, Tewkesbury much of Upton, half of Bewdley, and Worcester will be under water. Most of our cities will have shrunk to tiny hilltop settlements as the rain on the hills erodes the land below and washes away the houses. Roads, where drains can no longer cope with the torrents of running water become rubble strewn rivers themselves adding to real rivers breaking their banks and drowning all the adjoining land.

In Summer, the heat of the sun will evaporate all the water and England will be like Africa is now. There will be fires like they are experiencing in California and Australia, France, Italy and Spain, even the Arctic Circle, burning our food supplies and the timber we need for winter fires. Already, we have seen this happening in Yorkshire and Surrey, but it will be worse, much worse.

The heat will be so bad that we have to live underground during the day, with only fire watchers above the surface. We will have to carry out any work above ground in extreme temperatures just before dusk and just after dawn or during the short nights,then trying to sleep in airless bunkers during the day. Every household will live only by the electricity they can create, supplemented by firewood to heat the houses in winter when the continuous rain will mean we have no solar power, and the high river levels make hydro power inefficient.

To survive, you will need to know how to grow your own food and repair your own tools, even your own solar panels and turbines. You will need to be physically fit to work your land because there will be no fuel for the tractors, lorries and cars, not even electric vehicles because of the heat they create. You may return to horse power, but then you will need crops to feed your horse.

All the food we need to eat must be grown within our shores because any other countries that have survived will be like us with populations on islands, surviving on the food they grow. There will be none to spare. Imagine, such a restricted diet. No tea, no coffee, no chocolate. If there are no bees, there will be no honey. There may be no sugar either. The English craving for sweets will be unsatisfied. Can you imagine a future without sugar? It may be that we can find a way to breed bees that can survive the extremes of climate, but at the moment, no one is even thinking about it.

Our population will be more than halved as we fight for shelter and food. People will die in floods, in riots, in heathland fires. They will starve and many will be murdered for their food. It's going to be frightening beyond your worst imaginings. So, I suggest to you that, first, you ditch your cars. Tomorrow. Even if they are electric. Second you meet as a community, because as a group you are stronger than any individual and that you pool your expertise. And fill the gaps in the skills and knowledge you need. You need to have an emergency plan worked out to provide your own food, your own power, your own shelter. You need to plan to save winter water, stored where possible underground or within your homes. You may need boats to travel in winter, or even skis as the climate becomes more extreme and the country freezes in January and February.
The faster you prepare, the more chance we have of slowing the effects of climate change and the more chance you have

of being a survivor.

I don't really do politics, but I ask you to vote for people with practical skills or the ability to organise action rather than those who can only talk.

Vote for engineers in the solar and hydro electricity fields, farmers and naturalists who understand how one change impacts on other essential components.

By 2040, you will not need money because the computerised banking system will have collapsed along with the failure of mains electricity. The new economy will be based on those with skills and energy to keep us fed and sheltered. The rich will be a different set of people and they will not be rich in money, but in food and warmth and shelter and they will have these because they work as a community, pooling resources and knowledge and skills

I guess I've painted a pessimistic picture, but I say to you, you are at the beginning of a new kind of world. Embrace it, learn to work with the natural world and the communities that survive will be strong, and perhaps happier as they relearn the things that matter.

I have been lucky. My parents have learned the skills already of growing crops and rearing animals without chemicals that would have to be imported and that will no longer be available. My uncle is an engineer who understands how to borrow energy from the natural world rather than raping the planet for its failing resources. We have lived with the land, but we watch it change and have to keep relearning as the climate alters and crops which once thrived, fail so that we have to grow new crops that cope with drought or flood. It's a hard existence but every success is exhilarating. More exhilarating than any computer game you might win or football match you have watched. You know, in the world we are creating for 2045, there will be no sport because no one travels far, with no aeroplanes or trains, not even cars and mostly, there is no time to play between the tasks needed to keep the crops growing.

I wish I could tell you otherwise, but I'M SORRY, we have already left it too late and acted too slowly. If you want your children to survive, and perhaps rejuvenate the planet we live on, you can give them the gift of time and the gift of knowledge, for if you give them time, they may find a way to replant the deserts, make natural energy use more efficient, even control the heat that consumes us, but our generation needs time and the giving of that is within your power, if you live by all the slogans you have heard today. Live local, reduce travel, bike or trike NOT car, solar power for all, save water, reuse, recycle, buy to last. Love nature, Replenish what you take. I look around and I read your placards and I think, yes, you have understood the urgency of which I speak. Let us hope the rest of England, the rest of the world is watching and listening and will act with us".

Jemma stopped abruptly and found her eyes locked with her mother's. She flicked her gaze to her uncle who was jumping up and down, clapping his hands above his head. Her dad had stepped forwards, impulsively, and bumped Beth's shoulder as he cheered and waved his banner. Jemma broke her gaze as Beth turned to berate Carl. Jemma knew what would happen next. She felt tears in her eyes and desperately wanted to run to them, hug them and never let go, but the crowds were too vast. She would never find them at ground level, and anyway, what could she say? She turned away before the tears fell and walked blindly back into the speakers' tent.

Margot was gone. She tried to find someone who could give her a contact or address but there was a confidentiality policy. "Try through Greenpeace or The Soil Association," they

suggested. "She'll contact you if she wants to meet you."
 Jermma nodded glumly. She could hardly put on a public site, "I need to talk to you about travelling in time," could she?

She looked at the sandwiches, but found she couldn't eat. Too many emotions tumbling and rolling like seawater at the change of the tide. She took a drink of apple juice instead and sipped, watching the next speaker pleading with passion that we change now to save the natural world of which human beings were a part. Every message was the same, the need for urgency, the need to change now, this week. The need to prepare for what was to come. Some pointed out that the Green Party were no longer a minority party, that their policies covered everything from employment through schooling to housing and an end to poverty. They were no longer a party of nature nuts but a party which included accountants, bankers, engineers, scientists and logicians with expertise from industry to make things work. Others demanded an end to political parties altogether so that the many minorities that actually made a majority might be heard. Many side stepped politics altogether, even though it was a Green Party organised event and tried to appeal to all, regardless of party, only asking that they did not vote for a party that thought climate change was not important in their political agenda. Others asked that the voters demand from their candidates detail and fixed dates for steps towards achieving their aims to test the viability and sincerity of their written agenda, to find out what they really knew and understood about the challenge ahead.

Martin reappeared with Adrian at his side, their banner furled, and hugged her with big smiles. "You were great," Adrian said. "The whole crowd thought you were great."
Jemma felt exhausted. She had done the best she could and had run out of fight. History would roll on and, either she had changed it so that her mum and dad could survive in a better world, or she was already part of their world as it had

happened and they would live the lives Jemma had witnessed for nineteen, nearly twenty years....and they might have survived and be grieving only for their missing daughter. Was there still a way to leave a message for them in some alcove not yet explored? She had pen and paper now, even a computer if only she could work out how.

Martin was speaking as she refocussed on the world around her.
"I even heard one lady say, if she ever had a daughter, she would name her after you, and the guy next to her was pointing at his programme and saying to remember to spell it with a "J".
His smile was ecstatic, but as he looked at Jemma's face, he saw the lines of fatigue. "Come on," he said. "We had best eat and then we can go home. It's been a long day and this lot will be partying all night, I should think. They don't have a farm to run like we do."
He dragged Jemma back to the sandwich and cake table and filled her plate, insisting she needed the energy.
"I know it's mostly downhill but it's still a good length bike ride back home," he pointed out,
Jemma picked up a sandwich and took an unwilling bite, but then found that food was what she needed. They cleared their plates and left, wriggling through the throng. Jemma looked carefully for the four special faces but none came into view. Part of her wanted to stay, to sift through the whole crowd until they were found. Reason said, in a crowd of over three thousand, all moving about, she had no chance. She had to move on. There was an ache in her chest as she tore herself away, shutting the door on her access to the future.

She felt numb on the way back. The meeting had been successful beyond everyone's wildest dreams. Jemma had blanked the crowd while she spoke, taking Sara's advice and focussing on just the few known faces, but as she had finished, the crowd came into focus. Acres and acres of believers, people who cared about their families, the animals, the plants, people in different countries where climate change was already a killer,. These were people ready to make a difference. They had hoped for a thousand, adding to demonstrations in London and Liverpool, Leeds, Manchester and Bristol. They had tripled that, and more. Each city had different speakers from their local areas and video links for the national and international stars, pulling them all together. It was hard to believe she had played such a big part of it, and now she remembered her mum's words from over ten years ago. "There were three young speakers there who seemed to just know what would happen and told us what we must do......One of those girls looked a lot like my cousin. Quite odd, like I knew her from somewhere else..."

Now she understood that speaker was her. Was it her mum Martin had heard saying she would name her daughter, if she had one, after the speaker? And Uncle Seb telling her the spelling? If only Beth could realise it was her own daughter gone back in time, Beth would know she was OK. Martin was talking excitedly about all the other speakers and Jemma let it wash over her. As her dad had said. they had all done everything they could to save people. Now it was up to each individual to decide their own future. Jemma would slip into ambiguity and must be gone from Feckenham before her mum, dad and uncle completed the purchase of Shurnock Court. She might have just a few months longer. Stories of that first year had them working all hours and leaving the property only for supplies and equipment. Everyone in Feckenham thought they were a hippie commune and had left them alone until Beth attended a village hall talk four months later and showed her knowledge in quiet assurance and people began to listen and learn from three young adults with knowledge and foresight beyond their years, taking them more seriously as Beth's predictions were fulfilled.

They arrived home to smells of the evening meal being cooked. Sara looked over her shoulder at them.

"I watched you on television, and some of the other speakers, too. The news has the demos as its top story. They are praising the speakers and the crowds for their good behaviour. They say it's not just youngsters, not just students but pensioners with their grandchildren, professional people, the lot. I've been so proud of you all."

Martin laughed. "We may have made a mistake. We forgot the football was on at the same time. Hundreds of striped scarves going to Birmingham."

Sara laughed, too. "Nothing is more important than football to a fan. With luck, some footballer will get the hang of climate change and will speak out and then we'll get the fans onside......excuse the pun. Half an hour until we eat. OK?"

After they had eaten, Sara seemed distracted, as if she had something to say but didn't know where to start. It had been almost 2 months now since Jemma had arrived in 2024 and Sara had almost forgotten about unravelling Jemma's trauma. Jemma was happy, working on the farm and that was all that mattered. It was almost as if she had been unofficially adopted, but, while tidying a heap of bits and pieces that accumulated by the washing machine while emptying pockets of items to be washed, Sara came across the Organic Association card taken out of Jemma's filthy clothes when she had first washed them. She had seen the name, Beth Martin and done a computer search but it had led nowhere. Only now, she noticed the date of expiry, 06/2042. That was odd. Perhaps it was a typing error and should read 2024. Sara had never pushed Jemma for more information, afraid Jemma would close up, thinking she was being interrogated, but now she wondered what Jemma's dad's name was. His surname must be Martin. With time on her hands between news broadcasts, she searched under the name for a vet. There were hundreds of Martins, but as a christian name, not a surname, too many to search through. She added Worcestershire but got nowhere. The news was showing the demonstration. Hoards walking towards the square from all parts of Birmingham, a seething, waving ocean. Then a clip of the major speakers saying their piece and the crowds roaring in approval. Then Jemma appeared, so small, so shy. "You can do it, Jem," Sara whispered to the television, and Jemma began to speak. The crowd was awesomely silent as the words echoed around the square, and Sara found herself drawn in and listening to every word, the conviction and sincerity. When Jemma spoke of her family, properly for the first time since Sara had known her, they finally became real people, determined to live with the land, using the skills they had gained and Sara could not understand how Jemma could have left them. No way could she have fallen out with them. There must have been an accident, or....was that reference to murder of the food growers a clue? Sara wondered if she could use the speech to open the shell Jemma had kept clamped shut over her past.

With the evening ahead of them, Sara was trying to decide if this was the time. Was Jemma healed enough to speak of her past? Martin was on a high from the day, Jemma seemed happy but numb, as if the day's success was too much to take in. Sara lost her confidence. How could she spoil Martin's euphoria by trying to pry Jemma's shell open? Goodness knows what emotions would come pouring out. A small corner of her mind nagged. What if the card date was real? 2042. Jemma had said she wouldn't be believed and had said she changed times. That speech. It sounded just like Jemma had seen what would happen. But time travel? No. That had to be a psychological defence to explain some time Jemma experienced so much pain she could not think of it, but why was there nothing in the news? Sara had searched county by county, branching out from Worcestershire and Warwickshire over the last two year period and found nothing that fitted. She considered the police again, but really it was too late now. If she was going to tell them it had to have been done within a fortnight, not two months. Jemma's eyes were closing as they watched more broadcasts of the demonstrations, Jemma now focussing on the other speakers, but unable to stop herself searching the crowd for just another glimpse of her family. Would they be on facebook, or twitter? Could she contact them under a different name? Or even her own name, which they would have heard at the demo anyway. Then she remembered her mum saying facebook was a waste of electricity, her dad agreeing and gave up on the idea. There was snail mail, but what could she write? She figured they were all at university just now and she did not know their addresses, nor where her grandparents lived as they had all died in the pandemic. So many dead ends, but maybe it was for the best. She felt so tired. It was that "after" feeling when you had done something mega and your mind thought it could now relax.

"How about bed, Jem?" Sara asked, watching Jemma's nodding head. Jemma lifted her chin, startled and agreed. "Hot chocolate to help me relax, and then I'll sleep," she agreed. "Goodnight."

Her dreams were unsettled, speaking at demos about how to find your parents, flickering images of her parents looking for her. Sara and Martin applauding her for deciding to change times, and the last unbearable part, leaving Cassie behind.

She woke in tears, and crying out for Cassie, and struggled into her clothes, weeping, to go to her horse, the impact so great.

Cassie was there, looking patiently out of her box, perhaps surprised to see Jemma so early. It was Sunday. There would be few cars on the road. Jemma saddled Cassie, left a note on the table, "Gone riding. Back soon," and left, trotting up the gravel track to the barn on the hill, and then down the winding track to Shurnock. She took the bridle way and led Cassie into the deserted property from beyond the stables. Poor old house, she thought. It seems to be empty more often than it has people. She had come to be near her family, to send them messages through time and to think. If they had survived the marauders and returned, where could she leave a note that they had not yet discovered, but would discover soon? What might they sort and redecorate next that they had never done before? It had only to stay hidden for 24 years, not like leaving a note from 1601. The lawns were no good. By 2034 they were all pools or vegetable beds. The beams of the house looked like they had been recently renovated. No cracks to push notes into. Nothing on the front door and other woodwork had been sanded and repainted by the Martin family since 2026. The apple tree had been pruned and grown new branches every year. Same with the pear and the cherry. The swimming pool no longer existed. Just now, there were tennis courts but they were, in 2046 more pools and extension to the moat. The herb garden did not exist here, all slabs which Beth would yank up and replace with a new herb garden. She looked at the cellar, and froze, as if afraid to break the thought that was forming. No one had touched the cellar except to make a stairwell through the priest's hole. The doors of the cellar had, so far as Jemma knew, never been touched since her family arrived. The owners of this time had caulked them and painted them, replacing the iron hinges but there would be more work soon to do beyond 2046, and in the stonework, attaching the hinges to the wall, there was a gap. Jemma wrote quickly. "Hi Mum, Hi Dad, Hi Uncle Seb. I got away but ended up in a different time. You might have seen me in 2024! Don't know where I will be when you read this, but I know we don't meet. so....I love you. I will think of you often, Jemma PS Cassie is safe, too." She rolled the note tight, grimaced as she wrapped it in plastic to protect it from the damp and pushed it into the stonework. "Please find it, and know I'm OK." she thought, and, swallowing that lump of grief, again, returned to Cassie.

"There. That's done." she said. "Let's just ride some more, shall we? I need some time away from people and just with you, OK?"

Cassie gave a shake of the head in agreement and they set off south, not bothering too much about where they went, just enjoying the freedom and quietness of a Sunday morning. Jemma felt a smidgeon of guilt, She had not helped with the farm tasks. She hoped Sara would not mind this one day of spontaneous holiday. It was a day of patchy cloud and sun. Perfect for horse riding, even if the horse was a bulky shire rather than a flashy streamlined model. There were a few bees around, buzzing happily in the tree blossom and birds sang lustily, dashing about gathering food for their young. It was a beautiful sound and Jemma was glad to have been allowed back in time to hear it. There were even rabbits hopping about in a field of cows. It was beautiful, but she could see how much the animals had dwindled since the 1600's. No sparrows or woodpeckers. No starlings. Sara said that even the buzzards that had been increasing in numbers just a decade ago were almost gone, along with the hobbies and kestrels. They reached a road with a bridle way crossing the fields beyond and Jemma dismounted to lead Cassie across. Neither of them coped well with the noise of cars and lorries. That incessant rumble and hum, with the odd growl of a van or lorry was worse than the buzz of a mosquito. Always there in the background warning of trouble to come. It took a while to pluck up courage and cross. Then, just as Jemma was about to remount, there was a grumble in the sky, turning to a roar. Cassie danced on the end of her rein, and Jemma ducked as two jets belted over their heads. They were gone as quickly as they came, but it took minutes for Jemma and Cassie to regain their equilibrium. "What a stupid waste of fuel, eh Cassie?" commented Jemma. "All those silly men, practising for wars which just damage the whole world more. Why can't they just imprison the leaders instead of damaging the land and killing innocent people?.....I expect,being a horse, you don't understand what I'm talking about. I expect you are happier because of that, which is good." They rode on companionably. It was good to leave politics behind and concentrate on the moment and Jemma felt at peace. She had done what she needed to do and could now live each day as it came, helping Sara with the farm and letting the future take care of itself. They stopped on the top of a ridge and took in the patchwork of tiny houses and fields, the odd copse of trees, a church tower poking out of trees on Hanbury's hill, and another rising from the plain at Inkberrow. It was hard to believe so much of this would be under water in just 20 years, turning to dust in Summer. She felt lucky to have experienced the green-ness and a period of time when food was still easy to get. Although she hated the traffic noise and smell, it was an amazing thing to be able to order supplies and have them delivered in a lorry in just three or four days. Yes, the floods were getting worse. Yes, the Summer temperatures were soaring ever higher but they had not reached the point of desperation in England yet. There were another ten years to come before the fighting would begin.

They found a stream for Cassie to drink at and Jemma ate her picnic lunch before turning North and heading home, "Thanks, Cassie," Jemma said as she brushed her companion down and sorted her bedding and food. "You'll be able to stay out in the fields soon. Maybe just one more week for the grass to grow. I better go do some work."

Sara greeted her with a smile. "Good day?" she asked. "Yes," Jemma said. "I hope you didn't mind. I just needed some time to find peace. Yesterday was....too big. Too crowded. Too disturbing. Like, so much emotion, I nearly got swept away, but I'm alright now."

Sara nodded. "I was thinking about what you said. About self sufficiency. We do waste a lot of fuel buying food from the shops. It sounds like your mum taught you a lot about how to grow things. Could you help me here? I mean, tell me what crops we could grow and how to grow fruit and vegetables? My family has always done sheep. I don't know how to do anything else, but we have the land. It would be good to have our own supplies and I was working out about the brooks rising. This farm is high enough to not flood and has good

266

water run off. If we had a water store, maybe we could reduce the flooding downstream and help ourselves, too."

Jemma beamed. "Yes. Yes, I could. I was going to offer to check the sheep in the top field, but would you rather I started a plan now?"

Sara laughed. "Carry on," she said."You are relieved from physical duties for as much time as you need."

"I don't think it will take me long," Jemma replied.

With a mix of emotions impossible to describe, a thrill and shiver of the spine, she realised she knew already what the plan was like. She had walked this farm at the age of six and seen the plots laid out with a hydro plant built into the steep slope and reservoirs of water that could be covered, backing under the fields near the base of the slopes, but above the area of crops, vegetables and fruit laid out on the gently sloping land below. Her mum and dad had been with her and as they sat on the top of the hill and had a small picnic, Beth had pointed out the good things about the layout. How, having the reservoirs up-slope reduced winter soil erosion and meant water could be gravity fed to the crops below in summer. How one could rotate the different foods to stop disease and predation and keep the soil healthy and nutritious without the need for chemicals. Jemma had loved the way it all fitted together. So neat. "It's even good that the food is near the house so easy to harvest as its needed, and efficient in time for weeding. Look, its even near the stables for adding manure to the soil." Beth said.

It frightened Jemma a little that she seemed in some way to be teaching herself how to do things but shut the thought down quickly. "Live each day," she reminded herself, but it brought a glow to her insides that now she knew her mum was praising Jemma's work even without knowing she was doing it. It brought her family closer. Made her feel part of it again.

Sara found paper, ruler, pencils and pens and Jemma took them out to pace the fields, measuring by stride, rather than metres and centimetres, using a compass and triangulation as Seb had taught her and being grateful for his patient, clear instructions. Not caring that Beth said she was too young to manage it. "Your daughter's a genius," he informed her. "She might as well learn everything while she can." and gave his niece a proud hug.

The hardest part for Jemma was using pens and pencils. Her writing had always been appalling, her brain working faster than her hand. School had begun with everything being typed. Only when electricity became scarce had children reverted to pen and paper. Carl said her writing was so bad because she had missed the first five years of learning to write when skills were achieved sub consciously. Beth said she had just inherited the inability from her dad.

Anyway, the plan was done. She talked Sara through it, even advising on the priorities of what to change first – reservoirs to be dug, manure and sheep droppings to be saved to improve the fertility, clear the beds and alter the contours of the land. Only then would seed be sown and fruit trees and shrubs planted.
Martin had taken his exams by the time work was ready to begin and he and Jemma worked side by side, hiring a mini digger, ordering materials.,determined to get the work done over the summer before Martin left for University. Jemma used Cassie for transporting earth, watching the horse take pleasure in her efforts. It was what she was made for. Any one could see that she liked to earn her keep and use her muscles, almost showing off in her ability to pull heavy loads. She regained fitness that had reduced in the last few months of only riding out with Jemma, unable to be useful in transporting lambs or food, except to the barn field because of the busy road. It was frustrating. Jemma had taken responsibility for the sheep on the hired land around Shurnock

and on summer mornings had taken to spending five minutes, after checking the sheep, sitting watching the coots and geese on the moat. Occasionally, she was joined by a cat who came and rubbed around her, requesting a stroke around ears and chin. "Are you Marco's cat?" she asked it. In the enigmatic way of cats, it gave no response. It became a habit, a short chat while Jemma recharged her batteries for the day's energetic digging.

By August, the layout was completed, and Jemma drew up a planting board for sowing seed and harvesting, adding manure, and pruning for each section so that Sara would know what was to be done and could take control when she wanted. Learning on the job. Martin was preparing to leave. He had a place at Bristol. The course was more intensive than some, beginning in September and finishing at the end of July so that the students could qualify a year earlier.
Jemma was beginning to wonder what fate had in store for her. She was sure she would be gone before her parents arrived. Would she just move to another area of the country or was there going to be another jerk in time? She saw, now, that time was a patchwork. All fitting together, but needing each person to fulfil their role wherever and whenever it was due. If she had not travelled in time, she could not have laid out the farm design for her mum and dad to bring her to. If she had not spoken at the demo in Birmingham, even the baby born to Carl and Beth would have had some other name. She saw that, if time required her to travel, it would happen, whatever Jemma thought she wanted to do.

She was talking this through with the cat at Shurnock the day after Martin left for Bristol. The cat moved a little away from her and gave her a look of intensity. Unusually, he then stood up and walked fast, with great purpose towards the corner of the house, glancing back to check she was watching him, and, as he reached the corner, time blurred. Jemma saw the land beyond him change, the gravel disappearing, a sensation of someone wearing long colourful skirts and the cat vanished. Jemma found herself swallowing fast. The hollowness opened inside her and she remembered the lady smiling at her from the past, the cat at her feet. "Blimey!" she said. "He is Marco's cat." and she knew he was telling her that one day soon, now she was ready, he would take her to the time in which she next belonged. It was frightening, but in some way, also exhilarating. The last time it happened, she had not been prepared. She had had the theory of how to survive, back in time, but now she had experience. Her survival kit had saved her life, but now she could do it better. She gulped tears back, thinking that the cat was telling her she must leave Sara alone after all that Sara had done to support her and save her from breakdown, and what of Cassie? This place was perfect for Cassie. Shelter, food, work that she could enjoy, and Jemma even knew that she would come more into her own as cars were abandoned more and more in the five years that followed. Would it matter if two Cassies existed at once? Perhaps they wouldn't. Twenty two years she would have lived. A good life for a shire horse. Jemma would rather Cassie ended her life with good vets and medicines and a choice of whether she worked or not. Parting would be hard, so very hard, but it was better to leave her behind. Jemma thought about not going, refusing to follow the cat that invited her but she could feel, growing inside her, a sense of destiny not to be denied. She stood, feeling an extra weight on her shoulders and headed back to the farm.

Chapter 13

In the days that followed, Jemma tried to prepare the way for Sara, dropping hints about a young lad in the village looking for farm-work, eager to learn the ways of the land. Saying she might take a tour of talks around the country if Sara could cope without her for a while. The cat had met her every morning for his chat and stroke, never requiring food, only company, and did not seem to bother demonstrating the timeslip again. It was as if he knew she was still not ready and would be patient for a while.

Jemma decided she needed to do one more thing before she went. There was just one other person who could offer her advice, who wouldn't think she was crazy if she talked of time slipping. Margot. She was out there somewhere. Jemma spent time on the computer, facebook, twitter, blogs, and eventually decided to ask The Green Party and Greenpeace to put out a message that only Margot would understand. "A message from one time traveller to another who cares deeply about the planet. We both spoke at Birmingham this year. Do you have any advice? Do you know if we meet in time? Please contact Jemma via Greenpeace if you have any message for me."

She e-mailed Greenpeace and The Greens and asked them to send the message to Margot Bish and waited.

It took a week before a reply came back.
" I wasn't sure. You were so much younger in Birmingham, but your voice....All I can say, is I met you at Himbleton in 1564. You were older but fit, well, and, I think, content. I thought of you as The Wise Woman.

I find this difficult to think of and ask that we don't maintain a long correspondence. I think perhaps you are braver than me.

Thank you for the help you gave/will give me, Margot

PS If you have any urgent questions, I will do my best to reply".

Jemma sat back and pondered. If she went with the cat now, is that when she would find herself? So many things she could ask Margot, but she settled for two questions. "Is there anyone you can tell me of that I can ask for help or can trust? Did you by any chance also go forward in time to after 2046? That's where I started from. I want to know if my family are safe."

She hesitated over the send button. Would any answers change time? Was it OK to ask? She couldn't think of any reasons for not asking. Her finger dropped onto the key. There. Couldn't take it back now.

Next. Prepare for 1564. Same queen, but much younger. No potatoes or coffee. Jemma pulled a face. What on earth did they live on? Carefully she read how to grow the crops of the time, raised her eyebrows at the introduction of sheep, September, she thought. Warm clothes needed for the Winter. She might well take her ski thermals but she would also take a dress. Clothes to blend in. She would take seed, ready to plant and still take the survival foods she could buy now. Not as good as in 2046, but they would help her get through the winter.

Sara came into the room and gazed at the computer screen. "Now what are you researching?" she asked.
"Elizabethan styles of dress," Jemma replied. She swung round on the swivel chair. "Sara, I need to tell you the truth so that you won't feel hurt if I leave you suddenly, and …..and leave Cassie behind.".... Jeez, she thought. That was hard to say....

Sara looked alarmed. "You're not ill?.....or depressed?"
Jemma couldn't help smiling. "No. Come and read this first. It will help me convince you."
She switched to the e-mails with Margot, and while Sara read, said, " I really have travelled in time. Even I worried for a while that I had somehow gone crazy, but if I have gone crazy, so has this Margot. You heard us both talk at that demo and neither of us sounded crazy then, did we? I was born in 2026 and fell through time just before my twentieth birthday to 1601. Then time changed again and I ended up here, but in less than two year's time, I will be born just down the road, and I never met an older me, so......I know I somehow disappear, and," she waved her hand at the screen, "as I haven't yet been to Himbleton in 1564, that must be what happens."

She took Sara's hands and held onto them like a lifebelt. "I don't want to go. I feel safe and happy with you, helping with the farm, but I don't think I will have a choice, so thank you for everything you have done to help me, and .... and … and maybe it will be best if you don't tell anyone else about this in case everyone thinks you have done away with me. It's lucky, isn't it that you never got around to talking to the police. I mean, the villagers know that I'm here, and Greenpeace and such, but we never committed. If you just say I've gone away for a bit of peace and quiet, no one will question it because they know I never wanted to be in the limelight."

Sara was now gripping Jemma's hands. Holding tight and not wanting to let go. She tried to reject the things that Jemma was saying but the thoughts she had had on the demo day, about the certainty of the future, the membership card with the strange date and the inability to find Jemma's parents, even the strange mix of clothes Jemma had been wearing when they first met backed up her story and made more sense than anything Sara had cooked up to fit the facts, but she didn't want to lose Jemma with her steady knowledge and love of the land. She had watched her grow from a terrified child to a confident woman, each of them now supporting the other.

"How will I manage without you?" she asked, with tears coming to her eyes.

"Get Mark from the village. He's so keen to learn, and everything you need to know about the crops is on the planting board, and written on the seed packs. Cassie will help. You'll be fine. Maybe you could sign up for that Organic volunteer farming scheme, WOOF, or something like that," Jemma frowned, wishing everything wasn't clever acronyms these days. "Then you'll meet lots of keen eco warriors just like me, happy to be paid in board and lodging."

Sara leaned forward and gave Jemma a hug, "Oh Jem," she said, her voice breaking. "I'll miss you."

Jemma hugged her back. "Me too," she said.

The computer beeped. It was the return message from Margot.

"Throckmortons in conflict. Try not to get involved. You may meet Lady Jane. She might need your help. Vicar in 1564 is a nice vague kind of guy. Villagers welcome team work. Tramps and wanderers are not welcome.

Sorry, I only travelled to 1564. Once was enough and I have avoided Feckenham since I got back.

I think you may be there from a much earlier time. You were much older. Maybe thirty years!

Good luck and take care of yourself,

Margot"

They read it together, Sara finally fully accepting what must be. She gave a watery lopsided smile. "We'd better get you ready then. Have you any idea when or how this will take place?"

"Not exactly," said Jemma, "But I think it will be at Shurnock, and it will probably be orchestrated by Marco's cat."

Other books by Margot Bish

Tis The Irish Way   adult light hearted short story

A Moment In Time   adult the first in this series

Poems For Any Mood / Poetry For All Moods - same poems, one on high quality paper, one on basic quality

A Difficult Age   adult / teenage short story

Through The Storm   children's story age 8-12

Cats, Cats, Cats   3 cat stories in picture book style
for children aged 3-5

e-book only children age 3-5 picture books – cats,cats cats broken into separate books
The Long Day Out   cat story
How Could I Forget? cat story
The Perfect Home   cat story

There will be a third book in the A Moment In Time series called "Wise Woman"

Printed in Great Britain
by Amazon

81232786R00159